MacCallister
The Eagles Legacy
The Killing

MacCallister
The Eagles Legacy
The Killing

William W. Johnstone
with J. A. Johnstone

PINNACLE BOOKS
Kensington Publishing Corp.
www.kensingtonbooks.com

PINNACLE BOOKS are published by

Kensington Publishing Corp.
119 West 40th Street
New York, NY 10018

PUBLISHER'S NOTE
Following the death of William W. Johnstone, the Johnstone family is working with a carefully selected writer to organize and complete Mr. Johnstone's outlines and many unfinished manuscripts to create additional novels in all of his series like The Last Gunfighter, Mountain Man, and Eagles, among others. This novel was inspired by Mr. Johnstone's superb storytelling.

All Kensington titles, imprints, and distributed lines are available at special quantity discounts for bulk purchases for sales promotions, premiums, fund-raising, educational, or institutional use. Special book excerpts or customized printings can also be created to fit specific needs. For details, write or phone the office of the Kensington special sales manager: Kensington Publishing Corp., 119 West 40th Street, New York, NY 10018, attn: Special Sales Department; phone 1-800-221-2647.

PINNACLE BOOKS and the Pinnacle logo are Reg. U.S. Pat. & TM Off.
The WWJ steer head logo is a trademark of Kensington Publishing Corp.

ISBN-13: 978-0-7860-2481-0
ISBN-10: 0-7860-2481-X

First printing: March 2012

10 9 8 7 6 5 4 3 2 1

Printed in the United States of America

Prologue

Eight men had come to kill Duff MacCallister, and eight men now lay dead in the streets of Chugwater, Wyoming Territory. Before he headed back home, the entire town of Chugwater turned out to hail Duff as a hero. Duff had a few people of his own to thank: Biff Johnson for shooting the man off the roof who had a bead on him, Fred Matthews for tossing him a loaded revolver just in time, and Meghan Parker, who risked her own life to hold up a mirror that showed Duff where two men were lying in wait for him. Meghan also reminded Duff that Chugwater held a dance once a month in the ballroom of the Dunn Hotel.

It was about a ten-minute ride back home, and as he approached, he saw a strange horse tied out front. Dismounting, he was examining the horse when Elmer Gleason stepped out onto the front porch.

"Mr. MacCallister, you have a visitor inside. He is a friend from Scotland."

Duff smiled broadly. Could it be Ian McGregor?

He stepped up onto the front porch, then went inside. "Ian?" he called.

It wasn't Ian; it was Angus Somerled. Somerled was standing by the stove, holding a pistol that was leveled at Duff.

"Somerled," Duff said.

"Ye've been a hard man to put down, Duff Tavish MacCallister, but the job is done now."

Duff said nothing.

"Here now, lad, and has the cat got your tongue?"

"I didn't expect to see you," Duff said.

"Nae, I dinna think you would. Would you be tellin' me where I might find my deputy?"

"Malcolm is dead."

"Aye, I thought as much. Killed him, did ye?"

"Aye—it seemed to be the thing to do."

"There is an old adage: 'if you want something done right, do it yourself.' I should have come after you a long time ago instead of getting my sons and my deputies killed."

"That night on Donuum Road, I was coming to give myself up," Duff said. "None of this need have happened. Your sons would still be alive, Skye would still be alive. But you were too blinded by hate."

"We've talked enough, Duff MacCallister," Somerled said. He cocked the pistol and Duff steeled himself.

Suddenly the room filled with the roar of a gunshot—but it wasn't Somerled's pistol. It was a shotgun in the hands of Elmer Gleason. Gleason had shot him through the window, and the double load of 12-gauge shot knocked Somerled halfway across the room.

"Are you all right, Mr. MacCallister?" Gleason shouted through the open window. Smoke was still curling up from the two barrels.

"Aye, I'm fine," Duff said. "My gratitude to ye, Mr. Gleason."

Gleason came around to the front of the cabin and stepped in through the front door.

"Seein' as how I saved your life, don't you think me 'n you might start callin' each other by our Christian names?"

"Aye, Elmer. Your point is well taken."

"Sorry 'bout tellin' you he was your friend. But that's what he told me, and I believed him."

"And yet, you were waiting outside the window with a loaded shotgun."

"Yes, sir. Well, considerin' that the fella you went to meet in Chugwater was from Scotland, and wasn't your friend, I just got to figurin' maybe I ought to stand by, just in case."

"Aye. I'm glad you did."

Gleason leaned the shotgun against the wall and looked at the blood on the floor of the cabin.

"I reckon I'd better get this mess cleaned up for you," he said.

"Elmer, I'm sure you don't realize it, but you just did," Duff said.

Chapter One

One year later

Duff Tavish MacCallister was a tall man with golden hair, wide shoulders, and muscular arms. At the moment, he was sitting in the swing on the front porch of his ranch house in the Chugwater Valley of southeastern Wyoming. This particular vantage point afforded him a view of the rolling grassland, the swiftly moving stream of Bear Creek, and steep red escarpments to the south. He had title to twelve thousand acres, but even beyond that, he had free use of tens of thousands more acres, the perimeters limited only by the sage-covered mountains whose peaks were snowcapped ten months of the year.

He had once owned a cattle ranch in Scotland, but it wasn't called a ranch; it was called a farm, and he had only 300 acres of land. He was a Highlander, meaning that he was from the Highlands of Scotland, but compared to the magnificent mountains in the American West, the Highlands were but hills.

In the corral, his horse, Sky, felt a need to exercise, and began running around the outside edge of the corral at nearly top speed. His sudden burst of energy sent a handful of chickens scurrying away in fear. High overhead, a hawk was making a series of ever-widening circles, his eyes alert for the rabbit, squirrel, or rat that would be his next meal.

"I was talking to Guthrie yesterday," Duff said. "He said if I wanted to build a machine shed, he could get the plans and all the material together for me, but I'm not so sure I need another building now. What do you think, Elmer?"

Elmer Gleason was Duff's foreman and, at the moment, he was sitting on the top level of the steps that led up to the porch. Elmer was wiry and rawboned. He had a full head of white hair and a neatly trimmed beard. He leaned over to expectorate a quid of tobacco before he replied.

"'Pears to me, Duff, like you near 'bout got ever'-thing done that needs doin' in order to get this ranch a' goin'," Elmer said, as he wiped his mouth with the back of his hand. "I don't see no need for you to be buildin' a machine shed 'til you get yourself some cows."

"I expect you are right," Duff replied.

"I'll say this," Elmer said. "Once you get them critters here, there won't be a cow in Wyomin' livin' in a finer place than Sky Meadow."

Duff's house, which was no more than a cabin a year ago, was now as fine a structure as could be found anywhere on the Wyoming range. Made of debarked logs fit together, then chinked with mortar, it was sixty feet wide and forty feet deep, with a porch that stretched all the way across the front.

Duff's ranch was set between Bear and Little Bear Creeks, both streams year-round sources of good water. In an area where good water was scarce, the creeks were worth as much as the gold mine that was on the extreme western end of his property. Duff gazed thoughtfully across the rolling green pastureland to Bear Creek, a meandering ribbon of silver. He followed it with his eyes as far as he could see.

The insulating mountains not only made for beautiful scenery, but they tempered the winter winds, and throughout the spring and summer sent down streams of water to make the grass grow green. Over the past year, he had come to love this piece of ground, and had put in long hours each day getting it ready to become the ranch he knew it could be.

He had named his ranch Sky Meadow, not only because the elevation of the valley was at five thousand feet, but also because it kept alive the memory of Skye McGregor, the woman he would have married had she not been murdered back in Scotland.

"Where are you, Duff?" Elmer asked.

"Beg your pardon?"

"You been gazin' out over the land here for the last five minutes without sayin' a word. You been lookin' at the land, but I'll just bet you ain't a' seein' it. Your mind is some'ers else, I'm a' thinkin'."

"You're partly right and partly wrong," Duff said, his Scottish brogue causing the "r's" to roll on his tongue. "I was for seeing my land, for I find the view to my liking and soothing to my soul. But 'tis right you are that my mind was back in Scotland."

"You were thinking of your woman?" Elmer asked.

"Aye, the lass was much on my mind. 'Tis a shame I've all this, and no one to share it with me."

"You're a young man, Duff. You'll not be single all your life. I'm bettin'." Elmer chuckled. "What about the young woman who runs that dress shop in Chugwater?"

"Ye would be talking about Meghan Parker, I expect," Duff said.

"Who else would I be talkin' about? Of course I'm talking about Meghan Parker. She's all sass and spirit, with a face as brown as all outdoors, and yeller hair as bright as the sun. She's as pretty as a newborn colt and as trustin' as a loyal hound dog. Why, she could capture your heart in a minute if you would but give her the chance."

Duff laughed. "Elmer, 'tis a bit of the poet you have in that ancient soul of yours."

"I wasn't always a poor castaway creature of the desert," Elmer said.

Elmer was Duff's only ranch hand. When Duff came to take possession of his land last year, he'd heard stories of a ghost in the old, abandoned and played-out mine that was on his property. When he'd examined his mine, he had found the ghost who had kept others frightened away, and he'd also found that the mine was anything but played out. The ghost was Elmer, who was "protecting" his stake in the mine. At the time, Elmer was more wild than civilized, and had been living on bugs and rabbits when he could catch them, and such wild plants as could be eaten.

By rights and deed, the mine belonged to Duff, but he had wound up taking Elmer in as his partner in the operation of the mine, and that move was immediately vindicated when, shortly thereafter, Elmer saved Duff's life. The two men became friends then, and over the last year, Duff had seen occasional glimpses into Elmer's mysterious past.

Although Elmer had never told him the full story of his life, and seldom released more than a bit of information at a time, Duff was gradually learning about him.

He knew that Elmer had been to China as a crewman on a clipper ship.

Elmer had lived for two years with the Indians, married to an Indian woman who died while giving birth to their son. Elmer didn't know where his son, who would be ten, was now. He had left him with his wife's sister, and had not seen him since the day he was born.

And once, Elmer had even let it slip that he had ridden the outlaw trail with Jesse and Frank James.

Because of the gold mine, Elmer had money now, more money than he had ever had in his life. He could leave Wyoming and go to San Francisco to live out the rest of his life in ease and comfort, but he had no desire to do so.

"I got a roof over my head, a good friend, and all the terbaccy I can chew," Elmer said. "Why would I be a' wantin' to go anywhere else?"

Elmer stood up, stretched, and walked out to the

fence line to relieve himself. Just before he did, though, he jumped back in alarm.

"Damn!" he shouted.

"What is it?" Duff called from his swing. "What is wrong?"

"There's a rattlesnake here!"

Duff got up from the swing and walked to the front of the porch. "Where is it?" he asked.

"Right over there!" Elmer said, pointing toward the gate in the fence. "Iffen I had been goin' through the gate, I would a' got bit."

"I see him," Duff said.

Duff pulled his pistol and aimed it.

"You ain't goin' to try 'n shoot it from way back there, are you?" Elmer asked.

For his answer, Duff pulled the trigger. The gun flashed and boomed, and kicked up in Duff's hand. Sixty feet away, with an explosive mist of blood, the snake's head was blasted from its body. The headless body of the snake stretched out on the ground and continued to jerk and twist.

"Sum' bitch!" Elmer said. "I been to war, sailed the seas, and seen me a goat ropin', but I ain't never seen shootin' like that."

Elmer reached down and picked up the carcass and then, laying it on the top rung of the fence, pulled out his knife and began skinning it.

"What are you doing?" Duff asked.

"I'm goin' to make us a couple of snakeskin hatbands, and we're goin' to have us some fried rattlesnake for supper," Elmer said.

* * *

After supper that evening, consisting of batter-fried rattlesnake, fried potatoes and sliced onion, Duff pushed his plate away, then rubbed his stomach with a satisfied sigh.

"I never thought I would eat rattlesnake, but that was good."

"You can eat purt' nigh ever'thing if you know how to cook it," Elmer said.

"Aye, and I'm sure you do know how to cook it," Duff said.

"I et me a Tasmanian Devil oncet," Elmer said. "We put in to an island just off Australia. Tougher'n a mule, he was, and had 'im a strong stink, too. But after six weeks at sea with naught but weevily biscuits, molderin' fatback, and beans, why, it weren't all that hard to get around the stink."

The two worked together to wash the dishes and clean up the kitchen, then they went back out onto the front porch. To the west, a red sun moved heavily down through the darkening sky until it touched the tops of the Laramie Mountain Range. After the sun set, it was followed by a moon that was equally as red.

"Elmer, 'tis thinking I am that I'll be goin' back to Scotland," Duff said.

"What?" Elmer asked, surprised by the comment.

"Not to stay, mind you, but for a bit of a visit. I received a letter from Ian telling me that there are no charges against me, so there's no danger in my returning."

"When will you be leaving?"

"I'll ride to Cheyenne tomorrow, take the train

the next day. I'll leave from New York two weeks from today."

"How long will you be gone?"

"Nae more than two months, I'm thinking. Then when I come back, I'll be for getting some cattle on the place."

Elmer laughed.

"What is it?"

"I didn't want to say anything, you bein' the boss an' all. But I was beginnin' to wonder iffen I was goin' to have to tell you that in order to have a cattle ranch, you'll be needin' to have some cattle."

"Oh, I know we need cattle," Duff said. "That's not the question. The question is what kind of cattle we need."

"What do you mean, what kind of cattle do we need? Longhorns is the easiest. But lots of folks are raising Herefords now. Is that what you are thinkin'?"

"No, I'm thinking about introducing an entirely new breed."

"Really? What kind?"

"Black Angus. The kind that I raised back in Scotland."

"Is that why you are going back to Scotland? To get some of them black, what did you call 'em?"

"Angus. Black Angus."

"That seems kind of foolish, don't it? I mean goin' all the way back to Scotland to get some special kind of cow, when you can get Herefords here."

"That's not why I'm going back to Scotland. I'm going back in order that I might give a proper good-bye to those that I left so suddenly."

Elmer nodded. "A proper good-bye, yes, I can see that."

Scotland—Donuun in Argyllshire

Duff stood in the middle of the cemetery behind the Redeemer Presbyterian Church in Donuun in Argyllshire. Holding a spray of heather in his hand, he looked down at the grave.

SKYE MCGREGOR

1866 – 1886

Beloved Daughter of
IAN and MARGARET

*A light of love,
too quickly extinguished in this world
now shining ever brightly in
Heaven above*

Duff leaned down to place the flowers on the well-tended grave, then put his hand on the marble tombstone. Saying a silent prayer, he stood, then walked a half mile to the Whitehorse Pub.

The pub was filled with customers when Duff stepped inside, and he stood there unnoticed. Ian McGregor, the owner of the pub, had his back to the bar as he was filling a mug with ale. For just a moment, Duff had a start, for there was a young woman, the same size and with the same red hair as Skye, waiting on the customers. But the illusion was destroyed when she turned.

Ian had just handed the ale to the customer and was about to put the money into the cash register when he looked toward the door.

"Duff!" he shouted at the top of his voice.

Ian's shout alerted the others to Duff's presence, and so many swarmed toward him that he was immediately surrounded. All wanted to shake his hand or pat him on the back. Duff smiled and greeted each of them warmly as they escorted him over to one of the tables. He had just taken his seat when Ian placed a glass of Scotch in front of him.

"And would ye be for staying here now, Lad?" Ian asked.

"Nae, 'tis but a visit," Duff replied.

"For remember, 'tis no charge being placed against you. Three witnesses there were who testified that you acted in self-defense."

"Aye, 'twas explained to me in a letter," Duff said. "But I've started a ranch, I've made friends, and I've begun a new life in America."

"Then what brings you to Scotland?"

"As you recall, I had to leave very quickly," Duff said. "I had no time to say a proper good-bye to Skye. 'Tis ashamed I was that I was not here for her funeral."

"You were here, Lad," Ian said. "Maybe not in the flesh, but there wasn't a person in the church, nae, nor in the cemetery when she was lowered into the ground, that did not feel your presence."

Duff nodded. "Aye. For with all my heart and soul, I was here."

Ian had to get back to work, but for the next two hours, Duff was kept busy telling his friends about America. Finally, when the last customer had left, and the young woman, whose name was Kathleen, told the two of them good night, Duff and Ian sat together in the pub, dark now except for a single light that glowed dimly behind the bar.

"Have ye made friends, Duff?" Ian asked.

"Aye. Good friends, for all that they are new." Duff told Ian about Biff Johnson, whose wife was Scottish, and Fred Matthews and R.W. Guthrie. He told him about Elmer Gleason too.

"As odd a man as ever you might meet," Duff said, "but as loyal and true a friend as you might want."

"Have ye left anything out, Lad?" Ian asked.

"What do you mean?"

"You've made no mention of a woman. Is there no woman that has caught your fancy?"

"I don't know."

"Ye dinnae know? But how can it be that you dinnae know?"

"I have met a young woman, handsome, spirited, gritty."

"Handsome, spirited, gritty? Duff, ye could be talking about a horse. Surely there is more."

"I don't know," Duff said. "I—Skye, it's just that . . ." he was unable to finish the sentence.

"Skye isn't here, Laddie," Ian said. "And if she could speak from her grave, she would tell you nae to be closing your heart on her account."

"Aye," Duff said. "I believe that is true. But Skye is in a corner of my heart, Ian, and I cannae get her out."

Ian reached across the table and put his hand on Duff's shoulder. "There is nae need for ye to get Skye out of your heart, but keep her in that corner, so ye have room to let another in."

"You're a good man, Ian McGregor. 'Tis proud I would have been to be your son-in-law."

"Duff, sure 'n you are my son-in-law, in my eyes and in the eyes of God, if not in the eyes of the law."

Chapter Two

The next day, Duff visited Bryan Wallace. Wallace was one of the most knowledgeable men about cattle that Duff had ever met, and he was the same stock breeder who had provided him with the cattle he'd used to start his own small farm before he'd left Scotland. After a warm greeting, Duff filled him in on where he had been for the last two years.

"I've built a nice ranch, with good grazing land, water, and protection from the winter's cold blast," Duff said. "And now the time has come for me to put cattle upon the land. Most would say I should raise Longhorn, for surely they are the most common of all the cattle there, and they are easy to raise. But there are some who are raising Herefords, and 'tis said that I might try that as well."

"Aye, Herefords are a good breed, and they do well in the American West," Wallace replied.

"But I'm remembering with fondness the Black Angus I was raising here, and 'tis wondering I am if you could be for telling me a bit o' the background of the Black Angus."

"Aye, would be happy to, for 'tis a story of Scotland itself," Wallace replied. "A man by the name of Hugh Watson was raising hornless cattle in Aberdeenshire and Angus. Doddies, they were called then, and good cattle they were, but Watson thought to improve them. So he began selecting only the best black, polled animals for his herd. His favorite bull was Old Jock, who was born 1842 and sired by Grey-Breasted Jock. Today, if you look in the Scottish Herd Book, you'll be for seeing that old Jock was given the number 'one.'

"In that same herd was a cow named Old Granny. Old Granny produced many calves, and today, every Black Angus that is registered can trace its lineage back to those two cows."

"And how would the cows do in America?"

"Ye'd be thinkin' of raising Black Angus on the new ranch of yours, are ye?" Wallace asked.

"Aye, if I thought they would do well there."

"Ease your mind, Laddie, they do just foine in America, for they are there already."

"Really? In Wyoming?"

"Nae, I think there be none in Wyoming. But they are in Kansas, Missouri, and Mississippi. And there is already an American Aberdeen Angus Association, which has their headquarters in Chicago. If ye be for wanting information about the breed in America, I would say that's where you should go."

"Thank you, Mr. Wallace."

"You'll be going back to America then, will you?"

"Aye. I've set down my roots there, now."

"What do you think of the country?"

"'Tis as big and as wonderful as you can possibly imagine," Duff replied enthusiastically.

"Do me a favor, Lad, and drop me a line when you get your herd established. I have been keeping track of where all the Black Angus have been started. 'Tis a thing I do for the Scottish Breeders Association."

"I'll be happy to," Duff said.

Chugwater, Wyoming Territory

When Meghan Parker checked her mail, she was surprised and pleased to find a letter from Duff MacCallister. Excitedly, she started to open it, then just before opening the flap, she hesitated.

What if it was a letter telling her that he was not coming back? What if he was writing to tell her that he was going to stay in Scotland?

No, surely he wouldn't do that. He has a ranch here. He has made friends here.

But, he is from Scotland. And though Meghan didn't know all the particulars, she did know that he had been in love there and that the love, for some reason, was unrequited.

Of course, she was just being silly thinking about all this anyway. In the past year, Duff had made no overtures beyond being just friendly to her. He had even come to a few of the dances and, while there, had danced with her. But even then, he had been somewhat reticent, refusing to occupy too much of her time because the single men so outnumbered the single women that she was always very much in demand.

Still, it did seem that he went out of his way to speak to her or to find some reason to see her on his infrequent visits to town.

Was this a letter of good-bye?

There was only one way to find out, and that was to open it. Closing her eyes and breathing a little prayer of petition, Meghan opened the envelope and withdrew the letter. The writing was bold and neat, but she would have expected no less from him.

Dear Miss Parker,

Even as I pen the words upon the page of this missive, I am gazing out over the moors, lochs, and highlands of my beautiful Scotland, and I find myself wondering why I ever left its shores.

Meghan dropped the letter down and held it to her breast, afraid to read any further. Was he about to tell her that he wasn't coming back to America?

Then I think of the beauty of my ranch, Sky Meadow, and the joy of the friends I have made since I came there, and I know that America is truly my new home.

Again, Meghan dropped the letter to her chest, this time not in fear, but in joy.

"Yes!" she said aloud.

Looking around then to make certain that no

one was observing her odd behavior, she continued to read the letter.

I will be back within one month of your receipt of this letter. My visit here has been both personal and for business, and I now know the next step I am going to take with my ranch. I hope your memory of me has been kept green in my absence.

Yours Truly,
Duff MacCallister

The last time Duff had crossed the Atlantic from Scotland, he had done so as a crewman onboard the *Hiawatha*, a three-masted, square-rigged sail ship. This time, he was a paying passenger on the HMS *Adriatic*, a steamship that had already set a record in crossing. The trip was fast and pleasant, with good weather and good food. When he put in to New York, he visited with Andrew and Rosanna MacCallister, the famous brother-and-sister team of stage players, who were his cousins.

"You simply must tell me about your ranch," Rosanna said. They were having dinner at Delmonico's. Duff's train was due to leave Grand Central Station at eleven that same evening.

"Truly, it is a beautiful place," Duff said. "It sets between timbered hills that stretch down to the rolling green plains below, through which the Bear and Little Bear creeks run, shining like strands of polished silver."

"Oh, it sounds lovely," Rosanna said. "I should love to visit it someday."

"And I would love to have you as my guest," Duff replied.

"How many head of cattle are you running?" Andrew asked.

"Counting my milk cows," Duff said, pausing for a moment, then added, "two."

"Two? You have two cows on the entire ranch? Well, are you raising sheep?"

"Sheep? Oh, heavens no," Duff said, laughing. "I've taken enough teasing from the others for having no cattle. But I wanted to get the ranch exactly right before I introduced cattle, and also, 'tis a certain breed of cattle that I want. A breed that is not now in Wyoming."

"What breed would that be?" Andrew asked.

"Black Angus."

Duff explained what he considered to be the plusses of raising Black Angus, adding that he had raised the breed back in Scotland.

"And you will be the first to introduce them to Wyoming?" Andrew asked.

"Aye, as far as I know, I will be."

Andrew smiled and put his hand on Duff's shoulder. "Then you will be making history, cousin," he said.

Andrew and Rosanna went to the train station with Duff and waited with him until it was time for his train. With a final wave good-bye, Duff passed through the door that read TO TRAINS. Out under the train shed, he could smell the smoke and the steam and feel the rumble of the heavy trains in his stomach as he walked toward track number eight. Then he walked down the narrow concrete path that separated the train on track number eight from the train on track number nine. Half an hour later, the train pulled out of the station and began its overnight run to Chicago.

Chicago, Illinois

In Chicago, Duff looked up the address of the American Aberdeen Angus Association, and after a few preliminary questions, was directed to a man named Eli Woodson.

"Yes, sir, Mr. MacCallister, we are absolutely encouraging the expansion of Angus cattle in America," Eli Woodson said, when Duff told him what he had planned. "And you say that you have been around them before?"

"Aye. When I was in Scotland, I was growing the breed."

"Good, good, then I won't have to be selling you on them, will I? You know what a fine breed they are. Tell me, where will you be ranching?"

"In eastern Wyoming, a place called Chugwater Valley. It is just north of Wyoming."

"Oh, wonderful," Woodson said. "Wyoming is a big cattle area. It would be good to have the noble Angus represented there."

"My question now is where do I purchase the animals?"

"Well, I can set you up with a bull, and maybe ten heifers from here. You can ship them back on the train."

"Thank you, but I would like to start with a much bigger herd."

"How large is much bigger?"

"I want at least five hundred head," Duff said.

Woodson blinked. "You intend to start your herd with five hundred head?"

"Aye."

"Mr. MacCallister, do you have any idea how much something like that would cost?"

"I think no more than thirty dollars a head. Maybe a little less," Duff said. "And I can do the math."

Woodson smiled. "Well, now. If you are fully aware of the cost of starting a herd with such a number and nevertheless want to pursue it, I'm sure we can find enough cattle for you. How long will you be in Chicago?"

"I plan to take the train to Cheyenne tomorrow."

"Do you have a hotel for tonight?"

"I do. I will be staying at the Palmer House."

"Good. Enjoy your stay there, while I do some research. I will telephone the front desk at the Palmer House and leave a message for you when I get the information you need."

"Thank you."

The Palmer House was seven stories high. The room, compared to all the other hotel rooms Duff had occupied, was quite large and luxuriously decorated. It also had a private bathroom with hot and cold running water.

After taking a bath, Duff went downstairs, and into the barbershop to get a haircut. The marble tiles of the barbershop floor were inlaid with silver dollars. It, like the entire hotel, was well illuminated by electric lights. A wax recording machine sat in the back of the barbershop and one or more of the barbers kept it playing all the time Duff was in the barber chair.

From the barbershop he went into the restaurant, where he saw Angus steak on the menu, and ordered it. By the time he finished dinner, it was dark but still too early to go to bed, so Duff decided to take a walk around the city. He wound up at the Chicago River and stood there by the bridge for a while, watching the boat traffic.

"No! Please, no!"

The voice was that of a woman, and she sounded frightened. The sound was coming from under the bridge, but when Duff looked underneath, it was far too dark to see.

"Oh, please, don't hurt me. I am but a poor woman, I have done you no harm."

Moving quickly, Duff climbed over the railing of the bridge, then down the embankment.

"Miss?" he called. "Miss, where are you?"

"Help, oh please help!"

Duff started toward the voice.

"We've got one, Percy, don't let him get away!" a woman's voice said excitedly. It was the same woman who had been calling for help.

Duff realized at once that he had fallen for a trap. And in the time it would take others to figure out what was wrong, Duff was already reacting. He knew that where he was standing would make him stand out in silhouette against the reflections off the Chicago River. He moved quickly to step farther under the bridge, and to put the dark part of the embankment behind him.

"Where the hell did he go?" a gruff voice asked.

Duff looked toward the sound, using a trick he had learned when fighting on the desert in Egypt at night. By not looking directly at an object, but slightly to one side, a person could see better at night. Duff saw a shadow moving toward where he had been but a moment earlier.

"Find him, Percy!" the woman's voice said. "Don't let him get away!"

Percy was holding one arm out in front of him.

"I'm going to cut him up good," Percy said.

Duff breathed a sigh of relief, knowing that it wasn't a gun. He wasn't armed, and under the circumstances, he thought it would be a lot easier to deal with someone who was holding a knife, than it would be to deal with someone with a gun.

"I'm over here, Percy," Duff said.

"What?" Percy said. He moved quickly toward where Duff had been when he spoke. But Duff had stepped to one side, and he felt, heard, and saw Percy make a wild, unsuccessful swipe with his blade.

Duff reached out at the exact moment when Percy's arm was most extended. Putting one hand on Percy's elbow, and the other on Percy's wrist, he jerked the arm back, breaking it in the elbow.

"Ahhh!" Percy screamed in pain.

Duff heard the knife hit the ground and reaching down quickly, he picked it up, then tossed it into the river, hearing the little splash as it went in.

"Percy!" the woman shouted.

"He's here," Duff said.

"Percy, what happened?"

"The son of a bitch broke my arm!" Percy said, his voice strained with pain.

"Aye, but ye should be glad 'twas your arm I broke, and not your neck," Duff said.

"You son of a bitch! You broke Percy's arm!" the woman cried angrily.

"Tch, tch, such language from a lady," Duff said. "Sure now, Lass, an' I'm beginnin' to think ye were in nae danger at all, now, were ye?" Duff asked.

"Kill him, Percy! Kill him!" the woman said, her voice rising in fear.

"Kill him? I can barely move, you dumb bitch! How am I going to kill him?"

"I would be for betting that I'm nae the first ye have invited down here by your ruse," Duff said. "But 'tis thinking I am that I might be your last."

"I need a doctor," Percy said. "M' arm is about to fall off."

"Aye, if I were you, I would get that arm looked at," Duff said. Stepping out from under the bridge, he climbed back up the embankment. Behind him, he could hear Percy and the woman arguing.

"I got him down here for you. The rest was up to you, but you couldn't handle it."

"He broke my arm," Percy replied. "Can't you understand that? He broke my arm. I need a doctor."

Their angry and accusing voices faded behind him as he walked through the night back toward the hotel.

* * *

"Mr. MacCallister," the hotel clerk called to him as he crossed the lobby.

"Aye?"

"You've a message, sir, from a Mr. Woodson." The clerk handed a note to Duff.

"Thank you," Duff said.

Duff took the message over to one of the sofas in the lobby and sat there as he unfolded it to read.

The Kansas City Cattle Exchange can make all the arrangements to provide you with Black Angus cattle. Good luck with your enterprise.

Woodson.

Smiling, Duff put the note in his pocket. As soon as he got back to Wyoming, he would contact the Kansas City Cattle Exchange and make whatever arrangements might be necessary.

Chapter Three

It was dark when Duff rode into Chugwater, returning home after an absence of nearly two months. Although there had been some discussion of it in a few of the town council meetings, Chugwater still did not have streetlights. The reason they had decided against them was that Chugwater had not yet been "electrified," and it was felt that it would be a waste of money to put gas lamps in, only to have to convert them at a later date.

As a result, the only light on First Street was that which spilled out in little golden squares through the windows of the lighted buildings. Because it was after dark most of the citizens of the town were inside somewhere so the street was nearly deserted. Duff could hear the hollow clopping sounds Sky's hooves made as he moved down the street toward the Fiddler's Green saloon. He could hear the tinkling of the piano and a burst of laughter as he drew closer.

Passing by Meghan's Ladies' Emporium, he looked

upstairs toward her apartment, which was over the store, to see if a light was burning. It was, and he asked himself if she would welcome a visit from him before he went back out to the ranch. He might call on her.

Then, as he thought about it further, he realized that it would probably be best that he not call on her now, since it would be considered improper for a man to call upon a single lady after dark. And though he wanted to see her to let her know that he was back, he did not want to do anything that could, in any way, sully her reputation.

Tying his horse off at the hitching post in front of Fiddler's Green, he stepped up onto the porch and pushed his way through the batwing doors to go inside.

"Duff!" someone shouted, and, just as they had done so at the White Horse Pub back in Scotland, all the patrons of Fiddler's Green began crowding around him.

After a universal greeting, Duff settled at a table in the back corner, where he was joined by R.W. Guthrie, Fred Matthews, and Charley Blanton, editor of the *Chugwater Defender.* These were some of his closest friends. He counted Biff Johnson as one of his friends as well, but because Biff owned the saloon, and because it was particularly busy tonight, he was unable to find time for much more than occasional short visits.

The men had dozens of questions, and Duff answered all of them as best he could. He told them about Scotland, and about his visit with old friends in the pub there. He did not tell them about visiting

Skye's grave at the cemetery. That was something that seemed a little too personal to discuss.

"Hey, you, piano player!" one of the cowboys at the bar called. "Play 'The Gal I Left Behind Me.'"

The piano player complied, and the cowboy and two of his friends sang along.

After the song, the piano player started to play something else, but the drunken cowboy yelled at him.

"I said, play 'The Gal I Left Behind Me.'"

The piano player repeated the song, and again the three drunken cowboys sang along.

When the song was over and the piano player started to play something else, once more the drunken cowboy called out.

"Play 'The Gal I Left Behind Me'!"

This time, the request was greeted with groans from others in the saloon, and the cowboy pulled his gun.

"By God, I aim to sing some more," he said.

Now the saloon grew quiet as everyone looked on in concern as to what was about to happen.

"Now, that I got ever'body's attention," the drunken cowboy said, "I'll say it again. Piano player, play 'The Gal I Left Behind Me.'"

"Drop that gun, Woodward," Biff Johnson said.

When Woodward and the others glanced toward Biff, they saw that he was holding a double-barrel twelve-gauge shotgun leveled at the drunken cowboy.

For a long moment, the scene could have been a staged tableau, with all the principals holding their places. Then, slowly, a smile spread across Woodward's face and he put his pistol back in his holster.

"Sure thing, Mr. Johnson," he said. "Me 'n Case 'n Brax here was just havin' a little fun singin', is all. But if you don't like our singin', why, I reckon we could go somewhere else."

"I think that would be a good idea," Biff said.

"Come on, boys. Looks like they don't appreciate good music here."

The two cowboys with him laughed, as the three left the saloon. Within a moment, the saloon was back to normal.

When Duff left the saloon and started back toward his ranch later that night, he again passed by the front of Meghan's Ladies' Emporium. The apartment over the shop was dark now.

Meghan was standing at the front window of her apartment as Duff rode by. She felt a sense of joy that he was back, coupled with a sense of disappointment that he had not called upon her. But, she knew that Duff was a man of great propriety and never would have subjected her to any possible gossip about receiving a male visitor after dark.

Two days later

As had become their normal custom after a hard day of working, Duff and Elmer Gleason were sitting on the front porch of Duff's house.

"Elmer, 'tis thinking I am that tomorrow I'll ride into Cheyenne," Duff said.

"You'll be back come Saturday, won't you?"

"Aye, I am thinking that I will be. But what is so important about Saturday?"

"They's the Firemen's benefit dance at the Dunn Hotel Ballroom on Saturday."

"Aye. Being as I've been gone for two months, I'd nearly forgotten about that."

"Maybe you forgot it, but you can be certain that Miss Parker ain't forgot it. More'n likely she's plannin' on you askin' for to take her. Especially since you been gone for two months."

"I'll be back before Saturday, but I'm not for sure exactly when it will be. Mayhaps you can ask Miss Parker to the dance for me."

"Duff MacCallister, I may have spent the last twenty years in the desert, the mountains, or at sea, but even I know that ain't right. You need to ask her yourself, is what you need to do."

"Aye, you are right, I'm sure. But let me ask you this. Would you be for deliverin' a letter to her for me?"

A broad smile spread across Elmer's face.

"Well now," he said. "That I'd be willin' to do."

It was before dawn when Duff awakened the next morning and, unexpectedly, he could smell coffee and bacon. Dressing quickly, he walked into the kitchen and saw Elmer leaning over the stove, looking into the oven.

"The biscuits will be done in a few minutes."

"Elmer, you did not have to go to all that trouble," Duff said. "I was just going to make myself a cup of coffee and then be gone." Although Duff had been a tea drinker when he first came to Wyoming, he had managed to develop a taste for coffee as it was so much more available than tea.

"And that don't make no sense a' tall," Elmer said. "You got a long ride ahead of you. You need somethin' that'll set good in your stomach. I got some good bacon grease here. I'll make us some gravy to go with the biscuits."

"It does look good," Duff agreed.

"Do you have the letter?"

"Aye."

"Leave it there on the sideboard," Elmer said. "I'll ride into town and deliver it today."

Duff laid the letter on the sideboard, then sat down at the table to enjoy the breakfast.

Dawn was just breaking when, having eaten more than he really wanted, but not wanting to seem ungrateful for Elmer's efforts, Duff walked out to the barn and saddled Sky, his big bay. As he rode out, he threw a wave toward Elmer, who was standing on the front porch holding a cup of coffee in one hand, and with his other, leaning up against one of the porch roof support beams.

As Duff rode south that morning, the notches of the eastern hills were touched with the dove gray of early morning. Shortly thereafter, a golden fire spread over the mountaintops, then filled the sky with light and color, waking all the creatures below.

Stopping at noon, Duff shot, skinned, and cleaned a rabbit, then spitted him over an open fire.

He had brought a few of Elmer's biscuits with him, and the biscuits and rabbit made a tolerable meal. Sky found some sweet grass, and they both enjoyed water from Horse Creek.

It was mid-afternoon by the time Duff reached Cheyenne. The capital city of Wyoming was a town of considerable importance, not only in the territory, but in the entire Northwest. No more than a tent town in 1867, just over twenty years later it had become a bustling city with substantial buildings, many built of brick and three stories high. There were over ten thousand souls in the town, and that number represented over half of the total population of Wyoming.

Boardwalks ran on either side of every street, and at the ends of each block, planks were laid across the road to allow pedestrians to cross to the other side without having to walk in the dirt or mud. Mounted, Duff waited patiently at one of them while he watched a woman cross the road, holding her skirt up above her ankles to keep the hem from soiling. After she was clear, Duff clucked Sky on, and the big horse stepped gingerly across the plank as they headed toward the J.C. Abney livery stable at the far end of the street.

"Hello, Mr. MacCallister," the eighteen-year-old youth who worked for Abney said, as he stepped out of the barn to greet him. "Is Sky going to stay with us for a while?"

"Hello, Donnie. I'll probably just be here overnight," Duff answered. "Two at the most."

The two knew each other because, on Duff's frequent visits to Cheyenne, he always boarded Sky there. Duff swung down from the saddle and handed the reins to Donnie, who began talking soothingly to Sky as he led him into the barn.

Kansas

Earlier that same morning, a stagecoach left Turkville, Kansas, bound for Haye City, which was the nearest railroad connection. There were no other coaches and few wagons or other conveyances on the road. It was hot and dusty, and only those whose business, whether professional or personal, was important enough to get them out into the dust and the heat, ventured to make the trip.

There were four passengers in the coach, and though it was designed to carry nine, the fact that there were only four made the trip somewhat more bearable, if not comfortable. One was Dooley Long, a gambler who was headed to the nearest railroad depot with the intention of taking the cars to what he hoped would be more profitable pickings in San Francisco. Mildred Luke, a pretty, ruby-cheeked, blue-eyed, young auburn-haired girl, was only seventeen, but was put on the coach by her father, the sheriff of Dawson County, for a visit with her grandparents who lived in Plumb Creek. Dr. Philip Rosen and his wife intended to take the train east to Chicago to attend a medical convention there.

Though it would get hot later in the day, it wasn't so bad now, for the morning air was dry and relatively cool. A stream of cold, clear water ran swiftly by the roadside, and earlier the coach had stopped to fill a water barrel. There might be some hardships brought about by the travel, but thirst would not be one of them, for the stream would accompany them for the rest of the way into Plumb Creek.

Up on the box, Sam Schaeffer, the driver, and Vernon Westbrook, the shotgun guard, kept their eyes peeled for any danger they might encounter. The passengers were occupied with their own thoughts or engaged in light and sporadic conversation, and thus unaware of the stage driver and his shotgun guard, who were scanning the road and the adjacent trees and brush on the watch for would-be robbers.

"I could not help but notice that your mother and father came to see you off back at the stage depot," Dr. Rosen said to Mildred. "Are you going a long distance?"

"No, sir," Mildred answered brightly. "I'm just going to spend a few days in Plumb Creek with my grandmother and grandfather."

"Oh, that sounds nice," Mrs. Rosen said. "I do hope you have a very good time."

At noon, the stage stopped at the Armada way station, where the passengers and stage crew had their lunch. Then, after a lunch of bacon, fried potatoes and biscuits, the coach rolled out of Armada in a cloud of dust, to the rattle of harness and the drum of hoofbeats.

"I don't like this part of the trip," Mrs. Rosen said, shortly after they left Armada. "This is where Crack Kingsley held up the stage last month."

"He didn't kill anyone, did he?" the gambler asked.

"No," Dr. Rosen replied. "But he well could have. You never know with someone like Crack Kingsley. He served five years in the penitentiary, but he didn't learn anything. He's still riding the outlaw trail. But I reckon that all started during the war. He was an irregular then, robbing, burning, and killing without compunction."

"Which side was he on?" the gambler asked.

"He rode with Doc Jennison, so you might say he was a Union man, but from what I've heard, the Jayhawkers were no better than the Bushwhackers who rode for the South," Dr. Rosen said.

Dr. Rosen's observation had everyone in the stage on edge, and they looked out the windows as vigilantly as did the driver and guard. Up ahead by the side of the road was a single, rather large rock, ideally positioned to shelter a road agent, should one wish to take advantage. Schaeffer was well aware of this part of the trip, for that very rock had hidden Kingsley last month. Schaeffer cracked his whip to hurry the team by.

"Oh!" Mildred said, frightened. "What was that?"

"Not to worry, child," Dr. Rosen said. "That was just Mr. Schaeffer, popping his whip over the heads of the horses."

The stage rolled on by the rock, then passed a grove of aspens and cottonwood trees that were ideal for harboring a robber or robbers. The road angled down from there, still paralleling the stream running clear and cold among the rocks. Then the road started up, a long, slow ascent, with the stream dropping off so that one could look down upon it breaking white over the rocks and sparkling brightly in the sunshine.

As the coach continued to climb, Mildred felt cold shivers run down her spine. From every bush, stump and rock, she expected a masked man to leap out before them. Whereas the coach had been traveling as fast as a man could run, it was now slower than a crawl as the horses labored up the long hill, a hill that was haunted by the ghosts of travelers who had been murdered there in at least half a dozen robberies in the past.

Finally reaching the top of the hill, the horses were allowed to rest a few minutes, and the passengers were encouraged to step out to stretch their legs. It was not mere coincidence that here, too, were two privies, the ladies' on the left side of the road, the men's on the right.

Crack Kingsley had been waiting behind a clump of bushes about twenty yards from the ladies' privy. Hearing the coach laboring up the hill, he discarded his half-smoked cigar, called a "Long Nine," and ground it out under his heel. Subconsciously, he rubbed his finger across the puffed-up purple scar tissue on his face, and waited until the coach reached the top of the hill. He made no further move until he saw the passengers step out, the driver get down to check the harness, and the shotgun guard leave his gun on the seat while he went into the toilet to relieve himself. Kingsley had waited in this place for just such an opportunity, and he walked up to the right side of the team so he would be able to keep an eye on the men as they came back to the coach.

The driver, having found a loose line, was so busy adjusting it that he didn't notice Kingsley until he spoke.

"Now, gents, this is what I want you to do," Kingsley said, his voice startling all of them. "Drop your guns right here on this side of the log." He was referring to a fallen tree of about four feet in diameter.

The driver and shotgun guard pulled their pistols and dropped them as Kingsley ordered.

"I'm a doctor," Dr. Rosen said. "I don't carry a gun."

"What about you?" Kingsley asked the gambler.

Dooley Long pulled his pistol from the holster and dropped it alongside the log. "You look to me like the kind of person who carries a holdout," Kingsley said. "Let me see it."

Long hesitated a moment, and Kingsley pointed his pistol at him and cocked it.

"I'll just shoot you now and be done with it," he said.

"No!" Long said. He pulled a small pistol from his jacket pocket and dropped it with the other weapons.

At this time, Mildred and Mrs. Rosen emerged from their privy and, seeing a robbery in progress, Mrs. Rosen gave a loud gasp. "Kingsley!" she said.

Kingsley jerked his pistol over in her direction.

"Damn, have I gotten famous?" he asked. He

waved his pistol toward the stage. "Get over here where I can keep an eye on you."

"You'll never get away with this, Mr. Kingsley," Mildred said. "My daddy is the sheriff of Dawson County."

Kingsley chuckled. "Is he, now? Well, you tell your daddy that Crack Kingsley sends his regards. Now, you, driver, climb up there and throw down the money box."

"Mr. Kingsley, maybe you should've scouted this out a little better than you done," Schaeffer said. "We ain't carryin' no money box on this trip."

"What do you mean, you ain't carryin' no money? You always carry money."

"No, sir, we don't always. Lots of times now, what money there is goin' back and forth to the railroad is took by courier. We ain't carryin' no money a' tall, and that's the Lord's truth."

"You!" Kingsley said, pointing his pistol at Mildred. "You, the sheriff's daughter. Climb up there on the driver's seat and take a look around."

Frightened, Mildred did as she was instructed, climbing with some difficulty because of her dress, up onto the driver's seat.

"Now," Kingsley said, "look under that seat and throw down what you see."

Mildred looked under the seat, then rose up again.

"There is nothing under the seat," she said.

"Don't you be lyin' to me girl, 'cause I'd as soon kill you as any of the others. Now, throw down what you see up there, whether it be a pouch or a box."

Kingsley pointed his pistol right at her and pulled the hammer back.

"Please!" Mildred said, her voice almost a scream. "There is nothing up here!"

Swearing in frustration, Kingsley ordered the girl back down.

"Come here," he said, calling her over.

Mildred did as ordered.

Suddenly and unexpectedly, Kingsley grabbed the top of her dress and jerked it down, exposing her bare breasts. Crying out in shock and terror, Mildred folded her arms across her breasts in an attempt to restore some modesty.

"Now," Kingsley said to the others. "If you don't want to see this girl hurt, you'll empty your pockets of any money you're a' carryin', and put it right here in my hat."

Dr. Rosen had a ten-dollar and a twenty-dollar gold piece. Dooley Long put one twenty-dollar gold piece into the hat.

"Mister, the way you're dressed, I don't think this is all the money you got," Kingsley said. "I'm goin' to ask you again to empty your pockets. Then I'm goin' to come over there and reach down in your pocket my ownself, and if I find any money you was holdin' out on me, I'll kill you."

Nervously, the gambler produced three more twenty-dollar gold pieces.

The driver and guard came up with thirty dollars between them.

"What about you?" Kingsley asked Mrs. Rosen.

"She's my wife. I carry our money," Dr. Rosen said.

"How much money do you have?" Kingsley asked

Mildred, who was still standing alongside the coach with her arms folded across her bare breasts.

"I have five dollars," Mildred said, her voice quaking with fear.

"You're travelin' and you only have five dollars?"

"I don't need any more," she said. "I'm going to see my grandmother and grandfather."

Kingsley smiled at her. "Well, I'll tell you what, honey," he said. "For lettin' me get a peek of them little titties, I'll let you keep your money."

"You are a despicable human being," Mrs. Rosen said angrily.

"Yeah, I reckon I am," he said. "All right, all you folks climb up into the coach now. Driver, you get on out of here. I'll just stay here and keep an eye on you 'til you're gone. Guard, you go up first and toss your scattergun down. Pick it up by the barrel. If I see your hand anywhere else, I'll shoot."

Westbrook climbed up onto the box, then tossed the shotgun down. Kingsley ordered the others into the coach, and as it drove away, he lit another cigar. He stood there wreathed in cigar smoke, watching until the coach was at least a mile away. Not until then did he count his money.

"One hundred forty dollars," he said aloud. He had thought he might get as much as five hundred from a cashbox, but given that he had less than twenty dollars before he had begun this afternoon's adventure, he was satisfied enough.

Chapter Four

Chugwater

There was no bridge across Chugwater Creek, but there was a ford, and Elmer rode through it on his way into town. The swift-running creek broke white over rocks that had been polished smooth by centuries of running water. It was less than ten feet wide, but it provided enough water to give its name not only to the town of Chugwater, but to the entire Chugwater Valley.

Fred Matthews was standing out on the front porch of his mercantile store, seeing to the offloading of some groceries he had bought, and he waved at Elmer as Elmer rode by.

"You heading for Fiddler's Green?" Fred called out to him.

"I'll be by in a bit," Elmer replied. "I'm runnin' an errand for Duff."

Elmer acknowledged the greetings of a few others as he continued his ride toward Meghan's Ladies' Emporium.

* * *

Meghan Parker was twenty-three years old, quite pretty, with blond hair and blue eyes. At the moment she was in the Ladies' Emporium, a dress shop that she owned, on her knees, with her mouth full of pins as she pinned up the hem of the dress she was making for Mrs. Abernathy.

"We're going to Philadelphia," Mrs. Abernathy said. "My sister-in-law thinks that all the women out here wear dresses made of buckskin and flour sacks. I simply must have a dress that will make her pea green with envy. My niece is getting married next month."

"Turn to the left," Meghan said, and Mrs. Abernathy complied. "You look beautiful in this dress. You'll be the belle of the wedding. Next to the bride, of course. Turn a little more to your left."

Again, Mrs. Abernathy complied. "So when are you?"

"I beg your pardon? When am I what?" Meghan replied.

"When are you getting married?"

Meghan laughed. "I don't know. But shouldn't I be engaged first, before I start thinking about such a thing?"

"You mean Duff MacCallister hasn't asked you to marry him?"

"No, whatever gave you that idea? Mr. MacCallister and I are just good friends, that's all."

"Uh, huh, just good friends. Or so you say," Mrs. Abernathy said with a smile.

"There," Meghan said. "I've got it all pinned up.

Now, go back into the dressing room and take it off, but be very careful that you don't lose any of the pins."

"You don't want to talk about it, do you?" Mrs. Abernathy said.

"Talk about what?"

Mrs. Abernathy laughed. "Never mind, if you don't want to talk about it we won't. But you know that I am right."

The melodic tinkling of the bell on the front door got Meghan's attention, and she walked into the front with a smile to greet her customer. When she saw Elmer Gleason standing there, the smile left her face, and she gasped.

"Elmer! Is something wrong? Did something happen to Duff?"

Elmer began shaking his head and he held his hand out, palm forward. "No, ma'am, no ma'am, ain't nothin' a' tall like that. I'm sorry if I put a fear into you, Miss Meghan."

Meghan relaxed, then forced a little laugh. "No, I'm the one who should apologize. I have no idea what might have made me think such a thing."

"What it is, is I brung you a letter from Duff. He bein' in Cheyenne for a couple of days, he asked me to bring it to you."

Elmer pulled the letter from his shirt pocket and held it out toward her. "I tried to keep it clean as best I could," he said. "But what with the ride 'n all, well, it might 'a got a little smudged up."

"It's fine," Meghan said. "Thank you very much. Oh, would you like some coffee and cookies? I have some made for my customers."

"Thank you kindly, ma'am, but bein' as they are for your customers, why, I wouldn't want to get in to 'em. Besides which, I done promised Mr. Matthews I'd meet him down at Fiddler's Green."

"All right. Thank you, Elmer. Thank you very much for bringing Duff's letter to me."

"Yes'm, you're welcome," Elmer said as he touched his fingers to the brim of his hat. Just as he reached the door, he turned back toward Meghan. "You know, ma'am, he puts a great deal of store in you." The doorbell tinkled again, as he left without waiting for a reply.

"So, you are just friends, huh?" Mrs. Abernathy said.

The words gave Meghan a start, because she had no idea that Mrs. Abernathy had come up behind her.

"Didn't mean to startle you," Mrs. Abernathy said. She was holding the carefully pinned-up dress in her hands, and she extended it toward Meghan. "I was real careful with the pins."

"Good," Meghan said. She purposely avoided commenting on Mrs. Abernathy's observation about Meghan and Duff being "just friends."

"So, what is in the letter? Will he be coming to the Firemen's Ball this Saturday?" Mrs. Abernathy asked.

"I'll have your dress ready before four tomorrow," Meghan said.

"Thank you dear, that will be very nice," Mrs. Abernathy said. Knowing that she wasn't going to get an answer, she smiled again and departed.

Meghan waited until she was absolutely certain

Mrs. Abernathy was gone before she opened Duff's
letter.

Dear Miss Parker,

*It may seem strange to have a missive from me
presented to you by Elmer Gleason, but he has
generously offered to act as a means of posting
this letter. By the time you read this I shall be in
Cheyenne. While in Cheyenne, I intend to make
arrangements to bring cattle onto my land so that,
after a year of preparation, Sky Meadow will truly
become a cattle ranch. I am sure that the news of
my establishing a ranch is important to you only as
a matter of the friendship that exists between the
two of us. However, there may come a time when
this information would be of much greater interest
to you.*

*I am told that there is to be a dance on the
evening of Saturday next, the purpose of which
is to raise funds for the volunteer fire brigade.
Because I deem this a worthy purpose, I have every
intention of attending the function, and I hope
that you do as well. If so, I would be delighted to
share a few dances with you, should you grant me
that opportunity.*

Sincerely,
Duff Tavish MacCallister

After Mrs. Abernathy left, Meghan sat at her sewing
machine, working the treadle with her foot as the
needle plunged in and out of the bright blue material of Mrs. Abernathy's dress. Was Mrs. Abernathy cor-

rect in her appraisal of Duff MacCallister's regard for her? It was certainly no secret to her friends—though Meghan had not told anyone—that she had feelings for Duff. But her sense of propriety dictated that she say nothing to him before he declared himself to her. And her sense of self-preservation prevented her from investing too much of herself in the relationship until she knew that there could actually be such a thing.

She had seen him only briefly since he'd returned from his trip to Scotland. He had stopped in her shop the next day to visit with her. And what made the visit particularly pleasant was that he had brought her something from Scotland. It was a souvenir plate with a traditional Scotsman playing the pipes in front of Edinburgh Castle, with "Edinburgh" at the top of the plate. She treasured it, not so much for what it was as for the fact that he had thought to bring her something.

She had been pleased to get the letter today, but it had seemed oddly impersonal. Though, there was one intriguing part of the letter, a couple of sentences that she had been playing and replaying in her head all day. She stopped sewing for a moment, then picked up the letter and reread the sentences that had particularly caught her attention.

I am sure that the news of my establishing a ranch is important to you only as a matter of the friendship that exists between the two of us. However, there may come a time when this information would be of much greater interest to you.

What did that mean? Why would there ever be a time when information about his ranch would be of much greater interest to her? Could it possibly mean that Duff might think of her as a part of his future?

Meghan was fully aware that such a relationship might never develop between them. There was much about Duff MacCallister to admire. He was handsome, yes, and in less than one year he had earned the respect and esteem of just about everyone in the valley.

But there was something else about him too, something deep and dark. It took a while before Duff was comfortable enough with Meghan to tell him about the love he had lost in Scotland. That had left this otherwise very powerful man with a wounded and vulnerable soul. And as much as she wanted to have a deeper relationship, the thought of doing further emotional damage to him was more than she wanted to deal with.

She would have to go slow.

Meghan finished the hem, then hung the dress up so it would be ready for Mrs. Abernathy tomorrow. After that, she went upstairs to her apartment, which was over her shop. She had baked cookies today, as she did every day, to provide a treat for her customers. She took one of them, then walked out onto the front balcony. The sky was filled with stars, from those so bright that she felt almost as if she could reach up and pluck one down from the sky to those of lesser and lesser brilliance, to those that could not be seen as individual stars but provided a blue haze against the black velvet vault of night.

From across the street, she could hear Mrs. McVey's baby crying. From down the street she could hear the piano and laughter coming from Fiddler's Green. She could also hear choir practice from St. Paul's Episcopal Church, which was right next door.

What did he mean by "there may come a time when this information would be of much greater interest?"

After Elmer delivered Duff's letter to Meghan Parker, he stepped into Fiddler's Green. He was feeling pretty good about things because, while he hadn't read the letter, he knew from their conversation that Duff was going to ask her about the dance.

Sky Meadow needed a woman on the place, and Duff needed a wife. Elmer knew about Skye McGregor, and he could understand a man grieving over the loss of a true love, but Duff needed to get on with his life. Otherwise he would wind up wasting it away, the way Elmer had.

He had not started out to waste his life. When he was young, he'd had plans like every other young man. All he wanted to do was have a farm, marry Alma Dumey, and raise a family.

But all that changed with the war.

* * *

"Alma's dead, Elmer," Jesse James told him. "A bunch of red-legged bastards from Kansas killed her and her whole family."

Elmer gripped the handles of the plow so hard that he could feel the blisters forming.

"Was it Doc Jennison?"

"Worse," Jesse said. "They were led by one of our own. Crack Kingsley."

"Kingsley? Kingsley did this?"

"I heard it from Alma's dying lips."

So far, Elmer had managed to avoid the war. He was in Missouri and he knew that there were men of good conscience fighting on both sides. But avoiding the war did not mean he was avoiding its price. He had already lost a brother, two cousins, and several friends. And now Alma Dumey, the girl he had intended to marry, was dead.

Elmer pinched the bridge of his nose to keep himself from crying in front of this man, who had been his boyhood friend and was now an experienced warrior.

"I know you haven't ever had any trouble with him before, but never did like the son of a bitch," Jesse James said. "So, to be truthful with you, I wasn't all that surprised when he crossed the border to join up with the Kansans. But I never thought he would do anything like this to one of his own."

"It's my fault. She wanted to marry this spring, but I wanted to put it off 'til after the crops were out. If she had been here with me, she would still be alive."

Jesse James reached out and put his hand on Elmer's shoulder. "You can ride with us, Elmer," he offered. "I guarantee you, we'll find the sons of bitches who did this, and we'll make them pay."

* * *

Elmer did ride with Frank and Jesse James, and with Quantrill, and they did find some, but not all, of the men who had murdered the Dumey family. Crack Kingsley, the one who had led the Jayhawkers, got away.

When the war ended, most of the soldiers were able to go home again to pick up their lives from before. But Elmer couldn't, because he and many of the men who had ridden with Quantrill and Bloody Bill Anderson were not considered soldiers.

It didn't seem right. The men who rode with Doc Jennison, whose personal depravities equaled anything anyone who ever rode with Quantrill did, were regarded as heroes. But Elmer became a wanted man, unable to reenter society. As a result, he continued to ride with Jesse and Frank James. Then, after the debacle of the Northfield Raid, Elmer, who was nursing a bullet wound in the thigh, left the outlaw trail so he could heal up. Once he was healed, he decided not to go back on the trail. Instead, he went west.

Elmer became a wanderer after that. He spent a year with the Brule Sioux, where he took a squaw, and then left after she died. Then he went to San Francisco and, trying to rescue a Chinese prostitute, ran afoul of the Tong. He killed two Tong members and, to escape retribution, found his way to a sailor's hall. There, though he had never been to sea in his life, he signed on to the *Harriet Sutton*, a clipper ship bound for the Orient.

It had been quite a ride for Elmer since then, including a long period where he had lost his soul and nearly his life, only to be rescued by Duff Mac-Callister. He had been a loner for as long as he could remember, and it was good to have a friend like Duff.

Chapter Five

As Elmer stood at the bar in Fiddler's Green, nursing his beer and wrestling with his thoughts, he became aware that someone at the opposite end of the bar was staring at him. It was a young man wearing a black hat with a silver headband, from which protruded a small red feather. He was also wearing a pistol, with the holster hanging low on his right side. The man was slender, with dark hair and narrow, obsidian eyes.

When he realized that Elmer had caught him staring, the young man tossed his drink down and wiped the back of his hand across his mouth. Then he turned to face Elmer.

"Hey, you, old man."

Elmer turned toward him, and by way of greeting, lifted his beer.

"Would you be Elmer Gleason?" The tone of the young man's voice was anything but friendly, so Elmer didn't answer.

"Didn't you hear the question? I asked if you are Elmer Gleason."

"I'm Gleason."

"They tell me you rode with Jesse James. Is that right, Mister—Gleason?"

The young man set the last word apart from the rest of the sentence, and said it with a sneer.

Again, Elmer didn't answer.

"You know what? I don't believe you rode with Jesse James at all. I think that's just a lie you've been spreadin' around, hopin' it would make people think you are somebody."

Elmer picked up his beer, then walked around behind the bar. He sat the beer down on the bar and looked at the young man.

"It 'pears to me like you 'n me got started on the wrong foot," Elmer said in as friendly a voice as he could muster. "Suppose I buy you a drink. What will you have?"

"I don't want nothin' from you, Mr. Outlaw," the young man. "Is there a price on your head for riding with Jesse James? If there is, how big is the reward? I might just collect on it."

"I don't think there is any paper out on me," Elmer said.

"You don't think? Well, Mister, that might be the truest thing you have said so far. You gotta have a brain to think, and since you don't have no brain, then you don't think."

Elmer sighed and shook his head. "Doesn't look to me like I'm goin' to be able to get onto your good side, does it?" Elmer said.

The boy chuckled. "Now, that there is a good one," he said. "Mister, maybe you don't know this, but I ain't got no good side for you to get on. Most especially with old, cowardly outlaws like you."

"What's your name, boy?" Elmer asked.

"The name is Clete. Clete Wilson," the boy said with an arrogant smile. "I reckon you have heard of me."

"No, sir, I don't reckon I have."

The smile left the boy's face. "You're lyin'. You've heard of me, and even now you're quakin' in your boots."

"You think so, do you, boy?" Elmer asked.

"Don't call me boy! I just told you what my name is. If you want to talk to me, call me by my given name."

"All right, Wilson," Elmer said. "I'll call you by name, because it is important that you hear what I've got to say. I don't know what your problem is, but I'm plumb worn out, and one thing about reaching my age is that I don't have to put up with assholes like you if I don't want to."

Even though Elmer's words were spoken calmly, they were clearly heard and understood by everyone else in the saloon. By now, everyone had grown quiet as they sat, nervously, to see where this was going.

"Well that's just too bad, Mr. Gleason, because you're goin' to have to put up with it whether you want to or not."

"Just what is it that you've got stickin' in your craw?"

"You, Mister. You are stickin' in my craw," Wilson said.

"Have I killed someone close to you? Your father, your brother, perhaps?"

"No, nothin' like that," Wilson answered. "I just want my name in the paper. And I figure that killin' someone that used to ride with Jesse James will get my name in the paper."

"You know what else will get your name in the paper?" Elmer asked.

"What?"

It had not been mere restlessness that had caused Elmer to walk around to the back of the bar. Nor was it to offer to buy Wilson a drink. Elmer had walked around to the back of the bar to stand in front of the double-barrel Greener twelve-gauge shotgun that Biff kept there. In a smooth and non-threatening motion, Elmer reached under the bar, wrapped his hands around the shotgun, and brought it up. He pointed the gun directly at Clete Wilson and watched as the arrogant, overconfident smile faded.

"You can also get your name in the paper by dyin'," Elmer said. "And I'll be glad to oblige you in that."

"What?" Wilson shouted, the expression on his face now one of pure terror. He put his hands up. "No, no, wait! This ain't fair! You ain't even given me a chance to go for my gun!"

"Fair? Who's talkin' about fair?" Elmer asked. "You don't understand, do you, boy? I ain't no gun-fighter like you are, so there ain't goin' to be nothin' fair about this. This here is just goin' to be a killin', plain and simple. So if you've got 'ny prayers, boy, you better say 'em."

Elmer pulled the two hammers back, and the

deadly click of them coming into position sounded exceptionally loud.

"Please, Mister, I—please, don't kill me."

"Elmer," Biff said sharply.

Elmer glanced over toward him.

"Before you kill this little piss ant, make him move away from the bar. That Greener is going to open up a hole big enough for you to drive a freight wagon through him, and that's goin' to mean a lot of blood. It'll clean up pretty easy over there behind the stove, but it's harder than hell to clean up here, right in front of the bar."

"Yeah, you're right, Biff. I don't see no need to put you through all the trouble. All right, boy, you heard the man. He wants the killin' to be done over there behind the stove," Elmer said. "So I reckon we had better move on over there."

Elmer's words weren't angry or threatening. On the contrary, they were as quiet and as calm as if he were just suggesting that they change tables to drink a beer. And the more terrifying because of the lack of emotion.

Elmer came back around to the front of the bar. By now, all the others who had been standing at the bar had moved over to the side wall. Those who had been sitting at tables moved as well, so there was nobody left on center stage except Elmer and Wilson. And Wilson was shaking uncontrollably. He sank down to his knees, then clasped his hands in front of him.

"Please, Mr. Gleason, don't kill me," he begged.

Elmer let both hammers down, and Wilson breathed a sigh of relief.

"I'm goin' to let it pass, this time," Gleason said. "Almost," he added.

Still gripping the shotgun by its stock, Elmer brought the barrel around in a vicious arc, landing on the side of Wilson's head. Two teeth and a stream of blood spewed from Wilson's mouth as he fell forward, flat on his face.

"Damn it, Elmer, you went and got blood on the floor anyway," Biff said.

"A little piss, too," someone else said, pointing to Wilson's pants, which were now obviously wet.

"I'll give a free beer to anyone who will drag this boy's sorry ass out into the alley behind my place and leave him there," Biff said.

Two men responded immediately to the offer.

"Take his gun belt off and leave it with me," Biff said. "I don't want him comin' back in here, blazin' away."

Business returned as usual in the saloon as the two men, one on each leg, dragged Clete Wilson across the floor and out through the back door.

Kansas

Crack Kingsley had been riding for eight hours. Behind him, like a line drawn across the desert floor, the darker color of hoof-churned earth stood out against the lighter, sun-baked ground. Before him the Kansas plains stretched out, not in hills but in motionless waves, one right after another. As each wave crested, another was exposed, and beyond that another still. The ride was a symphony of sound: the jangle of the horse's bit and harness, the squeaking leather as he shifted his weight upon the saddle, and the dull thud of hoofbeats.

He had filled his canteen in a creek this morning, and it was already down by a third. He had no idea how far it would be to the next dependable water hole, and already his tongue was so swollen with thirst that, in a condition that was rare to him, he did not have a cigar clenched between his teeth. As a means of preserving his water, he allowed himself no more than one swallow of water per hour.

Squinting at the sun, he guessed that an hour had passed since last he'd last allowed himself a drink, so he stopped his horse, mopped his brow, then reached for the canteen. He had just pulled the cork when the shot rang out.

The bullet hit his horse in the neck, and blood gushed from the wound. Without a sound, the animal went down. Kingsley jumped clear to avoid being pinned beneath it. As he did so, however, he dropped the canteen and water began running out. He scurried to pick it up, not knowing how much of the precious fluid he'd lost.

Crack pulled his rifle from its sheath, then ran to a nearby arroyo. Jumping down into it, he was not only concealed from the approaching posse, but he also had the advantage of cover. He cocked his rifle, then slithered up to the top, lay his rifle on the parapet and waited. There were three men approaching.

"Ha, lookie here!" one of the men said. "I told the sheriff he was turnin' back too fast. We got 'im now. We'll teach that son of a bitch not to treat women they way he done the sheriff's daughter."

"I wouldn't be all that sure if I was you, Poke," one of the other men said. "All I'm seein' there is the horse. Don't see him nowheres."

"Well, he's got to be around here some'ers," Poke said, sliding down from his saddle. "He sure ain't goin' to get far without his horse."

Poke dismounted, then holding his pistol at the ready, walked over to the horse and gave it a kick.

"Damn! Where'd he go?"

Poke put his pistol back into its holster.

"I reckon 'bout the only thing we can do now is start back."

When Poke put his pistol back in its holster, that meant that not one man of the three had a weapon in his hand. With a huge, triumphant smile spread across his face, Kingsley stepped up out of the arroyo. His rifle was raised to his shoulder and he was pointing it at Poke.

"You boys give up too easy," Kingsley said.

"Son of a bitch! It's him!" Poke shouted. He made a panicked grab for his pistol, but even before his hand reached his pistol, Kingsley fired. Pumping the lever of his rifle, he fired two more times, and all three men lay dead or dying on the ground.

Crack started toward the horses, aiming to capture one of them, but they were all frightened by the gunshots and bolted away. He still had no horse, but he also knew, now, that there was nobody else on his trail. That meant he no longer had to avoid the towns, but could go into the next one he saw. He had no choice now but to walk.

It was hard going. An hour or so into his walk, his feet began to swell inside his boots. As the day wore on, he began tiring, and he started breathing through his mouth. The hot, dry air created a tremendous thirst, and the more he thought about it, the thirstier he got. His throat grew more and more parched, and his tongue swelled. He tried to keep up the schedule of one swallow of water per hour, but he was working much harder now than he had been when he was riding, and it was nearly impossible to wait for an hour between swallows. In addition, there wasn't much water left. He drank the last of his water at about five in the afternoon. He started to throw the canteen away, but decided to keep it in case he did stumble across a water hole somewhere.

Then, just before dark, a scattering of weathered buildings rose from the plains before him, somewhat distorted in the shimmering heat waves. Gathering what strength he had remaining, Kingsley started toward it. Staggering into the little town, he saw a pump beside a horse watering trough, and hurried to it. Moving the handle a couple of times, he was rewarded by seeing a wide, cool stream of water pour from the pump mouth. Putting his left hand in front of the spout, he caused the water to pool and, continuing to pump, drank deeply. Never in his life had anything tasted any better to him. With the killing thirst satisfied, Kingsley rose up from the pump, stuck a cigar into his mouth, lit it, then looked around the town. Just down the street, a door slammed and an isinglass shade came down on the upstairs window. A sign creaked in the wind, and flies buzzed loudly around a nearby pile of horse manure.

These sounds were magnified because the street was silent. No one moved, and Kingsley heard no human voice, yet he knew there were people around. There were horses tied here and there, three of them in front of a building which was identified by a sign as the Silver Dollar Saloon. Kingsley walked over to make a closer examination of the horses, looking at their teeth and their eyes, and feeling their legs. He also examined the saddles, realizing that the more expensive the saddle, the more likely the horse is of good stock.

Across the street from the saloon, in Millie's Café, Deputy Sheriff Stuart Mosley was having a piece of chocolate cake and a cup of coffee. Because of his position near the window, he saw a man come walking into town, then drink water from a pump as if he were dying of thirst. When he finished drinking the water, he came farther into town, and Mosley got a good look at him. When the man reached the front of the saloon, he stopped and looked at the horses. He did much more than look. He made a very thorough examination of them.

Mosley knew every horse the man examined, and knew their owners, but he had no idea who the man was who was showing so much interest in the horses. He was looking at them as if he were about to buy one of them.

Or steal them!

Mosley got a real strong feeling, in his gut, that that was exactly what the man was planning. After all, he did walk into town, and that meant he needed a horse. And if he was planning on buying one, he would have gone straight to the livery, where a huge sign announced clearly: HORSES FOR SALE.

Thinking this needed further looking into, Mosley finished the last bite of his cake and the last swallow of his coffee, then stood up.

"Deputy, you sure you don't want another cup of coffee?" Millie offered. "Second cup is free."

"Thank you, no, Miz Turley," Deputy Mosley answered. "I'd better be getting on."

For Kingsley, the horses were inviting, and he thought about getting on one and just riding away right now. But the horses would still be here, and even more inviting for the moment was the thought of a cool beer. He had made his selection and, giving that horse a pat on the neck, he stepped up onto the porch, then pushed through the batwing doors to go inside.

The shadowed interior of the saloon gave the illusion of coolness, but it was an illusion only, for the heat was just as oppressive inside as it was outside. Kingsley stepped up to the bar and slapped a dime onto the counter.

"Beer."

The bartender drew the beer, then made change for the dime. Kingsley left the nickel on the bar, then picked up the beer and drained it without even putting the mug down. Finished with the first beer, he used his finger to slide the nickel across the bar toward the bartender.

"I'll have another one," he said.

"Mister, you sure come in here with some kind of thirst," the bartender said. "What you been doin' that's got you so thirsty?"

"What business is that of yours?" Kingsley replied, and, stung by the unexpected hostility of the retort, the bartender said nothing else. He merely refilled the mug.

Kingsley put another dime onto the bar. "I'll have ten of them Long-Nine cigars," he said.

Taking the dime, the bartender turned to the glass cabinet that contained loose pipes and chewing tobacco, makings for roll-your-own cigarettes, various kinds of snuff, and a box of long black cigars. Taking ten of those from the box, he handed them to Kingsley, who put all ten of them into his shirt pocket. He had just put them away when he heard a loud, accusing voice from just inside the door of the saloon.

"Mister, what was you doin' lookin' at them horses so close?" The questioner's voice sounded a little like a locomotive letting off steam. Turning toward the front door, Kingsley saw a big man, easily six feet four inches tall, staring at him. The man was also wearing a badge.

At first the badge startled him, then he realized that if the lawman knew who he was, he would have called him by name. Instead, he was only questioning Kingsley's interest in the horses.

"I'm a man that appreciates horses," Kingsley said. "I was just lookin' at them."

"You walked into town, didn't you?" The man had a mustache that curved up at each end, like the horns on a Texas steer. He was wearing a long-barreled Colt sheathed in a holster that was tied halfway down his leg. He had an angry, evil countenance, and looking directly at him was like staring into the eyes of an angry bull.

"Suppose I did?"

"It just makes me wonder, is all," the lawman said. "I mean, you havin' such an appreciation for horse flesh."

"My horse stepped into a hole just outside of town. He broke his leg and I had to shoot him."

"Why didn't you bring your saddle into town?"

"It's ten, maybe twelve miles out of town. Too far to be carryin' a saddle."

"Well, I'm a generous man," the lawman said. "Why don't I hitch up a buckboard, and we'll just go out there and get your saddle?"

Kingsley thought of the three men he had just killed, lying out there by his dead horse. At least one of them, he knew, was wearing a deputy's badge. It wouldn't be good for this lawman to see that.

"No need," Kingsley said. "I'm pretty tired from the walk. I plan to just leave it out there for now. Thought I might go back after it tomorrow."

"That ain't no problem, Mister. You don't have to go. I'll go get it for you."

"No, you don't have to do that."

There were only six others in the saloon, and that was counting the bartender. By now all conversation had stopped as the six men watched the interplay between Deputy Mosley and the stranger who had just come into town.

"Mister, seems to me like Deputy Mosley is offerin' to do you a big favor, ridin' out there to get your saddle for you. What you got against that?"

"I'll tell you what he has against it," Mosley said. "He don't want me goin' out there 'cause he knows there ain't no saddle out there. There ain't no saddle at all." He looked directly at Kingsley. "He don't have a horse, he never did have a horse, and he come into town with no other purpose than to steal one. Now, that's the truth of it, ain't it Mister?"

Kingsley didn't answer.

"Ain't you got nothin' to say?" Mosley asked.

"Seems to me like you're the one doin' all the talkin'," Kingsley replied. "Go on, if you think you got it all figured out."

"I got it all figured out, all right. By the way you was lookin' over them horses out front, I know you was plannin' to. Which one was you goin' to take? Calhoun's horse? I seen the way you was a' lookin' at him."

"My horse?" one of the men in the saloon said. "You son of a bitch! You was plannin' on stealin' my horse?"

"I ain't stole no horse," Kingsley insisted.

"Tell you what. Why don't I just put you in jail? Then when the judge gets here next month, you can tell him that you wasn't plannin' on stealin' a horse," Deputy Mosley said.

"You ain't puttin' me in no jail."

Kingsley started for his gun and, seeing him, Deputy Mosley made his own move. The lawman was exceptionally quick for his size, and his hand moved toward the long-barreled Colt as quickly as a striking rattlesnake.

Kingsley was almost caught by surprise. He hadn't expected the deputy to be that fast. But as it turned out, the deputy wasn't fast enough. Kingsley's draw was smooth, and his practiced thumb came back on the hammer in one fluid motion. His finger put the slightest pressure on the hair trigger of his Colt. There was a blossom of white, followed by a booming thunderclap as the gun jumped in his hand. The deputy tried to continue his draw, but the .44 slug caught him in the heart. When the bullet came out through his back, it brought half the deputy's shoulder blade with it, leaving an exit wound the size of a twenty-dollar gold piece.

"Son of a bitch! This feller just kilt Deputy Mosley!" Calhoun said.

Out of the corner of his eye, Kingsley saw the bartender reaching under the bar. Knowing that many bartenders kept shotguns under their bars, Kingsley swung his gun around and fired a second time. The bartender, with the unfired shotgun in his hand, fell back against the liquor shelf, bringing it down and causing a dozen or more bottles to come crashing to the floor.

Kingsley turned his gun toward the others in the saloon, but, with their hands up, they backed away.

"Don't shoot, Mister!" Calhoun shouted. "We ain't a' plannin' on stoppin' you."

Kingsley glared at them, then turned and ran out the front door. Mounting the horse the deputy had identified as Calhoun's, he turned his pistol on the other two and shot them down, to slow down any immediate pursuit.

   As Kingsley galloped out of town, he left heading west. But once out of town, he made a wide turn, then circled back to the east and south, pausing just long enough to light up a cigar. If a posse came after him, they would be looking for him in west Kansas, but he was planning to go to Missouri. He hadn't been in Missouri since the war, and as far as he knew, nobody was looking for him there.

Chapter Six

Cheyenne

The Cheyenne Club on the corner of Seventeenth Street and Warren Avenue was established in 1880 by twelve Wyoming cattlemen. Equipped with two wine cellars, double parlors, a dining room, library, smoking room, and billiard room, it was "the" place to be for cattlemen from all over Wyoming. At the moment, Duff was in one of the club's parlors, enjoying his cigar and a Scotch as he engaged in convivial conversation with some of the other cattlemen.

While in Cheyenne, Duff always stayed at the Inter Ocean Hotel which was advertised, with some justification, as the finest hotel between Chicago and San Francisco. Built by Barney Ford, a black man and former slave, the hotel had hosted such notables as President Grant and General Sherman, and writers Charles Dickens and Samuel Clemens, as well as actors Edwin Booth, Sara Bernhardt, and Andrew and Rosanna MacCallister. The latter two happened to be Duff's cousins.

"How is your cattle ranch coming along, Duff?" W.C. Irvine asked. Irvine, who was one of the top cattlemen in Wyoming, was with the group of cattlemen enjoying their evening at the club.

"I've grass and water," Duff replied. "Aye, and there is shelter from the winter's blow. I have everything on my cattle ranch that you might want, except for one thing."

"And what would that be?" one of the other ranchers asked.

"I don't have cattle."

All the others in the parlor laughed.

"Ah, but 'tis a small oversight," Duff assured them.

"You think no cattle on a cattle ranch is a small oversight?" Irvine asked. "So tell me, Duff, would no apples in an apple pie be but a bit of an oversight as well?"

"It is a condition soon to be remedied," Duff said. "I intend to purchase cattle from the Kansas City Cattle Exchange."

"Duff, why would you buy stock from the Kansas City Cattle Exchange when you can buy all the cattle you might need, right here in Wyoming to start your ranch?" Francis Warren asked. Like Irvine, Warren was one of the leading cattlemen in the territory.

"Yeah," Joe Carey said. "Isn't that a bit like carrying coal to Newcastle?"

"*Och* . . . Newcastle is in England," Duff replied. "What care I about Newcastle?"

The cattlemen laughed at Duff's response.

"But, to answer the question you have posed.

Kansas City is the only place I can buy a certain breed of cattle, a breed that does not now exist in Wyoming, but one which I shall introduce."

"If you're talking about Herefords, I'm running them on my own ranch," Converse said.

"So am I, along with the Longhorns," Irvine said.

"No, I'm talking about Angus. Black Angus. Developed in Scotland, they were, and an animal far superior to that English breed, Herefords."

"Black Angus? Black cows? You're going to fill the range with black cows?"

"Aye."

"And they are all black, you say?" Converse asked.

"Aye, black as a raven's wing, and shining in the sunlight. Beautiful animals, they are. I had them on m' place in Scotland."

"You make 'em sound so pretty you may have to keep a look out for bull buffalo," Warren said. "A big buff might come along and make a cuckold of your seed bulls."

The cattlemen laughed again.

"When are you going to Kansas City?" Converse asked.

"'Tis not my plan to go to Kansas City. 'Tis my plan to have them put the cattle on the cars and ship them here to Cheyenne. Then I will drive them up to my ranch."

"Well, I wish you good luck with it," Irvine said. "Wyoming is a big and empty territory. I expect there's room here for about ever' breed of cow there is. And the more the merrier, I say."

"How many head you plannin' on buyin'?" Converse asked.

"Five hundred head, I think."

Warren whistled. "Five hundred? Damn, you're getting a running start, aren't you?"

"Aye, with this many I expect that within five years, I'll have five thousand head."

"That's going to cost you a ton of money to get started," Warren said. "If you need to borrow some, and are willing to take a note on your property, I'd be happy to make you a loan."

"'Tis grateful I am for the offer, Francis, but I'll be all right."

If the ranch had not made Duff any money yet, his gold mine had, though he had never shared with any of these men the secret of the mine. He knew that the other ranchers had speculated that he may have come from a wealthy family in Scotland, and though it was not true, Duff did nothing to dissuade them from that belief. The fewer people who knew about the mine, the better off he would be.

At that moment, one of the employees of the club came into the parlor. "Gentlemen," he said. "Dinner is being served."

As Duff went in for dinner at the Cheyenne Club, a few blocks away in the Eagle Saloon on Fifteenth Street, Tyler Camden was playing a game of Ole' Sol. Actually, he would have preferred to be playing a game of poker, but no one would play with him, for he was known to have a vicious temper. Last year, he'd killed a man in a poker game after the man accused him of cheating. Of course he had been cheating, but he couldn't let the accusation go unchallenged. Quicker than anyone could react, Camden had reached across the table, grabbed the man by his shirt front, lifted him up, and plunged his knife in through the man's ribs. Quick and silent. The man was dead before most of the people in the saloon even knew what had happened.

The man Camden had killed had made the mistake of saying, "Where I come from, cheaters get shot."

Others at the table had heard him say that, and while that wasn't a direct threat, the quickly assembled court had declared it sufficient justification for a case to be made of self-defense.

There was a very strong rumor that Camden had also stabbed a man down in Colorado last year, and though neither of the two men he had killed were known to be gunfighters, they were, nevertheless, victims, and that was enough give Camden the reputation of someone to be feared.

Camden counted out three cards, but couldn't find a play. The second card of the three was a red nine. There was a black ten on one of the stacks where he could have used the red nine, but the nine was one card down, and thus, useless to him.

Or was it?

With a shrug of his shoulders, Camden slipped the red nine out from under the black queen, and played it on the black ten.

Dingus Camden and Lee and Marvin Mosley

came into the saloon then, and seeing his brother playing solitaire, Dingus walked over to him.

"Me and Lee and Marvin is goin' to take the cars over to Laramie," Dingus said. "They got some new sportin' girls in at the Rocky Mountain House. You want to come along?"

"Nah," Tyler said. "I reckon I'll spend a little time with Libbie."

"She done told you she didn't want nothin' to do with you," Dingus said. "Why don't you come along with us?"

"She'll come around," Tyler said.

"All right, but you're goin' to be missin' out on a good time," Dingus said. "All right, boys," he said to his two cousins. "The next local is no more'n half an hour from now. Let's go."

Tyler watched them leave, then thought about Libbie. He had seen her go upstairs with a cowboy about half an hour earlier and had tried to get her attention, but she wouldn't look at him. He wasn't worried, though. Once she was through with the cowboy, she'd have to come to him. He had already intimidated everyone else into staying away from her, so if she wanted to make a living with her whoring, she would have no choice but to accept him.

And it was damn well going to be on his own terms, too. He would see to that.

Examining the cards he had spread out on the table, he found a needed black five. It didn't matter where it was, it was where he was about to put it that counted.

Camden had just played his card when he heard laughter at the top of the stairs. Looking up, he saw

Libbie coming down the stairs, arm-in-arm with the cowboy who had taken her up.

"I tell you what, darlin', that was just a real fine time me 'n you just had," the cowboy was saying as they came down the stairs side by side. "Damn me if I don't believe that the next time I have me enough money, why, I'll just be comin' back to see you again."

"Anytime, cowboy," Libbie said.

Camden waited until the cowboy left, then he walked over to Libbie.

"Let's me 'n you go upstairs now," he said.

"I told you, I ain't goin' with you no more," Libbie replied.

"What do you mean, you ain't goin' with me no more? I got the money. I got the money right here."

Camden stuck his hand down in his pocket and pulled out a fistful of dollars. "See? This here is more than enough for you to go upstairs with me."

"I don't want nothin' to do with you anymore, Camden. And neither do any of the other girls who work here. You get drunk and you hit us. We ain't gettin' paid to be beat on."

"Yeah, well, I ain't drunk now," Camden said. "I'm sober as a judge."

"I told you, I ain't goin' upstairs with you, and that's that."

"All right, fine. Try and make it without me," Camden said. "Because here's the truth: 'ceptin' for that cowboy that just left, there ain't nobody else goin' to touch you with a ten-foot pole. And while you're wastin' away to nothin' over here, I'll be takin' my business to the Tivoli."

"Ha! The Tivoli?" Libbie said. "Lots of luck with that. There won't be a woman over there who will have anything to do with you," Libbie insisted.

After dinner was served at the Cheyenne Club, most of the members returned to the parlor for conversation or cards or billiards, but Duff decided he would visit the Tivoli Saloon. He did this not only because it reminded him of the White Horse Pub back in Donuun, but also because he enjoyed being among a more diverse group of people than could be found at the Cheyenne Club.

There were several saloons in Cheyenne, from the Eagle Saloon, which was in a part of town frequented by rough men and soiled doves, to the Tivoli, which was an exceptionally nice establishment. The Tivoli featured an elaborate wood backbar, a shining brass footrail, and customers' towels hanging from bass rings on the front of the bar. The towels were kept fresh by frequent changing. The saloon also had electric lighting, a feature not enjoyed by some of the more pedestrian saloons.

Upstairs in the Tivoli, there were several rooms called "visiting parlors." In these rooms, gentlemen could enjoy a conversation with some of the women who worked at the Tivoli, as long as they understood that it was conversation only. A printed sign on the wall of each of the visiting parlors laid that out.

> *We select our young women*
> *from the best backgrounds.*
>
> *They are attractive, intelligent,*
> *and well versed in enough subjects*
> *to provide stimulating*
> *conversation with our guests.*
>
> ☞ *There is a three drink minimum*
> <u>*required*</u>
> *to use one of these rooms.*
>
> *Please act as* GENTLEMEN,
> *and respect the* LADIES,
> *who are here to make your visit*
> *with us more pleasurable.*

Tyler Camden, having made good on his promise to come over to the Tivoli was, at the moment, in one of the visiting parlors. He had already exceeded his three-drink minimum, and things were not going well for him. He was with two girls, Cindy McPheeters and Polly Fenton, but it seemed that the only thing they wanted to do was talk. Finally, he decided to take matters into his own hands.

"Look here, ain't there some rooms up here where we can go?" Camden asked.

Cindy laughed. "What do you mean, are there any rooms up here? You are in a room up here, silly."

"Nah, I ain't a' talkin' about that. What I'm a' talkin' about is a room with a bed, so me 'n one of you," he smiled at both of them, displaying a mouth full of yellowed and broken teeth, "could go split the sheets. An' I don't care which one 'tis, 'cause either one is fine by me."

Polly and Cindy looked confused.

"Mr. Camden, is it possible that you don't understand?" Polly asked.

"Don't understand what?"

"We don't do that."

"What do you mean you don't do that? That's what all whores do, ain't it?"

"We wouldn't know about that," Cindy said. "We aren't whores."

"What do you mean, you ain't whores? What the hell are you doin' up here, if you ain't a whore?"

"Didn't you read the sign on the wall?" Polly asked, pointing to the sign.

"No, I didn't read no sign, on account of I cain't read. What does it say?"

"It says we are here for conversation only."

"Look here, I done spent me three dollars since I come up here."

"Yes, you have. You spent it on drinks for you and for us."

"Well, what the hell? You say I've spent it on drinks for you two, why would I do that iffen I wasn't plannin' on gettin' somethin' out of it?"

"You have gotten something out of it," Cindy said. "You've had our company and our conversation."

"That ain't enough. One of you get out of here. The other'n stay. If you ain't got no place else to go, we'll just do it here."

"We will both leave," Cindy said.

As the two women started to leave, Camden

reached out and grabbed the nearest one, who happened to be Cindy, by her arm.

"You ain't leavin,' bitch, 'til I tell you you can leave!" he said angrily.

Reacting quickly, Cindy used her free hand to rake her fingernails across his cheek, leaving four deep and bleeding scratchmarks.

"Damn you!" Camden shouted. Pulling his knife from its sheath, Camden made a quick, totally unexpected slash, cutting open Cindy's throat.

With her eyes opened wide in shock and the realization of what had just happened, Cindy put her hands to her throat. Polly watched in horror as blood gushed through Cindy's fingers. Cindy's eyes rolled up in her head, and she fell.

Polly screamed.

Chapter Seven

Duff had been at the saloon for about half an hour, during which time he was nursing a single beer and visiting with some of the other customers. He drank only one beer, not because he was cheap, but because he didn't want to get drunk. He was about to leave when a woman's scream brought all conversation to a halt. A moment later, Duff and all the other patrons of the saloon looked up and saw a woman appear at the railing on the balcony that overlooked the grand floor. There was a man behind her, and he was holding a knife to the woman's neck.

All conversation stopped as everyone in the room stared up at the man and woman who were standing at the railing.

"Polly, what is it? What's going on?" the bartender shouted.

"Please help me," Polly said, her voice quivering in fear. "I'm so scared."

"Who is that with her?" someone asked.

"I know him," another said. "His name is Camden."

"Polly, where is Cindy?" the bartender asked.

"She—she's dead! He just killed Cindy. He cut her throat."

"Is that true, Mister? Camden, is it? Did you kill Cindy?" the bartender asked.

"Yeah, the name is Camden. And yeah, I killed the other woman."

"What did you go and do that for?" one of the saloon customers asked.

"I killed her 'cause I wanted to. And I'm goin' to kill this one, too, unless all of you empty your pockets and put your money there in the piano player's hat. Piano player, once they do that, you bring it on up to me."

"I'll just take my tips out first," the piano player replied.

"Huh-uh," Camden said. "Them tips you got in your hat will be your contribution."

One of the men near the front of the saloon started toward the door.

"Hold it right there, Mister!" Camden yelled. "Unless you want to see me cut this woman now."

"Stay there, Ed. I think he means it," the bartender said.

"You damn right, I mean it. Now, all of you, do like I said," the man shouted down to the others. "If I don't see some money goin' into that hat right now, I'm goin' to start cuttin'!"

Slowly and deliberately, Duff drew his pistol and pointed it up toward the man who was holding the knife.

"Mr. Camden," Duff called. He voice was neither

loud nor nervous. On the contrary, it was as calm as if he were inquiring about the time. "I'll be for asking you now to let the woman go," he said. Though his voice was quiet, it was possessed of a deep resonance that made it easily heard and understood. Somehow, the others in the room sensed the danger in this man.

"What's the matter with you?" Camden asked. "Are you crazy, Mister? Ain't you got eyes? Can't you see that I am holding a knife to this woman's throat?"

"Aye, I can see that. But if you will lower your knife and let her go, I'll let you live," Duff said as calmly as before. "If you do not lower your knife, I am afraid I shall be forced to kill you."

"You're goin' to shoot me from down there? Hell, if you was to try, you'd more'n likely hit the woman." Camden chuckled, an evil-sounding cackle. "Truth is, they ain't nothin' none of you can do."

"I'll not be for asking you again."

"No? Well, that's good. Now, put down the pistol or I'll . . ."

Nobody had any idea what the rest of Camden's sentence would have been, because that was as far as he got. Duff squeezed the trigger right in the middle of the man's bluff and bluster.

The pistol roared in Duff's hand, and the woman screamed as blood spewed onto her face.

"You son of a bitch! What did you do that for? You shot her!" someone shouted angrily.

"No, I did not hit her," Duff answered calmly. He slipped his smoking revolver back into his holster. It was only now that the others noticed that the man who had been holding the knife was no longer behind the girl, but was lying on his back.

"Look at that! Camden's lyin' on his back!"

"Polly! Are you all right?" the bartender shouted.

"I . . ." Polly started. She felt around on herself, then, realizing she was unharmed, let out a little cry of relief. "Yes, I'm fine!" She ran her hand across her face, then pulled it down and looked at the blood on it. "Ohh," she said. "His blood! I've got his blood on me! I've got to get it off, I've got to get it off!"

Turning, she ran back down the hall of the upper balcony so that she could no longer be seen by those below. Several of the saloon customers hurried up the steps then to examine the man who had been holding the knife. Duff didn't watch them. Instead, he turned back to the bar and continued to drink his beer. One of those who had gone upstairs stepped over to the railing to call down to the others.

"He's dead! He's shot clean through his right eye!"

"Damn! How long of a shot was that?" someone asked. Immediately, the saloon was a bedlam with everyone talking at once. Ironically, there were as many condemning Duff as there were those congratulating him.

"Mister, that was a hell of a chance you took with Polly's life," someone said. "Don't you know you could have hit her?"

"Yeah, did you even give it a second thought before you fired?" another asked.

"No, I dinnae need a second thought," Duff said. "If I dinnae think I could hit him without hitting her, I would not have fired."

"Wait a minute. Are you telling me that standing here, shooting up like you done, with a target no bigger'n a man's hand and it bein' better 'n a hundred feet away, that you knew you would hit him, and not her?"

"Aye."

"Mister, you are lying. You took a dumb chance, and you know it."

Duff's eyes narrowed. "I do not think I like it being said that Duff Tavish MacCallister tells lies."

"Duff MacCallister?" One of the others said. "Wait a minute. Are you Duff MacCallister?"

"Aye."

"Conley, if I was you, I wouldn't be calling Mr. MacCallister a liar," the man said.

"Oh, yeah? Well now, suppose you tell me why not."

"Because in the first place, when you think about it, Mr. MacCallister isn't just runnin' a bluff here. He said he thought he could hit that feller without bringin' any more harm to Polly, and that's just exactly what he did."

"That's pure, dumb luck, Stewart, and you know it," Conley said.

"And in the second place, this is the same Duff MacCallister who cleaned house up in Chugwater 'bout this time last year," Stewart said. "Mr. MacCallister went up against eight outlaws who were holding the town hostage, and he killed every one of them. No sir, I expect he is a man who is good for what he says."

"'Tis thanking you I am for the vote of confidence, Mr. Stewart. But with a foine Scottish name like you have, 'tis no surprise that you be a man of integrity," Duff said.

It had been over a year since Duff MacCallister had left Scotland, but even now, when he spoke, he sounded as if he had just walked in off the moors.

"No, Mr. MacCallister, it's you that deserves thanks, not just from me, but from all of us," Stewart said. "You killed a monster. And there is no doubt in my mind that he was prepared to, and probably would have, killed Polly."

"Aye," Duff said. "From the moment he held the knife to the lass's neck, she was all but dead. He could not let her go before he left the pub, or he would have been fair game for any of us. And 'tis not likely that he would keep her with him while he was running from the law, so I'm thinking the only thing he could possibly do is kill her once he got out of our sight. I did the only thing that could be done for savin' the poor lass."

"Here, here!" the bartender shouted. "Drinks are on the house!"

A few minutes later a couple of Cheyenne's finest, two police officers in uniform, complete with badges and high-domed hats, came into the Tivoli.

"You fellas are too late; it has already been taken care of," Stewart said.

After that, everyone started talking at once until, finally, the police officers were able to restore enough calm to get the story straight.

What happened was made evident soon enough, and the police left without so much as issuing a warrant or citation.

"But I wouldn't be so quick to use that pistol if I were you," one of the policemen said before leaving. "You were lucky this time."

"Thank you, Constable. I'll consider that," Duff said, not wanting to argue.

When Nathan Baker, the editor of the *Cheyenne Leader*, heard about the shooting in the Tivoli, he delayed putting out the paper until he could write the story himself. There were frequent shootings in Cheyenne, and though the newspaper reported all of them, no shooting prior to this one had justified holding up a printing. This story was special because, while shootings were relatively common in the Eagle and other saloons of similar ilk, the Tivoli was rarely involved in such a thing.

The other reason the story was worth delaying the print run was the skill it took to make the shot. This was the kind of shot that people would be talking about for some time.

Baker set the last letter of type, then made a quick read for his final edit. The fact that the letters were backward, and the sentences and paragraphs also ran backward, caused no impediment, for he had worked with the reverse settings needed for printing for many years. He could read the copy backward as quickly and with as much comprehension as the average person could when reading it forward.

He made a quick check of all the pages, making

certain that he had every ad in its proper place: Coleman's Drugstore, Dace Leather Goods, Union Mercantile. People read the newspaper for the news, but it was the advertisers who paid the bill.

The editor put the first form in, adjusted the platen, applied the ink, and made the first impression. He held the page up for perusal, smiling in satisfaction at the way the lead story dominated the page.

Magnificent Shot
Fired From Thirty Yards

THE BALL HAD DEADLY EFFECT.

Tyler Camden, a man of known disreputable character, met his end last night in a most memorable way. A habitué of the soiled doves, Camden was known to ply the saloons and cheap hotels of Fifteenth Street. Last night he came instead to an area of town that was far above his poor station, and while there attempted to practice his debauchery with one of the young serving women he encountered. To his dissatisfaction, he learned that the ladies who are employed by the Tivoli are not of the same low character as the denizens of his normal haunts. When his advances and entreaties were denied, Camden became angry and murdered Cindy McPheeters, a young lady hired for serving and genteel conversation only. He then stepped to the head of the balcony with Polly Fenton as his hostage, holding a knife to her neck.

Camden demanded as payment for her safe release the contribution of money from everyone in the saloon, said donations to be deposited in the hat of the piano player. However, Camden did not consider the presence of one Duff MacCallister, a resident of Chugwater who is visiting our fair city. Mr. MacCallister, from a distance of over one hundred feet, didst raise his revolver and fire, the ball entirely sparing Miss Fenton, while striking Camden with deadly effect. Many witnesses who have observed skillful shooting before have stated that never had they seen so skillful a demonstration of marksmanship as that displayed by Duff MacCallister in his heroic rescue of Miss Polly Fenton.

The current hot spell not being conducive to a prolonged delay of interment, Miss McPheeters's funeral will be conducted at St. Mark's Episcopal Church on Nineteenth and Central at three o'clock tomorrow afternoon. It is expected that much of the city will attend.

Laramie

Dingus Camden and Lee and Marvin Mosley were downstairs in the Rocky Mountain House after having enjoyed some time with some of the establishment's "companions for gentlemen," as the house described them.

"Say, Dingus, why do you think Tyler didn't want to come with us?" Lee asked.

"Why you askin' me?" Dingus asked.

"I'm askin' you, 'cause you're his brother. Me an' Marvin ain't nothin' but his cousins."

"Well, you know him as well as I do. I don't know why he didn't want to come with us."

"I know why," Marvin said.

"Why?"

"He didn't want to come with us 'cause he's stuck on that whore back at the Eagle. What's her name?"

"Libbie," Lee said.

"He ought to know better 'n to get stuck on a whore," Marvin said. "All whores is the same."

"No, they ain't," Dingus said.

"What do you mean, they ain't the same?"

"Some whores is better'n others. When we get there, I think I'll get me a little black-eyed Mexican girl. I like them the best."

"Not me, I like my whores to be American," Marvin said.

"With big tits," Lee added. "Besides, there ain't no difference between a Mexican whore and a Injun whore."

"Yeah," Dingus said. "Sometimes it is hard to tell the difference. I got me a woman one time back in Arizona Territory . . . thought she was Mexican but she turned out to be Injun. You ever had a Mexican whore?"

"Nope, never had one. Had me a Injun once, though," Lee answered.

"Really?" Marvin said. "I never knew you had you no Injun woman."

"You don't know ever'thing I've ever done," Lee replied.

"Well, how was she?"

"What do you mean how was she? She was Injun," Lee replied, as if that explained what he'd said without elaboration. "Why don't you ask Dingus how his Injun woman was?"

"She pissed me off. She told me she was Mexican, but I knew better. That's why I kilt her."

"Ahh, you're lyin'. You didn't kill her."

"Yeah, I did. And I can prove it."

"How you goin' to prove it?"

"I've got her tit," Dingus said.

"You've got her tit?" Lee asked. "I don't believe it."

"You don't believe it, huh? What do you think this is?"

Dingus reached down into his pocket and pulled out a dry, leathery-looking bag and handed it over to Lee.

Lee took it, thinking at first it was simply a rawhide bag. But then he saw a spongy little nub and realized that he was looking at a nipple. This really was a woman's breast.

"I'll be damn! Look at this, Marvin," Lee said, handing it to his brother. "It really is a tit!"

"I told you it was."

"What are you goin' to do with it?" Marvin asked, as he examined it more closely.

"I don't know. I was goin' to make a tobacco pouch, but I don't think I'm goin' to."

"Would you sell it?"

"I reckon I would. What will you give me for it?"

"Two dollars?"

"Yeah, all right, give me two dollars and it's yours."

One of the girls came over toward the table, carrying a newspaper. "Honey," she said to Dingus. "Don't you have a brother named Tyler?"

"Yeah, why?"

"You might want to read this," she said, handing the paper to him.

The headlines jumped out at him.

Magnificent Shot Fired From Thirty Yards

THE BALL HAD DEADLY EFFECT.

"Son of a bitch!" Dingus said.

"What is it?"

"We have to go back to Cheyenne."

Chapter Eight

Back in Cheyenne, Duff continued to take care of his business. He went into Union Mercantile, where he bought a hay mower.

"Yes, sir, Mr. MacCallister, you are buying the finest hay mower on the market," Elliot Whipple said. "This one machine, pulled by a team of horses, can do more in one day than a whole field full of farmhands can do in a week."

"I will need to have it transported to Chugwater," Duff said. "Can you disassemble it for me?"

"I can disassemble it, and have it shipped for you. I have an arrangement with Rollins Freight."

"Thank you, but I will make shipping arrangements from Chugwater."

"Very well. I will see that it is ready for shipment," Whipple promised.

Duff's very good friend, R.W. Guthrie, owned not only the lumberyard and building supply company in Chugwater, he also owned the town's only freight-wagon company. But it wasn't only because R.W. was

Duff's friend that he wanted to use him. Duff believed that because he lived in Chugwater it was incumbent upon him to patronize the Chugwater business establishments, and he did that whenever it was possible.

After buying the hay mower, Duff visited the Cheyenne office of the Kansas City Cattle Exchange, where he intended to make arrangements to buy a herd.

"Well, I don't know," Terry Conn said. "Most of the business I do is with the local cattlemen, arranging to buy their herds. I've not had to deal with selling cattle before."

"But your company does this, do they not?" Duff asked. "I was informed by the American Aberdeen Angus Association in Chicago that I could make arrangements to purchase a herd of Angus cattle through the Kansas City Cattle Exchange company."

"Oh, yes, we can do that. It is just , as I say, a little unusual. Though, as you want a specific breed, I suppose it isn't all that unusual. Black Angus, you say? Well, I know they are doing well back in Missouri and down in Mississippi. I think you would be the first to run them out here. They aren't as hardy as Longhorns, you know. Could be you are biting off more'n you can chew."

"Aye, they can be a bit troublesome, 'tis true, but this won't be the first time I've raised the breed."

"You've raised Angus before?"

"Aye. I did so back in Scotland."

Conn smiled. "Scotland, is it? Well, I'm not all that surprised. I thought you sounded like a foreigner. All right, how many do you want?"

"I'd like five hundred head: four hundred and eighty cows and twenty bulls."

"That's quite an order. Let me see what that would cost," Conn said. He walked over to the ticker-tape machine, a glass half-globe that enclosed the device itself. It made a constant clicking sound, all the while spitting out a long, narrow strip of paper. Conn picked up the paper and ran it through his hands as he looked at the symbols printed thereon.

"Ah, here it is," he said. "The latest price is twenty-seven dollars and fifty cents a head for mature cattle. You want five hundred head. Let's see, that would be . . ." he paused for a moment as he figured the cost, "thirteen thousand seven hundred and fifty dollars. Then, of course, there is the fifteen percent handling and service fee." Conn put a pencil to paper and did some figuring. "That will bring it to fifteen thousand, eight hundred twelve dollars and fifty cents. I'd advise you to make arrangements with your own bank for the loan, as the Cattle Exchange cannot extend credit."

"Aye, so I have been told," Duff replied.

"Now, what do you say we get your order written up?" Conn said. He sat at his desk and took out a pre-printed form. "And what is your name, sir?"

"MacCallister. Duff MacCallister."

"MacCallister? Of course, I read about you in the

Cheyenne Leader this morning. You are the one they were writing about, are you not?" Conn asked.

"Aye, 'tis me. I had no idea 'twould be the stuff of newspapers."

Conn chuckled. "The stuff of newspapers? My good man, it is stories like this that become the stuff of legends."

"I've no wish to be a legend, I wish only to be a rancher."

"Well, with this," Conn held up the order document, "it would seem you have made a favorable start."

"Aye," Duff said. "Would that my trip had been only to tend to business for my ranch, and none of the other."

"It is obvious that you saved the young lady's life by what you did, Mr. MacCallister. There is no need for you to feel remorse over it."

"It had to be done, that is true."

"The young woman who was killed . . . will you be going to her funeral?" Conn asked.

"I have been asked to do so by her friends at the Tivoli," Duff said. "I feel that I must."

"From what I've been hearing, the whole town will be turning out for it," Conn said. "It is to be held in St. Mark's Episcopal Church. That's a large enough church, but I don't know if it has enough room for all who wish to attend. You'll need to get there early if you want a place to sit."

Saloons, cheap hotels, and restaurants lined Fifteenth Street along the two blocks west of the Union

Pacific Depot. It was not an area that genteel women frequented, though there was no shortage of women for the soiled doves did business in the saloons, hotels, and even in small cribs that they maintained in the alley behind the buildings.

Between the Western Hotel and Lambert's Café was a whitewashed building with a high false front. The name of the establishment, painted in large black letters, was Eagle Saloon. Unlike the Tivoli, which had a fine mahogany bar and gleaming electric chandeliers, the Eagle was illuminated by kerosene lanterns and candles.

Dingus, Lee and Marvin, having returned from Laramie on the next train, were now in the Eagle, sitting at a table near the back, close to one of the two coal stoves that heated the building from early October to late May. Although the stove was cold, the smell of coal still hung around it, and the floor immediately around the stove was stained black with ground-in coal dust.

"He should'a gone with us when we asked him," Dingus said. "If he had gone with us, he'd still be alive now."

"When are you buryin' 'im?" Lee Mosley asked.

"I talked to the undertaker this mornin'. I told him to go ahead and bury Tyler today. May as well get it over with, ain't much sense in letting him just lie around 'til he starts stinkin'."

"Ain't you goin' to have no funeral or anythin' for him?" Marvin asked.

"Nah, Tyler prob'ly wouldn't want nothin' like that, anyway. Beside which, I don't know nobody that would come 'cept me an' you two."

"They're goin' to have a big funeral for the whore that Tyler kilt," Lee said. "I seen it in the paper. The whole town is goin' to turn out."

"Don't seem right that ever'body's goin' to be cryin' and blowin' snot over the whore, when there ain't goin' to be nothin' done to remember Tyler," Marvin said.

"Oh, there will be somethin' done to remember him all right," Dingus said.

"What?"

"I aim to kill the son of a bitch that kilt Tyler."

"That ain't goin' to be all that easy to do," Lee cautioned. "They say he was more'n a hundred feet away when he shot Tyler. And what's more, Tyler was standin' behind a woman, so this fella MacCallister didn't have all that much to shoot at."

"I didn't say I was goin' to challenge him to a duel in the street or nothin' like that," Dingus said. "What I said was I aim to kill him."

As the three carried on their conversation, a small man dressed all in black came into the saloon. He approached the table, then halted a few feet away and cleared his throat to get their attention.

Looking up, Dingus saw the undertaker.

"Yeah, Welch, what do you want?"

"If it is all the same to you, Mr. Camden, I mean, seeing as you said that you don't want a funeral or anything, I wonder if we could go ahead and bury your brother's remains now. I think it would be best if we got everything taken care of before Cindy McPheeters's funeral. I expect a rather substantial crowd of mourners for her, whereas your brother's interment will be, uh, rather simple."

"Yeah, go ahead and do it, I don't care," Dingus said dismissively.

Dingus Camden and his two cousins were the only ones in the graveyard as the two gravediggers, using ropes, lowered Tyler Camden's body into the hole. One of them looked over at Dingus.

"Do you want to say a few words?"

"Nah," Dingus said. "Cover 'im up."

The two gravediggers started shoveling the dirt in, and as Dingus, Lee, and Marvin left Lakeview Cemetery, they could hear the sound of the dirt falling on the wooden coffin behind them.

There could not be a bigger contrast between Tyler Camden's burial and the funeral that was going on for Cindy McPheeters. St. Mark's Episcopal Church was filled to capacity, and those who could not find seats stood along the walls on each side and at the rear of the church. Even the narthex was filled, and several more waited out front, ready to accompany the funeral cortege to the graveyard.

Duff, perhaps thinking of the way his fiancé was killed, attended the funeral and, as a guest of the owner and employees of the Tivoli, was afforded a seat up front. Cindy's coffin sat on a catafalque in the transept, covered with a black pall that had a white cross worked into it. When the music stopped, the priest stepped up to the pulpit and looked out over the congregation, and began to speak. His voice was richly timbred, and it resonated throughout the room. Every eye was turned toward him, every ear attuned.

"We have come today to bury Cindy McPheeters. Cindy was employed by the Tivoli saloon in a position that some may find unseemly for a young woman. But who are we to pass judgment upon her?

"Regardless of how Cindy made a living, I want all of you to know that she was not abandoned by our Lord. And those who knew Cindy have all testified that she was a woman with a good heart, truly a child of God. Therefore, we can rejoice with Cindy, because we know that our sister is in Heaven today."

It had started raining during the service, a torrential downpour that drummed on the roof and beat against the windows of the church. Two of the vestrymen, who had gone about earlier using long, hooked poles to pull the tops of the windows down to provide a breeze, now used those same long poles as they hurried to close the windows. That did keep the rain from coming in but it made the inside of the church grow hotter and muggier. Those who had been waiting outside the church with the intention of accompanying the funeral cortege to the cemetery left. The priest, trying to outlast the rain, dragged the service on as long as he could. But when some of the mourners got up and left the church, then more, and more still until the narthex and wall space, and even some of the pews were empty, he realized that he could not drag it out any further.

The hearse, polished black ebony with glass sides, was backed up against the front door of the church. The team of black horses stood stoically in the rain, their black feather accoutrements hanging down and dripping with water. The pallbearers carried Cindy's body through the nave and narthex, then slid it into the back of the hearse. By the time the cortege reached the cemetery, only the priest, Polly, the owner of the Tivoli, and Duff remained of the funeral attendees. The two gravediggers who had found a tree to provide them with some shelter from the downpour were present as well. The driver of the hearse waited until Cindy's coffin was offloaded, then he snapped his reins against the backs of the soaked team and drove away.

Because of the rain, the committal ceremony was brief. As soon as the graveside service was over, the priest nodded at the two gravediggers. They came over from their improvised shelter and lowered the coffin into the ground, then started closing the grave.

"It was good of you to come, Mr. MacCallister," Polly said. "There were so many in the church, but nobody wanted to come out into the rain."

"You might say that the spirit was willing but the flesh was weak," the priest said, as the four of them returned to the carriage that had brought them from the church to the cemetery.

Chugwater

Charles Blanton, editor and publisher of the *Chugwater Defender*, read the article about Duff's "magnificent shot" in the *Cheyenne Leader*. Using the article as his guide, but embellishing it with personal and local information about Duff MacCallister, he rewrote it, then ran it in his own newspaper.

It had long been Blanton's habit to go down to Fiddler's Green shortly after his paper had hit the streets. He justified it by saying he needed a break from putting the paper together, getting it to bed, and finally out on the street. But the truth was he liked to hear the feedback on his articles, and the customers who frequented Fiddler's Green were not shy about commenting on the articles, whether they approved or disapproved.

Today was no different. Everyone in the saloon had already read the paper by the time Blanton arrived, ordered his mug of beer, then walked over to the table to join them.

"That must have been some shot," Fred Matthews said. "Don't know as one out of a hundred could have made it."

"It doesn't surprise me, any," R.W. Guthrie said. "I've seen him shoot."

"Well, yeah, we all have," Biff Johnson said. "I mean that display he put on here, last year, when he killed the eight men who came here after him."

"He only killed seven as I recall," Guthrie said. "You got one of them, Biff."

"Yeah, but still, he got seven," Biff said. "I tell you the truth, I've never known anyone quite like him. He is as generous and good-natured as any man you might ever want to meet. And to meet him, why you might even think he was a Sunday school teacher or something. But you go afoul of him, and he is as deadly as any man alive."

"And here's the thing," Matthews said. "Once he makes up his mind that a body needs killin', it doesn't bother him a bit to go ahead and do it. He's got that—well, I don't know what you call it, but what I mean is, he can just put it out of his mind."

"It's called a detached attitude," Blanton said. "And yes, he has something that is rare in men, an ability to recognize right from wrong, make an immediate and resolute decision, then act upon it without agonizing reappraisal."

Guthrie laughed. "I'm not all that sure what you said, Charley. But damn if it didn't sound good."

The others laughed as well.

Over in her dress shop, Meghan had read the same article. She was not surprised by it; she had seen Duff in action on the day he faced down the eight men who had come to Chugwater specifically to kill him. She also knew him well enough to know that if he was ever placed in a position of having to choose to act to save an innocent life, such as he had been in Cheyenne, that he would make the decision he'd made.

Meghan had never known anyone quite like Duff MacCallister. She was attracted to him by his rugged good looks, yes. And there was a dangerous excitement about him, yes. But underneath all that was a gentleness that defied all understanding.

Chapter Nine

Missouri–Kansas Border

Crack Kingsley was born and raised in Clay County, Missouri, but when the war started, he had left Missouri and ridden as an irregular with Doc Jennison and his Kansas Jayhawkers.

The Jayhawkers told themselves that they were a military outfit, and they were organized as one, though none of them wore uniforms. And, since they were what Doc Jennison called a "supernumerary military unit," which he explained meant that they were not really a part of the Union army, they were responsible for supporting themselves. That was actually the part that Kingsley had enjoyed the most. They supported themselves by stealing from the Confederate sympathizers, whether they were banks, stores, or individuals.

It had meant nothing to Kingsley that the banks, stores, and individuals they stole from had been his own neighbors. Kingsley's mother had been abandoned by Kingsley's drunken father, and they had survived during Kingsley's formative years due to the kindness of their neighbors. Rather than endearing them to him, though, it had generated a sense of inferiority, jealousy and envy. Thus when the war started, he'd had no problem crossing over to the other side.

When Crack Kingsley crossed the border into Missouri today, he realized that this was the first time he had been back in the state since the war. Like the rest of Missouri, the citizens of Clay County had been divided in their loyalties, and as many of the men of the county had fought for the North as fought for the South. What upset the citizens of Clay County about Kingsley was that he had joined the Kansas irregulars.

And, he had raided and killed his neighbors.

Looking around him, he knew exactly where he was. This was the old Dumey place. The house had not changed. The huge, scarred oak tree was still there. So too was the meandering creek. He smiled as he recalled the raid, the first raid he had ever led.

Clay County, Missouri, 1862

The raid had started under Doc Jennison, but they ran into a unit of Confederate soldiers led by General Sterling Price. Badly outnumbered, they paid a high price and Jennison ordered his men to split up and make it back to Kansas on their own.

Because Kingsley was a native of the area and knew it well, seven men attached themselves to him when they separated. At first, Kingsley was irritated by it. Then he realized that they had not only attached themselves to him, they were following him, listening to his orders. That gave Kingsley an idea. He would conduct his own raids, but with only seven men attached, he would have to be careful in selecting his targets.

He didn't have to look far. As he and his men rode north away from Kansas City, they came across the Dumey farm. Kingsley knew the man others called "The Dutchman," and had a strong dislike for him. He had tried to come on to Alma, Dumey's daughter, but she was engaged to Elmer Gleason, one of the other young men of the county. Not willing to take no for an answer, he attempted to force himself upon her, and when she cried out in protest, her father heard her.

Although Chris Dumey was twice as old as Kingsley, he was a big man and incredibly strong. He beat Kingsley to within an inch of his life, then ordered him off his farm.

He had not come back until today, and now he was leading seven men.

"Boys, how would you like to have some roast pork, and maybe some fried chicken?" he asked the others.

"Where we goin' to get that?" one of his riders, a man named Byrd asked.

"Right here on Chris Dumey's farm."

"You know this farmer?" Byrd asked.

"Oh, yeah, I know him."

"That sounds good to me, too," one of the other men said.

"All right," Kingsley agreed. "Let's go get 'em."

"What if the farmer ain't willin' to sell 'em to us?"

"Who said anything about buyin' 'em?" Kingsley said. He slapped his legs against the side of his horse. "We're just goin' to take 'em."

Kingsley kept his eyes peeled as they rode down the small hill to the farmhouse, but he didn't see anyone. Dismounting just inside the gate he took another look around, but saw no one.

"All right, boys," he said with a casual wave of his hand. "Start gatherin' 'em in."

Three of the men started chasing down the chickens, while the other four started toward the pigpen. The chickens began cackling loudly.

"Who are you men? What's going on here?" a loud, stern voice called.

Looking toward the porch, Kingsley saw the man who had fired him two years earlier.

"Hello, Dumey," Kingsley said.

"Kingsley! What do you want here? I told you to never come to my farm again."

"I know what you told me, old man. But times have changed, and I'm givin' the orders now. We're goin' to take the loan of some of your chickens," Kingsley replied.

A pig let out a squeal, and Kingsley laughed.

"And your pigs," he added.

"The hell you will!" Dumey said. "Martha, bring me my shotgun!"

Kingsley drew his pistol and waited until the man's wife appeared on the porch, carrying a double-barreled shotgun. Then he shot them both.

"Mama!" a voice called from inside. Alma, a young woman of no more than eighteen or nineteen, came running through the back door. She knelt beside her slain parents. She looked up at Kingsley. "Crack! You would do such a thing?"

Byrd raised his pistol to shoot the girl.

"No!" Kingsley shouted.

"What do you mean, no?" Byrd asked. "What the hell, Kingsley, have you done gone soft on us?"

"Soft ain't exactly the word that comes to mind right now," Kingsley said as he reached down to rub himself.

When they rode away from the farm later that day, they were carrying with them twelve chickens, two live shoats, a sack of flour, and a sack of beans. Behind them lay the three members of the Dumey family: Chris and Martha dead, and Alma, who had been raped eight times, barely clinging to life.

Kingsley later learned that she had died, but not before telling her neighbor, Jesse James, who was responsible.

If it had been Sterling Price's men who had found Alma Dumey and her slain parents, there would have been a charge of murder and rape filed against him that would have resonated with the civil authorities despite the divided loyalties of the war. But it wasn't Price's troops; it was Jesse James and his band of guerrillas, and Jesse James had his own brand of justice in mind. Because of that, no charges were ever brought against Kingsley for that particular raid, and unlike the other irregulars who had ridden for the South, Kingsley had left the war with no wanted papers on him.

Now, as Kingsley thought back upon that incident so long ago, he lit a cigar and stared down at the house. Jesse James had boasted that he would find Kingsley and make him pay. But he never had.

"Where are you now, Jesse James?" Kingsley asked, speaking aloud. "You and your big mouth? Oh, that's right. You're dead, ain't you?"

Slapping his legs against the side of his horse, he laughed as he rode on toward Kansas City, his head wreathed in smoke from his cigar.

On the trail between Cheyenne and Chugwater

"You sure he is going to come through here?" Lee Mosley asked.

"The newspaper said he lived in Chugwater, didn't it?" Dingus asked.

"Yeah."

"Then he will be coming through here. This is the only way he can get back home."

"Yeah, well we been here two days now, and he ain't showed up yet," Marvin said.

"He prob'ly didn't leave yesterday because of the rain," Lee said. "That was some rain. We most drowned our ownselves. We should'a found a place to wait it out."

"And maybe miss MacCallister? No, sir. I ain't willin' to take that chance. By leavin' when we did, we're sure to be ahead of him, and when he comes . . ."

"He's comin' now," Marvin said, interrupting the conversation.

"What?"

"There's someone comin', one man on a horse. I

would say that is more than likely him, wouldn't you?"

"Where are the horses? Are they out of sight?" Dingus asked.

"They are down in the coulee, just where you told me to put 'em," Lee said. "If that's MacCallister, he ain't goin' to see 'em."

"That's MacCallister all right," Dingus said.

"How do you know?"

"I had someone point him out to me yesterday," Dingus said. He pointed to a little jut of rocks about thirty yards in front of them. "Lee, you get down there and stay out of sight until he passes you. That way when he gets here, you'll be behind him. Marvin, you get over there behind that rock on the left, and I'll be here. That way we'll have him from three different angles."

"How will we know when to shoot?" Marvin asked.

"I'm goin' to shoot first," Dingus answered. "And if I'm lucky, there won't any of us have to do any more shootin' a'tall after that."

"I sort of hope you miss," Lee said. "I'd like a crack at that son of a bitch myself."

"Hurry, get in position before he gets any closer. I don't want to take a chance on him seein' any of us," Dingus said.

Duff started back home to Chugwater the day after he'd made arrangements to buy the Angus cattle. The heat was intense, and what little wind there was exacerbated more than alleviated the situation because it blew in his face like a blast from the mouth of a furnace. The land, familiar to him now because he had traveled it many times over the last year, unfolded before him in an endless vista of rocks, sage, and hills. The sun heated the ground, sending up undulating waves, which caused near objects to shimmer and nonexistent lakes to appear tantalizingly in the distance. It was always a hard day's ride from Cheyenne to Sky Meadow, and it seemed even more so now because of the heat.

Suddenly there was the crack of a pistol and a bullet whizzed by, taking his hat off, fluffing his hair and sending shivers down his spine.

Realizing that he was a perfect target while mounted, Duff slipped down quickly from his horse, then slapped Sky on the rump.

"Get out of here!" he shouted at the animal, but his warning wasn't necessary because Sky, sensing the trouble, galloped out of the way. The last thing he needed was to have his horse shot out here.

Bending over at the waist, and running in a zig-zag path, Duff got out of the open as quickly as he could, diving for the protection of a little outcropping of rocks. As he did so a second shot came so close that Duff could hear the air pop as the bullet sped by.

Duff was a big man, but he made himself as small as he possibly could, wriggling his body to the end of the little ridge topped by rocks. Once he was in position he lifted his head to take a cautious look around.

He saw a little puff of smoke drifting east on a hot

breath of air. That meant the shooter was a little to the west, so he moved his eyes in that direction. There, he saw the tip of a hat rising slowly above the rocks.

Evan Webb was returning to Cheyenne, having made a visit out to the Claymore Ranch, when he heard the shot. At first he feared someone might be shooting at him, then he heard a second shot and its echo, and realized that he was in no danger. Curious as to what it might be, he set the brake on the buckboard, then climbed down and scurried up the side of a bluff to look down on the other side. From here he saw clearly that three men were accosting one.

Webb had no weapon with him, but even if he did have one, he would have been reluctant to intervene. Although it looked clearly as if the big man was the one in the right, one couldn't always tell by first impressions. He decided to wait right here, stay out of sight, and see what would happen.

Duff wished he had taken time to snake his Winchester out of the saddle sheath, but he hadn't. All he had with him was his pistol, and that would have to do. As he stared across the opening he saw a hat appear. Duff aimed and fired. The hat sailed away.

"Damn, you're pretty good," a voice called from the other side of the rocks. "If you'd'a waited a few seconds longer, you would've got me."

"Who are you?" Duff asked. "And would you be for tellin' me why it is that you are shooting at me?"

"Tell me, Duff MacCallister, are you really so damn dumb that you didn't stop to think that if you kill someone, he might have a brother somewhere?"

"Would your name be Camden?" Duff asked.

"Yeah. Dingus Camden. Tyler was m' brother, and you killed him. So now I'm plannin' on killin' you."

"I suppose it did not make any difference to you that he was holdin' a knife to a young lady's neck. I had no choice. I had to kill him."

"You had a choice. You could'a waited 'til ever'-one put their money in the piano player's bowl like ever'one else was goin' to do. You didn't have to be no hero."

Duff fired again, this time at the sound of the voice. His bullet sent chips of rock flying and he was rewarded with a yelp of pain.

"Did that hurt?" Duff asked.

"Yes, it hurt, you son of a bitch! You sprayed rock into my face."

"That's the way it is, Camden. You play this kind of game, you are goin' to be hurt."

"Hold it!" a voice suddenly yelled behind him, and when Duff turned, he saw someone standing about sixty feet behind him, holding his gun leveled at Duff.

"Marvin, Dingus, come on out! I've got 'im!" the man yelled.

"Good job, Lee," Dingus replied. Dingus stood up from his position behind a rock about seventy-five feet away and directly in front of Duff. The one called Marvin stood up to Duff's right, and he was somewhat farther away, at least one hundred feet.

"MacCallister, do me a favor, will you?" Dingus said. "When you see my brother, tell him I said hello."

"I'm afraid I can't do that," Duff said.

"Oh? And why not?"

"For one thing, your brother is in hell, and I don't plan to go there. Better you tell him yourself, for you're about to see him."

"Ha! There are three of us and one of you!" Dingus said.

"That's not a problem," Duff said.

Suddenly and unexpectedly, Duff dropped to his knees. Startled, Dingus fired, but his bullet passed over Duff's head, and Duff heard a grunt of pain from behind him.

"Dingus, you dumb son of a bitch! You shot Lee!" Marvin shouted.

Dingus had no time to reply to Marvin's angry shout, because almost immediately on top of Dingus's shot, Duff fired, and saw a black hole appear in Dingus's forehead. Dingus went down.

By now, Marvin realized two things. He knew that he was all alone against Duff, and he realized that he had not yet fired. He pulled the trigger, but one hundred feet was too far away for him to be accurate.

Duff had no such problem. He fired back and Marvin dropped his pistol, grabbed his neck, then fell forward.

Duff stood up then and looked at the three

bodies lying in a triangular formation around him. He heard a groan from the one Dingus had called Lee, and when he went back there, saw that Lee was still alive, though barely so.

"Damn," Lee said, grunting through the pain. "I told Dingus this was a dumb idea."

Duff looked at the wound and realized that it was fatal.

"I'm done for, ain't I?"

"Aye, I think so."

"Damn," Lee said. He took a couple of wheezing gasps, then surrendered his life in a wheezing death rattle.

Duff didn't want to leave them lying here, because this was the road between Cheyenne and Chugwater. But he had no shovel, either, so he couldn't bury them. He pulled all three of the bodies together, laid them alongside the road, then marked the spot in his mind.

Evan Webb watched everything from his position, and debated whether or not he should reveal himself to Duff MacCallister. He knew who it was, because he had heard one of the men call him by name. And it was a name he recognized, because he had read of MacCallister's exploits in the *Cheyenne Leader*. And he knew that a man who could shoot as well as MacCallister would have no problem in shooting him, even from this distance. Of course, he represented no threat to MacCallister, but in the heat of the moment, would MacCallister know that?

Webb chose the safer of the options. He remained out of sight watching as MacCallister positioned the bodies along the side of the road, and waiting until MacCallister left the scene.

Chapter Ten

Kansas City Cattle Exchange

The building was divided into two parts. On one side, there was an area that everyone referred to as "the bull pen." It was so called because there were six desks crowded rather closely together. Behind the desks toiled the inventory clerks, men who came to work and buried their heads in endless rows of numbers. The irony was that every day they added, recorded, transferred, and were responsible for tens of thousands of dollars, and they did all that for the sum of twenty-five dollars per week.

There was a long counter that separated the bull pen from the much larger and better-decorated director's room where Jay Montgomery had his desk. On the back wall was a large blackboard upon which figures were written, the figures representing the latest quotes from the cattle market. In the corner was a ticker-tape machine, and at the moment one of the clerks was standing by it, holding the tape in his two hands, reading it as it came from the machine.

As soon as he got all the numbers, he would transfer them to the blackboard.

On the opposite side of the counter from the ticker-tape machine, one of the toiling clerks, Hodge Denman, watched his fellow employee examine the tape until he started transferring the numbers to the blackboard. Then Denman took off his wire-rimmed glasses, removing them very carefully from one ear at a time. Blowing his breath on the lenses, he polished them with his handkerchief, then hooked them back onto his ears, one at a time, just as he had taken them off. With his glasses cleaned, he reread the paragraph that was causing him such distress.

> *We regret to tell you, Mr. Denman, that as the expected repayment of your loan did not occur as agreed upon, we are being forced to take further action. If the loan is not satisfied within sixty days, we will have no alternative but to foreclose upon the property you used for collateral.*

The loan was for four thousand dollars, and it was secured by his father-in-law's property. Neither his wife nor her father realized that Denman was in such debt. Denman was afraid to tell his father-in-law of the crushing debt, because Denman knew that the man had little sympathy for anyone who could not manage his own affairs.

What his father-in-law also did not realize was that his own property was in jeopardy. That was because Hodge Denman had forged his father-in-law's name in order to use his land as the collateral backing his loan. Denman was in debt because he had a gambling habit, a habit that had taken every cent he had, and now threatened to break not only him, but his father-in-law as well.

Leaning back in his chair, Denman pinched the bridge of his nose. How could he have let himself get into such a mess? What could he possibly do to extricate himself?

"Mr. Denman?"

Looking up, Denman saw his boss, Jay Montgomery, coming toward his desk. Denman stood.

"Yes, Mr. Montgomery?"

"We just got a telegram from Mr. Conn in Cheyenne. There is a Mr. Duff MacCallister, from Wyoming, who has requested to buy a herd of cattle. Specifically, he wants five hundred Black Angus. I want you to handle all the details. Gather the cattle, arrange to have enough cars in the lot to move the cattle, and of course, handle the transaction. He has been quoted a price of thirteen thousand, seven hundred and fifty dollars, plus a fifteen percent handling charge."

"I'll get right on it, Mr. Montgomery."

Denman computed the amount of money Mac-Callister would be charged, counting the cost of the cattle and the handling charges. The total came to fifteen thousand, eight hundred twelve dollars and fifty cents.

Denman put the pencil down and drummed his fingers as he looked at the figure. That was a lot of money. It didn't seem fair that some people could raise that much money when he was so desperate.

He drafted the letter.

Dear Mr. MacCallister:

This is to inform you that we have received your order for five hundred head of prime Black Angus cattle. We will undertake to collect and process the cattle, then load them on the cars for shipment to you in Cheyenne. Before shipment can be completed, however, we must have in our hands a bank draft for the fifteen thousand, eight hundred twelve dollars and fifty cents. This sum will cover all costs attendant to this transaction, to include the price of the cattle and our handling fees.

Thank you for choosing to do business with us.

> *Sincerely,*
> *Jay Montgomery, President,*
> *Kansas City Cattle Exchange*

Denman was about to put the letter in the envelope when he suddenly got an idea as to how he might extricate himself from his problems.

Putting the letter in his pocket, he walked outside. Because the Cattle Exchange consisted of several acres of feeder lots, the odor was so strong that every morning as he came to work, he could smell it for half a mile before he reached it.

"How does one ever get used to the stink?" he asked one of the cowboys whose job it was to move the cattle from pen to pen.

"It's all a part of the cattle business." The cowboy laughed out loud. "I heard someone ask Mr. Montgomery about the smell once, and you know what he said?"

"What did he say?"

"He said, 'It might smell like cow shit to you, but to me it smells like money.'" The cowboy laughed out loud and slapped his knee. "Yes sir, it smells like money, he says."

The cowboy was named Rob Howard, and he was who Denman was looking for now. He walked down a narrow path that ran between two very large feeder pens. Here the smell was even more intense, with the smell of the animals themselves adding to the odor of the feces.

He saw Howard standing on the top rung of one of the feeder pens, watching as others, who were mounted, drove several cows through the open gate of the pen.

"Mr. Howard!" Denman called.

"Yeah?"

"A word with you, please?"

"Walt!" Howard shouted. "Get up here and make sure the cows don't hurt themselves comin' into the pen!"

Walt rode over to the fence, then climbed up on it as Howard jumped down.

"What do you need?"

"I'm going to need five hundred Black Angus at a ratio of one bull to twenty-five heifers. That will be twenty bulls and four hundred eighty heifers."

"I can do cipherin', Denman," Howard said.

"Of course you can," Denman said quickly. I did not mean to cast any dispersions on your mathematical acumen."

"My what?"

"Your ability to do math."

"Five hundred Black Angus?"

"Yes."

"That's a pretty big order," Howard said.

"Yes, it is. Evidently some rich man from Wyoming is wanting to introduce Black Angus out there."

"All right, I'll get 'em put together for you."

Howard turned to go back to the holding pen.

"Mr. Howard?" Denman called after him.

Howard turned. "Is there somethin' else?"

"Yes, but, this is not company business. This is personal."

"What do you want?"

"That man you said you met a few days ago. I would like to meet him."

"I meet a lot of men," Howard said. "Which one are you talking about?"

"The one you said that was a, uh, I believe you put it, dangerous man. Kingman, or something like that."

Howard looked at Denman with a surprised expression on his face, then he laughed. "Do you mean Kingsley? You want to meet Crack Kingsley?"

"Yes."

"Why in hell would you want to meet him? Didn't you hear what I said about him? He was a border raider during the war. He's probably killed more men than you have mosquitoes."

"I have a proposal for him."

"No, you don't," Howard said.

"Yes, I do."

"Listen to me, Denman. Kingsley is not the kind of man I would want to have anything to do with. And if I don't want to be around him, you for sure don't."

"I would like to meet him," Denman repeated.

"You said you have a proposal for him. What kind of proposal?"

"I'm really not at liberty to say, right now," Denman said.

"It's somethin' illegal, ain't it? I mean, if you are wantin' to do business with Crack Kingsley, it has to be illegal."

"There's twenty dollars in it for you if you set up the meeting, and don't ask any more questions," Denman said.

"I tell you what, Denman, twenty dollars ain't enough money for me to mess with the likes of someone like Crack Kingsley. You go set up your own meeting."

Turning, Howard again started back to the feeding pen.

"Would you do it for one hundred dollars?" Denman asked.

Howard stopped in his tracks, then slowly and deliberately turned back toward Denman. "Damn, you are serious about this, aren't you?"

"I am very serious," Denman replied.

"One hundred dollars?"

"Yes."

"Why do you want to meet with Kingsley?"

"Part of the one hundred dollars is to keep you from asking me any more questions."

Howard stroked his chin as he stared at Denman.

"Where is the money?"

"You set up the meeting first. If he shows up, I'll give you one hundred dollars."

"You know where the Bucket of Blood Saloon is?"

"Heavens, you aren't going to tell me that's where you would have us meet, are you?"

"You want to meet him or not?"

"I do."

"Kingsley's pretty particular about where he goes. I reckon he's prob'ly made a lot of enemies in his life, so he goes where he feels comfortable. And the Bucket of Blood is that place."

"All right, if I must go to that dreadful place, I will. You just set up the meeting."

Howard cocked his head at Denman and stared at him for a long moment, then he chuckled quietly as he shook his head.

"I'd damn near set it up for free, just to know what this is all about," he said.

"Thank you. Let me know when you have the meeting set up."

Returning to his desk, Denman rolled two pieces of paper, separated by carbon paper, into the Remington typing machine. Using two fingers, he began to type a new letter.

Dear Mr. MacCallister:

This is to inform you that we have received your request for five hundred Black Angus cattle. We are now in the process of making the arrangements for you. However, it will be necessary for you to come, in person, to take delivery of your cattle. The amount of money due upon your receipt of the herd is fifteen thousand, eight hundred twelve dollars and fifty cents. This sum will cover all costs attendant to this transaction, to include the price of the cattle and our handling fees.

Too often, bank drafts drawn upon small anks in remote areas of the country have been non-processed due to the failure of the banks in question. Therefore, it is the policy of the Kansas City Cattle Exchange that all transactions must be conducted in cash, so we ask you to bring the money with you. We apologize in advance for any difficulty this may cause the buyer.

Please advise us by telegraph when you expect to arrive in Kansas City. Thank you for choosing to do business with us.

> *Sincerely,*
> *Jay Montgomery*
> *President, Kansas City Cattle Exchange*

Denman folded the letter carefully, put it in the envelope, sealed it shut, addressed it, then applied the postage stamp. He had just finished when Jay Montgomery came up to the counter that separated the two areas.

"Denman, did you take care of that Black Angus order?"

"Yes, sir, Mr. Montgomery," Denman said. "Mr. Howard is getting the herd assembled for me, four hundred eighty heifers to twenty seed bulls."

"That's an exceptionally large number of cows for a single order," Montgomery said. "But our percentage will make it well worthwhile. Good job."

"Thank you, sir," Denman said. He held up the letter. "If you don't mind, I'll carry this letter to the post myself."

"No, I don't mind at all. By all means, do so."

After he had delivered the letter, Denman stopped by the bank to talk to Rod Norton, the bank manager.

"This is serious business, Mr. Denman. Very serious business," Norton said, sternly.

"Believe me, sir, I am very aware of that," Denman said. "But I have come to tell you that I believe I have the situation under control. If you will but allow me thirty more days, I'm sure I will be able to pay off the loan, in full, plus any additional interest that will accrue in the next thirty days."

"Tell me, Mr. Denman, and I ask this not from idle curiosity, but from my position as president of the bank: what makes you think you have the situation under control?"

"I have just discovered that I have access to a rather substantial amount of funds," Denman said. "More than enough to satisfy all my debts. All I ask is for a little more time."

Norton leaned back in his chair and stroked his chin for a moment, then, sighing, came forward and picked up a pen. He wrote a few lines on a piece of paper, then handed the paper to Denman.

"Show this to Mr. Potter, the loan manager," he said.

Effective from this date, Hodge Denman is granted a thirty day extension on his loan.

Chapter Eleven

Though Sky Meadow Ranch had no cattle yet, they were raising their own pork and chickens, and Elmer was out feeding the chickens when he saw Duff approaching, still some distance away. He finished his chores, then went back into the house and made a pitcher of lemonade to have ready for Duff's return.

Duff dismounted in front of the house, but did not unsaddle Sky. Elmer met him on the front porch with a glass of lemonade.

"Thanks," Duff said, accepting the glass.

"Want me to unsaddle Sky for you?"

Duff took a swallow before he responded.

"Thank you, no. I'm afraid I'm going to have to ride on into town."

"Oh. Well, I'm sure Miss Parker will be glad to see you. I delivered your letter, by the way."

"Thanks, but it isn't to see Meghan that I'm going to town, though if she isn't too busy, perhaps I will stop by the store. I have to send a telegram," Duff said.

"I'll ride into town with you, if you don't mind."

"I don't mind at all. I'd appreciate the company."

On the way into town, Duff filled Elmer in on everything that had happened since he'd left, including the shoot-out he'd had on the road on the way back home.

"I left them there," he said, concluding his story. "So it's needing for me to tell the police back in Cheyenne where the brigands might be found."

"If there is any justice, the buzzards will have picked their eyes out by the time they find them," Elmer said.

When they reached Chugwater, Duff rode directly to the telegraph office. There, using one of the pre-printed forms, he wrote his message.

TO: *Chief Homer Davis, Cheyenne Police Department, Cheyenne, Wy.*

On my return trip from Cheyenne to Chugwater I was attacked by three men. I don't know their names, though one was the brother of Tyler Camden. I had no choice but to kill all three. You will find their bodies alongside the trail. Should you wish to speak with me, you can contact me at the address listed below.

Duff Tavish MacCallister, Sky Meadow Ranch, Chugwater, WT

Duff handed the message to the telegrapher, Dan Murchison.

"Well, Mr. MacCallister, let's see what the charges are," he said with a broad smile as he took the note. The smile left his face as he read the message.

"Oh, my, you had quite a frightening experience," he said. "And you killed all three?"

"Aye," Duff said. "It seemed the thing to do at the time."

"Yes, sir, I suppose it did."

"What are the charges?"

"That would be one dollar and twenty cents," Murchison said.

After sending a telegram to the police back in Cheyenne, Duff walked over to the city marshal's office. Jerry Ferrell, the marshal, had a chair drawn up to the bars of the jail cell, playing checkers with Perry Keith, who was serving a week in jail for drunk and disorderly conduct, to wit, "urinating in public."

Ferrell jumped three of Keith's men, then wound up on king's row.

"Crown me," he said.

"Oh, you're killing me here," Keith said as he placed a second checker on top.

"Damn, this is fun," Ferrell said. "Tell you what, soon as I let you out, how about peeing in the street again so I can put you back in jail? You're just too easy to beat."

"I told you, I don't remember peeing in the street," Ferrell said. "I was drunk."

"Yeah, well, that's sort of the whole point of you

being in here now, isn't it?" Ferrell said. He turned to Duff. "Yes, sir, Duff, what can I do for you?"

"I just thought I would let you know that you might get a telegram from the police chief down in Cheyenne," Duff said.

"About the fella you shot in the saloon there?" Ferrell said. "I already heard from him about that. He says there's no charges."

"No, not that. 'Tis another incident I'm talking about."

Duff told the marshal about his encounter with the three men on the way back to Chugwater, emphasizing that he was attacked first, and that one of the attackers was the brother of the man he had killed earlier in the saloon.

"Actually, I only killed two of them," Duff concluded. "One of them was killed by Camden, by a shot that was meant for me but missed. I left all three of them lying alongside the road, and I just sent a telegram to Chief Davis to tell him about it."

"I appreciate your coming to me," Ferrell said. "I'll send a follow-up telegram to Chief Davis to see what's going on."

"'Tis my thanks you have, Constable," Duff said. "I'll be around if you have need for me."

"All right," Ferrell said. "But if it happened the way you said, and I've no reason to doubt you, I'm sure nothing will come of it."

Thinking he wasn't being watched, Keith put his hand through the bars and repositioned one of his checkers.

"I saw that!" Ferrell said. "Damn it, Keith, you're cheating!"

"Of course I'm cheating," Keith said without any sense of shame. "I'm in jail. That's what people who are in jail are like."

Duff laughed as he left the marshal's office, then walked over to R.W. Guthrie's Building, Supply, and Freight Company to make arrangements for picking up his hay mower.

"You'll have the hay mower in two days," R.W. Guthrie said. "I'll even have my boys assemble the thing for you."

"Thank you, R.W.," Duff said.

"We heard of your adventure in Cheyenne," Guthrie said. "Charley Blanton picked it up from the *Cheyenne Leader* and reprinted it in the *Defender*."

"Did he, now?" Duff replied. Duff didn't mention his encounter with the three men on his way back home.

"You headin' down to Fiddler's Green?" R.W. asked.

"Aye, I thought I might."

"Well, hold on a minute. As soon as I get this order written up, I'll walk down there with you."

While R.W. was writing up the order, Duff stepped up to the big window in front of R.W.'s place and looked out over the town. A huge banner was spread across the street, tied to Kimberly's Dry Goods on one side of the street, and Holman's Drugs on the other side.

FIREMEN'S BENEFIT BALL SATURDAY NIGHT

He had not seen Meghan since coming back into town because he didn't want to barge in while she had a client. But he intended to see her before he went back out to the ranch today.

Fifteen minutes later, Duff and R.W. joined Fred Matthews, the owner of the Chugwater Mercantile, Charley Blanton, owner and publisher of the *Defender*, and Elmer, who had gone straight to Fiddler's Green as soon as he and Duff had reached town. The saloon owner, Biff Johnson, was sitting with them as well.

Biff Johnson was a former first sergeant in the army, and had been in the 7th Cavalry with Reno at the battle of the Little Big Horn. He had named his saloon Fiddler's Green after the old cavalry legend that "any trooper who has ever heard the trumpeter play 'Boots and Saddles' will, when he has died, go to Fiddler's Green, there to drink and visit with all the other cavalrymen until final judgment."

Elmer had already shared with them the story of Duff's encounter with the three men on the road, and Blanton was busy writing the story.

"Damn, Duff, you didn't say anything to me about that," Guthrie said.

"The subject didn't come up," Duff said.

The others laughed. "The subject didn't come up," Blanton repeated as he wrote it into his story. "That's a good line."

"Did you get the telegram sent?" Elmer asked.

"Yes, I told Chief Davis what happened, and where to find the bodies. Then I stopped down to the constable's office and told Marshal Ferrell. I also told him I would be available if either he or Chief Davis need me."

"They aren't going to need you," Murchison said, coming into the saloon then, carrying a telegram with him. "Chief Davis just sent this telegram to you and to Marshal Ferrell."

Duff read the telegram.

THE BODIES OF DINGUS CAMDEN, LEE AND MARVIN MOSLEY HAVE ALREADY BEEN RECOVERED. THE INCIDENT WAS WITNESSED BY MR. EVAN WEBB. HIS STORY CORROBORATES THE ACCOUNT TOLD BY MR. MACCALLISTER. NO FURTHER INVESTIGATION IS NEEDED.

"Good," Duff said. "'Tis glad I am to be done with that adventure."

"You weren't the only one with an adventure," Biff said. "Elmer, here, had an adventure of his own."

"Wasn't much of an adventure," Elmer said.

"The hell it wasn't," Biff said. "Folks in here are still talkin' about it."

"What happened?"

Biff told the others the story of how Elmer had backed down a young would-be gunman named Clete Wilson. He was very expressive as he told the story, and when he told how Wilson held his arms over his head, pleading with Elmer not to kill him all the while peeing in his pants, it left the others laughing.

"Have you seen him since then?" Duff asked.

"Ain't seen hide nor hair of him," Biff said. "If you want my thinkin', it's that he is plumb out of the territory now."

The conversation returned to Duff's intention to stock his ranch with Black Angus.

"I still don't understand why you want to go to all the trouble to get Black Angus cows," Fred said. "Longhorns have been just fine for as long as I can remember."

"Well, Herefords are better than Longhorns," R.W. said.

"If Sky Meadow is to prosper, it will have to stand out among all the other fine ranches in Chugwater Valley. And 'tis no better a way for me to do that than to be stocking my ranch with the best beef cattle in the world, and that would be Black Angus," Duff said.

"There is not a thing wrong with Longhorns. They are hardy creatures and they can live on dew and scrub grass. You go bringing in some high-toned cow, 'tis goin' to be nothin' but trouble, I tell you," Fred insisted.

"Fred, have you ever eaten an Angus steak?" Biff asked.

"And how would I have done that, I ask you, when I never even heard of the creatures until Duff came up with this wild idea of his?"

"Well, I have. Two years ago my wife and I took a trip back to Scotland to see her sister who still lives there. She served steak, and when I took my first bite I knew it was something different. Not tough like Longhorn, and never have I put a thing in my mouth that tasted better." Biff looked at Duff. "I say go for it, Duff, and when you take your first beef to market, I'll buy a couple myself and add some fine dining by serving my customers Angus steak."

"Ha! Fine dining in a saloon?" Fred asked.

"I'll build on to the side. I own the empty lot next door. I'll have a saloon in here and a fine restaurant next door."

"When will you actually get your cattle?" Fred asked.

"I don't know. I guess as soon as they get enough put together to make up the herd I want."

"Will they be shipping them to you? Or will you have to go after them?" Fred asked.

"Mr. Conn is the Kansas City Cattle Exchange representative in Cheyenne, and I asked him to arrange for them to be shipped by train to Cheyenne. I'll drive them down from there."

"Five hundred cows, you say?" R.W. asked.

"Aye."

"That's a lot of cattle for one man to be driving."

"I'll not be alone."

"Is Elmer goin' with you?"

"Damn right I'm goin'," Elmer said. "I've worked side by side with Duff for a year to get this ranch ready. Now that we are finally about to get some cows, I intend to be there from the beginning."

"Still, five hundred cows, even with two men, will be difficult."

"I'll hire some men before then," Duff said.

"Once I get the herd onto my ranch, I shall be needing a few more employees, anyway."

"If you have any trouble coming up with hands, let me know," Biff said. "I can probably find a few for you."

"Thank you, I appreciate that," Duff replied.

"I reckon you'll be goin' to the big shindig we got comin' up Saturday night, won't you?" Fred asked.

"Aye. I would not wish to miss it."

"Ha! You'd better watch it, Duff," Blanton said. "Fred is about to try and sell you a ticket. He is the head of the Fireman's Ball committee you see, so he's after every dollar he can get."

"It will cost you a dollar," Fred said. "And if you pay now, you won't have to pay at the door. We are going to charge a dollar and a quarter at the door."

"See what I mean?" Blanton said.

Chuckling, Duff pulled out his billfold and gave Fred a dollar. "Tell me," he said. "Has Miss Parker bought a ticket yet?"

"No."

Duff handed Fred another dollar. "Then I should like to buy one for her," he said.

"Well, now, I'm sure she will appreciate that," Fred said.

"Will you be taking your pipes to the ball?" Biff asked. He was asking about the bagpipes that Duff often played.

"I could be talked into it," Duff answered.

"And believe me, it doesn't take much to talk him into it, either," Elmer said. "He has those things caterwauling all the time."

"*Och*, Elmer, and would ye be for disparaging m' pipes now?" Duff asked.

"Oh, no, no, I'd never do a thing like that," Elmer said. "I know what them screechin' things mean to you."

Biff chuckled. "I will always remember the day you came into town to take care of Malcolm and his gang. You stood down at the end of the road and started playin' your pipes. It was a glorious sight to see him so afraid."

"*'Tis the pipes!*" *Malcolm said, standing up so quickly that the chair in which he was sitting fell over with a bang.*

"*The what?*" *Pettigrew asked.*

"*The pipes! MacCallister is playing the pipes! Everyone get into position, he's coming!*"

The others moved quickly to get into the positions they had already selected. Malcolm, with pistol in hand, moved to the batwing doors and looked out into the street as Pogue and Shaw went about clearing it.

"*Get off the street! Get out of the way!*" *Pogue and Shaw were shouting.* "*Get out of the street or get shot!*"

The pipes continued to play "Scotland the Brave," which only Malcolm recognized as the incitement to battle. The fact that pipes were being used against him gave him a chill, and though he wouldn't mention it to any of the others, it had frightened him.

"With your skill with a pistol, it won't be long before you'll have a reputation to match that of your cousin, Falcon MacCallister," Charley Blanton said. "I wasn't the only one to pick up the story of what happened down in Cheyenne when you shot Tyler Camden while he was holding a knife to that lady's neck. It has been run in papers all over the West. 'The shot,' they are calling it."

"There wasn't much to it," Duff said. "It wasn't as if I had to make a rapid extraction of my pistol."

Elmer laughed. "Quick draw, Duff. How many times do I have to tell you that it is not a rapid extraction, it is a quick draw."

The others laughed.

"Quick draw, aye, but whatever it be called, 'tis a skill with which I am not particularly proficient," Duff replied. "But as I said, in this case, swiftness was not required, just a bit of accuracy."

"A bit of accuracy?" Blanton said with a scoffing sound. "According to what they are saying, you took your shot from one hundred feet away, and hit a target no larger than a playing card."

"Why, pshaw, that ain't nothin' at all," Elmer said. "I oncet seen him shoot a gnat offen the hind leg of a fly from fifty feet away, and here's the thing, he didn't even hurt the fly."

Again, everyone laughed.

"Elmer, I spent thirty years in the army, and the army is full of people who can tell tall tales, but I ain't never heard no one that can top you."

"Those eight men came after you here in Chugwater last year, then you had an encounter with Camden in Cheyenne, and three more men on the road as you were coming back home. It's no wonder you left Scotland," Biff said. "Trouble just seems to have a way of followin' you."

Duff was silent for a moment. "I fear you may be

right," he replied, the tone of voice more somber than anyone expected.

"I'm sorry about mentionin' Scotland," Biff said. "I didn't mean to bring up old and painful memories." Biff was one of the few who knew about Skye, and how she was killed.

"You didn't bring the memories up, Biff. They never go away. And indeed, I just visited Scotland as you know," Duff said. He finished his beer and stood up. "Well, gentlemen, I have had a pleasant visit here with my friends, but I've some more business to take care of before I leave, so best I get about it."

"Do say hello to Miss Parker for us, will you, Duff?" Fred spoke up.

Duff had not said that he was going to call on Meghan Parker, but the way he smiled when Fred spoke proved that he had every intention of doing so.

"I will," he said.

Chapter Twelve

When Meghan Parker was twelve years old, both of her parents were killed in a riverboat accident. She could still remember the pain and sorrow of their loss. And the fear, the absolute, mind-numbing fear.

What would happen to her?

She needn't have worried, because even though her grandmother was already very old, she had stepped in and raised Meghan as if she were her own. It had been a wonderful relationship between Meghan and her grandmother, and when her grandmother died, three days after Meghan's nineteenth birthday, the pain and sorrow was as great as it had been when her own parents had died.

Meghan was in college at the time, and although losing her grandmother was a terrible emotional blow to her, it wasn't a financial blow, because she still had the money that had been left to her by her parents. And by selling her grandmother's house, she had been able to add to her coffer. As a result, she was able to finish her education without experiencing any financial burden at all.

She had gone to college to be a schoolteacher, but her grandmother, a seamstress, taught Meghan how to design, cut cloth, and sew women's clothes. It was a skill that Meghan picked up easily, and one that she enjoyed.

"I know you are studying to be a teacher and teaching is a good thing, but it is also good to have something to fall back on," her grandmother had told her. "That's why I think you should learn how to sew. Folks are always going to need clothes."

What Meghan especially enjoyed was creating original dresses and gowns. She had a great talent for it, and as it turned out, that advice may have been the most valuable thing Meghan Parker's grandmother had left her. Because though she had come to Chugwater to be a schoolteacher, she learned when she arrived that another woman had already been hired. She was about to return to St. Louis when she was given the opportunity to buy a dress shop, and she'd had just enough money left over to do that. That she had been successful in the enterprise was evidenced by the fact that her shop was now one of the most profitable business establishments in all of Chugwater.

Meghan had never been married, nor had she ever been serious about anyone before. And the question she asked herself now was: did she have a serious relationship with Duff MacCallister?

She couldn't answer that question. She did have a proprietary relationship with him, though, ever since she had saved his life in the gun battle that had taken place right here in Chugwater, on the street in front of her store. The gun battle had been between Duff and eight men, which certainly meant that the odds against him were almost in-surmountable.

Meghan had been an unintended witness to the battle from the window of her shop. *Seeing quickly what was going on, and understanding the odds against him, she was unwilling to stand by and watch the hand-some Scotsman, whom she barely knew at the time, be killed. She made up her mind right there to help him in any way she could.*

Meghan saw the two men behind the watering-trough cock their pistols and start to move toward the edge. If Duff had no idea they were there, they would have the advan-tage over him. Dare she call out to him?

Then she got an idea, and she hurried to the back of her shop.

"What is it?" Mrs. Riley asked from behind a trunk. "What is going on out there?"

"Stay down, Mrs. Riley. Just stay down and you'll be all right," Meghan said. She unscrewed the knobs that held the dressing mirror on the frame then carrying it to the front, she turned it on its side so that it had a length-wise projection. Holding it in the window, she prayed that Duff would see it.

Once he was safely behind the watering trough, Duff slithered on his stomach to the edge, then peered around it. He looked first toward the saloon to see if Malcolm was going to make another appearance, but the saloon was quiet. Then, looking across the street, he saw a woman in the window of the dress shop. It was Meghan, the same

*pretty woman he had seen step down from the stagecoach
the first day he rode into town and had actually met for the
first time at Annie's funeral. At first, he wondered what she
was doing there, then he saw exactly what she was doing.*

*Meghan was holding a mirror, and looking into the
mirror, Duff could see the reflection of two men lying on the
ground behind the watering trough that was directly across
the street from him. He watched as one started moving
toward the end of the trough in order to take a look. Duff
aimed his pistol at the edge of the trough and waited.*

*His vigil was rewarded. Duff saw the brim of a hat
appear, and he cocked his pistol, aimed, took a breath, and
let half of it out. When he saw the man's eye appear, Duff
touched the trigger. Looking into the mirror, he saw the
man's face fall into the dirt and the gun slip from his hand.*

Meghan was recalling that incident when she
heard the tinkling of the bell on her front door. Putting down the bolt of cloth she was examining, she
stepped out front. Duff MacCallister's visit wasn't
entirely unexpected, but seeing him come into her
shop did bring a broad smile.

"I saw you and Elmer ride into town earlier," she
said. "I was hoping you would stop by to see me."

"Sure now, Lassie, and ye dinnae think I would be
for leavin' without m' stoppin' by to tell you good-
bye, now?"

"Sure 'n t'was hopin' I was that you would nae be
for takin' your leave without so much as a visit,"
Meghan said, almost perfectly mimicking Duff's
Scottish brogue.

"*Och*, 'tis fun of me you be makin'," Duff said, though there was no anger in his voice.

Meghan laughed, her laughter like the lilting music of wind chimes. "I'm having a bit of fun, but I'm not making fun of you, Duff Tavish MacCallister. Have you had your supper?"

"I have not."

A fall of blond hair slipped forward to cover one of Meghan's eyes, and she brushed it back.

"I have some fried chicken and potato salad in the back room, if you would care to join me."

"I would be delighted."

They ate their meal on the same table Meghan used to lay out her material when she was cutting up cloth for her sewing projects. She had made lemonade to have with their supper, and Duff was on his second glass when Meghan cleared away the residue of the meal, then returned to sit across the table from him.

"Tell me about her," Meghan said.

"I beg your pardon?"

"Tell me about the woman back in Scotland. You never speak of her, but sometimes when you let your guard down, your eyes let me see all the way in to your soul. It is a good soul Duff Tavish MacCallister, but when I look that deep, I can see the scars and the pain. Tell me about her, Duff. I want to know."

Duff was quiet, so quiet that for a long moment Meghan feared she may have overstepped her bounds.

"I'm sorry, Duff, please forgive me for asking. I had no right to pry into your affairs. If you would rather not talk about it," she said, but Duff held up his hand.

"What can I say about Skye, Meghan? Would that I were a poet, that I could express myself in words that speak of a mist on the moors, of heather and cool lakes, and all that is beautiful about Scotland and she who was my love, I would do so, so that others might know her as I knew her."

"You words are eloquent enough for any poet, Duff."

"When she was murdered by Sheriff Somerled and his deputies, the self-same devils who came to America to try 'n kill me, I thought my world had come to an end."

"Oh, Duff, I'm so sorry. Please forgive me for causing you to have to recall such painful memories."

"There is nothing to forgive. The memory of her dying is painful, that is true enough. But the memories of Skye can never be painful. They can only be sweet."

"How lucky she was to have known your love."

"Not luck, I fear, but misfortune, for 'twas my love that got her killed."

"Better to have loved and died than never to have known love at all," Meagan said.

"For her sake, I pray that is true," Duff said.

Meghan reached across the table and put her hand on Duff's. "It is true, Duff," she said. "Believe me, it is true."

"Meghan, I . . ."

Whatever Duff was about to say was interrupted by a knock on the front door.

"Mr. MacCallister? Mr. MacCallister, are you in there?"

"That sounds like young Lonnie Mathers," Meghan said. "I wonder what he wants."

Lonnie Mathers was the seventeen-year-old son of a widowed mother and, for the last four years he had taken every odd job in town to help his mother meet expenses. Most of the time, he worked for Fred Matthews in his mercantile, but he had also done jobs for R.W. Guthrie at his lumber shed, and had even driven a freight wagon for him a few times.

"There is only one way to find out," Duff said, walking to the front of the shop and opening the door.

"Sorry to be botherin' you, Mr. MacCallister, but the fellers down at Fiddler's Green said you'd be here. And Mr. Murchison at the telegraph office said that, more'n likely, you'd be wantin' to see this here telegraph right away."

"Thank you, Lonnie," Duff said, handing the boy half a dollar.

"Oh my, thank you!" Lonnie replied, smiling broadly at the size of the tip. Turning, he walked away quickly into the dark.

"I don't like telegrams," Meghan said. "Too often they bring bad news."

"They're used for things other than bad news," Duff said as he opened the envelope. Pulling out the little yellow piece of paper, he read it, then frowned.

"You are frowning. Is it something bad?" Meghan asked, an obvious look of concern on her face.

"No, not really," Duff answered.

"Not really? That means it's a little bad, doesn't it?"

"It is a telegram from the Kansas City Cattle Exchange."

"Isn't that where you are going to buy your cattle?"

"Yes. They have received my order and are putting together a herd for me, but in order to ship the cattle I am going to have to go there to make arrangements. It says they have mailed a letter with all the details."

"That means you are going to have to go to Kansas City?"

"I'm afraid so."

"When will you go?"

"I don't know yet. Probably some time next week."

The look of concern on Meghan's face changed to a smile. "Oh. So you will be here for the Firemen's Benefit Ball?"

Duff smiled as well. "Aye, Lass, I'd not be for missing that."

"Good. I'll be there too."

"And would ye be for dancin' with an awkward Scot such as myself?"

"Nothing would please me more," she said.

"Good, being Scot as I am, I would not like to think I bought your ticket for naught."

"You bought my ticket?"

"Aye, that I have done. I was about to tell you that

when the young lad banged so loudly upon the door."

"Why, Duff MacCallister, how nice of you."

"I've been known from time to time to do nice things," Duff teased.

"Oh, of that, I have no doubt. But now, I've something to ask you, and I hope the question doesn't make you uncomfortable."

"Lass, I hardly think you can ask a question that would make me uncomfortable," Duff replied.

"In the letter that you had Elmer deliver to me, there was a paragraph that I found confusing," Meghan said. "I was hoping that perhaps you could clear it up for me."

"What was the paragraph?"

Meghan walked over to the sideboard to pick up the letter. Removing it from the envelope, she read aloud.

"While in Cheyenne I intend to make arrangements to bring cattle onto my land so that, after a year of preparation Sky Meadow will truly become a cattle ranch. I am sure that the news of my establishing a ranch is important to you only as a matter of the friendship that exists between the two of us. However," she paused and looked directly at Duff. "And this is the part that I wanted to ask you about." She continued to read, "*There may come a time when this information would be of much greater interest to you.*" She emphasized the last sentence.

Meghan folded the letter and returned it to the envelope.

Before Meghan could ask her question, they heard loud shouts from outside.

"Fire! Fire! Schoenberg's is on fire! Everyone turn out!"

Both Duff and Meghan went outside to join the others of the town as everyone hurried down to the hardware store, where flames were already leaping up through the roof.

Even with all the men of the town forming a bucket brigade to keep the pumper filled, it still took two hours for the fire to be extinguished, and everyone agreed that if the fire department had a second pumper, the fire would have been put out much quicker.

"Folks, this is as good a reason as I can think of for buying a ticket and coming to the Firemen's Ball this Saturday," Fred Matthews said.

"Look at Fred," R.W. Guthrie said. "No wonder he does so well with his mercantile store. The man is a born salesman."

Laughing at Guthrie's comment, Duff looked around and saw Meghan standing on the boardwalk in front of Dunnigan's Dry Goods. She and several other women had made lemonade and they were passing it out to the exhausted and thirsty men who had fought the fire. Duff walked over to join her, and, smiling, she handed him a glass.

"We didn't do much for Mr. Shoenberg's place I'm afraid," Duff said. "But at least we kept the fire from spreading."

"You look like a possum with all the black around your eyes," Meghan said, and she used a damp cloth to wipe his face.

"Thank you. Oh, you were going to ask me a question," Duff said.

"I was, wasn't I? Well, never mind, I've forgotten what it was, now. You must be exhausted. You need to get home and get some rest. I'll see you at the dance Saturday night."

Chapter Thirteen

Kansas City

"Are you sure this is where you want to go?" the hack driver asked Hodge Denman. The hansom cab had come into the most notorious street of the city and stopped in front of the most scandalous establishment on the most disreputable street. The sign on front of the building showed a bucket tipped over, from which streamed something red. The name beside the bucket was Bucket of Blood Saloon.

There were three people passed out drunk on the wooden porch in front of the saloon, and one of the three was a woman. The saloon, indeed the entire street, reeked of sour whiskey, stale beer, unwashed bodies, and even the unmistakable odor of urine.

"Yes, this is where I want to come. Wait here for me, please."

"Mister, I wouldn't wait in this place for Jesus Christ Hisself. When it comes time for you to leave,

you'd best find yourself another way out of here,"
the driver said. "I'll take my quarter fare, now."

"A quarter? It's fifteen cents anywhere else,"
Denman complained as he handed the driver a
quarter.

"Yeah, well, this ain't anywhere else, is it? It's
here. And a person could get his throat cut here."

The driver snapped his reins and the horse
started forward. He made a one-hundred-eighty-
degree turn in the middle of the road, then urged
his horse into a brisk trot.

Denman watched with a sinking feeling inside as
his driver left. He felt the hair standing up on the
back of his neck, and he was so frightened that he
was having a difficult time breathing. The driver was
right: a person could get his throat cut in this part
of town. Why did he agree to come here?

He agreed because Howard had told him that
this was the only place Kingsley would meet with
him.

Although Denman dreaded setting foot inside
the Bucket of Blood, he felt that it would be safer,
if only marginally so, if he were inside with other
people, rather than remaining out here in the dark.
So, steeling himself for the ordeal ahead, he
stepped up onto the front porch.

A bony arm reached up from one of the supine
figures on the porch. The hand grabbed his pants
leg, and Denman gasped out loud.

"Oh, my God!" Denman shouted, his voice a terrified shriek.

"Buy me a drink, honey," a besotted woman's
voice said.

Realizing that it was just a drunk woman and not some ruffian who wanted to kill him, Denman recovered enough to jerk his leg away from her. "Don't touch me!" he shouted. He moved quickly until he got inside.

Once inside, he stood for a moment looking around the room to see if he could find anyone who fit Kingsley's description. Denman was a small man, with delicate, feminine features and his hair was blond and thin, of a color and texture that made it look almost as if he were bald until one got closer to him. Anyone could look at him and know immediately that he was very much out of his element in a place like the Bucket of Blood Saloon.

To his frustration and no small amount of worry and fear, he did not see anyone who looked anything like the description Howard had given him of Kingsley.

"He is an ugly man, tall and scrawny," Howard had told him. "He has high cheekbones, and a scar that runs from the corner of his left eye down to just below the cheekbone where it curves up, sort' a like a fishhook. And you don't hardly ever see him without he has a cigar stuck in his mouth."

There were a lot of ugly men, and even uglier women, Denman thought. But he did not see anyone that he thought might be Crack Kingsley.

Aggravated that Kingsley had not gotten here when he was supposed to, Denman chose a table in the back corner of the room. He stayed as far away from the clientele as he could; this place was making him extremely uncomfortable. He was easily frightened by men like the ones who frequented this saloon, and their loud and boisterous talk made him even more so.

The bartender called over to him. "You want somethin', you got to come up here to get it," he said.

"I don't want anything. I'll just sit for a spell," Denman replied.

"Not in here, you ain't," the bartender said. "You sit in here, you better be drinkin'."

"Very well, I will have a beer."

"Come up here to get it, I ain't bringin' it to you," the bartender said.

Denman cringed as attention was called to him, but he walked up to the bar, paid for a beer, then returned to the table.

This seemed a most unlikely place for someone like Denman, certainly not a place that he or anyone in his circle of acquaintances would ever visit. On the other hand, he told himself that this was the one good point about having the meeting here. As long as he was here in the Bucket of Blood, he knew that the chances of seeing anyone who actually knew him were practically nonexistent. And he did not want to be seen and recognized when he had his meeting with Crack Kingsley.

Howard had laughed when Denman agreed to meet with Kingsley here.

"You ain't goin' to get all a' feared and pee in your pants or somethin' like that, are you?" Howard had asked.

"I shall be uncomfortable, that is true," Denman replied. "So tell him to please try to be on time."

Denman had hoped that Kingsley would be there when he arrived, but there was no such luck. Nervously, Denman checked his pocket watch as well as the clock that stood against the wall of the saloon, and nursed his beer slowly as he waited. Kingsley was already fifteen minutes late. Denman would give him fifteen minutes more, only; if he didn't show up by then, he would leave.

"Well, now, lookie here! Aren't you a cutie, though?"

One of the bar girls came up to him and began running one of her hands through his thinning hair. She was wearing a very low-cut dress, and as she leaned against him, one of her breasts threatened to spill out. She might have been pretty at one time, but the dissipation of her trade had taken its toll. Her eyes were hard, her face drawn and haggard beyond her years. She had a three-corner scar on her chin, and two of her teeth were missing.

"Please," Denman said. "I am waiting for someone."

"Well, honey, wouldn't you like to have a good time while you are waiting?" the girl asked. She threw one leg over his right leg, then straddled his thigh and scooted up against him, pressing against him. "Mandy can show you a real good time," she said.

"No, please, I am not the kind who indulges in such behavior."

"What's the matter, can't you get it up?" a man at

the next table over asked. His question was followed by loud laughter.

"Give it a pull, Mandy," the same man said. "Maybe if you work on it you can get it to come up."

"Please!" Denman said. "I am not one who associates with prostitutes."

"We can see that, Mister," his antagonist said. "We're just trying to figure out some way to help you is all."

Denman didn't know which he was feeling the most: humiliation or fear.

"Would you be Denman?" a cold, calm voice asked, cutting through all the laughter and ribbing.

"I beg your pardon?" Denman replied, surprised to hear his name mentioned in there.

"I was told to look for a scared-looking little shit, and that would be you, wouldn't it? Are you Denman?"

The speaker was an ugly man with a gaunt face and a long, disfiguring scar. It had to be Kingsley.

"Please, don't say my name so loud," Denman said. "I've no wish to be known by anyone who would habituate such a place as this. You would be Mr. Kingsley?"

"Mr. Kingsley?" Kingsley said. He laughed out loud again. "Yeah, I reckon that would be me."

"You are late," he said.

Kingsley pulled a long black cigar from his shirt pocket and held a match to the end. Not until his head was enwreathed with cigar smoke did he stare through the cloud at Denman. "Well, if I've interrupted somethin' you've got goin' on, I reckon I can wait until you're finished," he offered with a sardonic grin.

"No!" Denman said sharply. "I have nothing going on! I want to get our business taken care of, and then leave this—this horrid place!"

"Oh, honey, you aren't in that big of a hurry are you?" Mandy asked.

"Get offen his lap, girl. You've already seen that he ain't got nothin' for you."

With a pout, Mandy got off Denman's leg then turned toward Kingsley. "How about you, honey? Have you got somethin' for me?"

"Not now. Git," Kingsley said.

Mandy walked away, rejected and angry.

"Too bad I broke that up, Denman. I think Mandy was beginnin' to take a shine to you. And you ought to feel good about that. It takes a heap to get a whore to actually wantin' you."

"Please," Denman said. "I'm not interested in anything a prostitute might want or not want. And I don't like this place. I want to conclude our business, then leave."

"Get up, I'll be takin' your chair," Kingsley said.

"I beg your pardon?"

"I don't sit with my back to the room. Get up. I want that chair."

"Oh, uh, yes. All right, of course," Denman said, getting up from his chair and moving around the table so Kingsley could sit with his back to the corner.

"I'll have a whiskey," Kingsley said.

"A whiskey. Yes, of course," Denman said. "I'll be right back."

Denman walked over to the bar, being careful to

keep himself as separate as possible from the other customers and from Mandy, who was standing at the bar, still staring at him. She offered him a broken-toothed smile when he approached the bar, but dropped it when she realized that he wasn't coming toward her. He ordered a whiskey and another beer, then carried the two drinks back to the table, handing one of them to Kingsley.

Kingsley picked up the whiskey and tossed it down, then put the cigar back in his mouth, holding it clenched tightly in his teeth before he spoke again.

"All right," Kingsley said. "What is our business?"

"Is it true that you are an—uh, I don't know how to say this without coming right out and saying it—but, are you really an outlaw?"

"Why don't you come right out and say it?" Kingsley said. "You've got somebody you want me to kill. Is that it?"

"What? Heavens, no!" Denman said with a startled gasp. "That's not it at all. What would make you think such a thing?"

Kingsley chuckled. "What would make me think such a thing? Well, Denman, look at you and look at me. People like me and you don't never get together unless one has somthin' the other wants. I figure you got somebody that you think needs killin', and you're wantin' me to do it for you."

"Do you mean to tell me that if I did have someone for you to kill, that you would actually be willing to do something like that?"

"It depends on how much you would be willin' to

pay," Kingsley said. "It ain't something I do for fun. But I'll kill someone if I'm gettin' paid to do it."

"I have no wish for you to kill anyone."

"Then what do you want with me?"

Denman paused for a long moment before he answered. What if Kingsley agreed to do what he wanted, but then decided to cut Denman completely out of the picture? If he did that, what could Denman do about it?

The truth was he could do nothing about it. His only hope was in convincing Kingsley that if he played it straight with him, he could come up with other opportunities equal to, or perhaps even better than, this one.

"I have a proposition that I think would be mutually beneficial to us. A way to make some money."

"How much money?"

"Don't you want to hear what I want you to do first?"

"If there's enough money in it, I don't care what it is," Kingsley said. "And if there isn't enough money, it don't matter what it is."

"Your share would come to three thousand dollars."

Kingsley's eyes opened in interest. "Three thousand dollars?"

"Yes."

"That's my share, you mean. That's not the total amount?"

"No, the total amount is fifteen thousand, eight hundred and twelve dollars and fifty cents."

Denman had debated with himself as to whether or not he should tell Kingsley just how much money really was involved. He decided it would be best to go ahead and tell him, because Kingsley was going to find out anyway.

Now Kingsley's eyes narrowed in a squint. "Wait a minute. The total amount is over fifteen thousand dollars, but I am only going to get three thousand?"

"Isn't that enough? A moment ago, you seemed quite pleased with three thousand dollars."

"Yeah, well, that was before I learned that the total amount was over fifteen thousand. I want half."

"But I have had to do all the planning. I am the one who has set it up."

"But you need me for some reason, right?"

"Yes, of course, or I wouldn't have contacted you."

"What do you need me for?"

"I shall need you to actually, uh, take the money from the gentleman in question."

"In other words, you need someone to supply the muscle."

"Yes."

"Let me ask you this, Denman. What would keep me from just taking the money myself and leaving you out of it?"

"I would hope that you would have enough, uh," Denman cleared his throat before he continued, "honor to hold up to your end of the bargain."

Kingsley chuckled. "Honor, huh? You mean as in 'honor among thieves'? Something like that?"

Denman was very uncomfortable now, and he took out his handkerchief again, and, removing his glasses began nervously polishing the lenses.

"Something like that, yes," Denman said. "And of

course, a realization that I can supply you with many more opportunities to make money."

"But, and let me get this right, I am to get only three thousand dollars but you will get twelve?"

"On this particular job, yes." Denman had no intention of ever doing another job, but he had no reservations about dangling the prospect of more opportunities in Kingsley's face.

"Well, I'll tell you what. Three thousand dollars don't buy a lot of honor, but eight thousand dollars does."

"That's more than half," Denman said.

"Yeah, well, you said more than fifteen thousand, and my math ain't all that good. If the total is over fifteen thousand, then that's gettin' close to sixteen thousand, and half of sixteen thousand is eight."

Denman put his glasses back on, then cleared his throat before he spoke again. "Uh, yes, I believe that upon further reflection, I can see your point of view. Very well, your share will be eight thousand dollars. And if this particular arrangement works out all right, I'm sure I will be able to find other, let us say, opportunities for us to work together."

"Eight thousand dollars, you say?" Kingsley smiled broadly, but instead of making his face less frightening, it seemed to draw it into a bizarre harlequin-like mask.

"Yes, I will go along with eight thousand," Denman said. After all, he thought, eight thousand would more than clear up his own personal debts.

"All right, let's hear it. What is this opportunity?

"I don't know if Mr. Howard told you about me, but, like Howard, I work in the Kansas City Cattle

Exchange. We have recently closed a business deal with a rancher from Wyoming. He is coming to Kansas City to buy five hundred head of cattle."

"Haw! He's comin' to buy cattle? I thought people come here to sell *you* cattle."

"We both buy and sell," Denman said. "That's why we are called a cattle exchange. Anyway, I have been in contact with the gentleman in question, and I know that he will have on his person enough money, in cash, to make the purchase."

"Why would he be bringing that much money with him in cash? I thought rich folks wrote bank drafts and the like."

"Normally that would be the case, but Mr. Mac-Callister will be bringing cash because I made all the arrangements, and I told him that we will require cash on delivery."

"Wait a minute. You mean he don't really need to be bringin' cash, he's just carryin' it 'cause you told him to?"

"Yes."

Kingsley laughed and slapped his hand on the table. "Hot damn," he said. "It really is true what they say, ain't it? Some folks rob you with a gun, and some rob you with a fountain pen."

"Before I go any further with this, are you willing to undertake this operation?"

"Yeah, I'm in," Kingsley said. "But I do have a question. How am I going to know who it is?"

"His name is MacCallister. Duff MacCallister."

"What does he look like?"

"Oh, I don't have any idea what he looks like," Denman replied.

Kingsley got a perplexed look on his face. "Well, if you don't know what he looks like, just tell me how 'n the hell I'm goin' to know who it is I'm supposed to rob?"

"He is coming here by train from Cheyenne, Wyoming. He will telegraph us before he leaves Cheyenne. Since he cannot come here directly from Cheyenne, he will have to change trains in Fremont, Nebraska. You will be in Fremont, and I will telegraph you with information as to what day he will arrive there.

"The eastbound train from Cheyenne arrives in Fremont just before midnight, and the train from Fremont to here will not leave until one-thirty the following afternoon. Mr. MacCallister is a wealthy man, so that means he will not spend all that time in the depot. He will, no doubt, walk from the depot to the hotel. He will be alone, and it will be in the darkest part of the night. I think that if you get to Fremont before him, you will be able to find a place somewhere between the depot and the hotel where you might accost him and relieve him of his money."

"You still ain't told me how I'm goin' to recognize him."

"As I said, he will be carrying almost sixteen thousand dollars in cash, and in order to carry that much money, he shall require a small satchel of some kind. That is how you will be able to recognize him."

"So what you are saying is I am to go after ever'-one who gets off the train that's carrying one of them little satchels?"

"If necessary, in order to find the right one," Denman said. "But how many men do you suppose will exit the train at that time of night, carrying a briefcase and bound for the hotel?"

"All right, I guess you got a point there," Kingsley agreed. Again he smiled, and again the smile did nothing to ameliorate his foreboding countenance. "Me 'n you have us a deal. Now, let me ask you something else."

"Yes?"

"What about the whore?"

"I beg your pardon?"

Kingsley pointed to Mandy, who was still standing over near the bar. "The whore over there. Are you going to take her to bed or not?"

"Heavens, no!"

"Then you don't have no problem with me taking her?"

"You, uh, can have her," Denman said. "I must go."

Kingsley laughed at Denman as he hurried out of the saloon.

Chapter Fourteen

Sky Meadow

Even as Hodge Denman and Crack Kingsley were having their discussion, Duff was at Sky Meadow getting ready for the big Firemen's Ball. While in Scotland, Duff had been a captain of the Black Watch regiment. Because of that, he had a complete Black Watch uniform, which consisted of a Glengarry hat with the cap-badge of the Black Watch, Saltire, the Lion Rampant and the Crown, with the motto *Nemo Me Impune Lacessit* (No One Provokes Me With Impunity), a kilt of blue and green tartan, a black waistcoat, an embossed leather sporran which he wore around his waist, knee-high stockings, and the *sgian dubh,* or ceremonial knife tucked into the right kilt stocking, with only the pommel visible. He was also wearing the Victoria Cross, Great Britain's highest award for bravery, which was awarded him for his bravery above and beyond the call of duty during the battle of Tel-el-Kebir in Egypt.

At the moment, Duff was standing in front of the

hall mirror, making certain that all was as it should be, when Elmer came in, having just returned from the post office in town.

"You got that letter you was lookin' for, from the Kansas City Cattle Exchange."

"Good, let me see it."

Elmer handed Duff the letter and he read it, then nodded. "Yes, this confirms the telegram. They want me to bring the money there, in cash. And I'll have to make my own arrangements for the train."

"I tell you what, Duff, once you get all set up there in Kansas City, you send me a telegram tellin' me what time you plan on bein' in Cheyenne and I'll round up enough hands so's we can push the herd back here."

"All right," Duff said. "Thank you."

"Also, I've got the buckboard all hooked up and ready to go," Elmer said. "So let me know when—damn—pardon me boss for mentionin' it, but that sure as hell is some outfit you are wearing!"

"'Tis my regimental uniform," Duff said.

Elmer pointed to the kilts. "I'll say this for you. It takes a brave man to wear somethin' like that here. But I reckon anyone who makes fun of it will have to answer to you."

"There will be but few who would dare to make mockery o' the blue 'n green," he said.

Elmer shook his head. "I reckon that's so," he said. "And just so's you know it, Duff, I ain't makin' no mockery of it."

"I didn't think you were," Duff replied.

Elmer was wearing a brown four-button suit coat,

black and brown striped trousers, a rounded-lapel burgundy silk vest, and a saloonkeeper's tie that was a black neckband from which four three-inch strips of cloth were suspended.

"I must say that you seem exceptionally well turned out yourself," Duff said.

Elmer chuckled, then turned to show off his suit. "I bought this here suit from a mail-order catalogue," he said. "Would you believe this is the first suit I've ever owned?"

"Is it, now?"

"Ha! I'll bet the first time you seen me, you never thought you'd see me in a suit like this, did you?"

Duff thought of the first sight he'd ever had of Elmer. He was with his cousin, Falcon MacCallister, and they were examining the old abandoned Spanish mine that was on the land he had just filed upon. The rumor was that, though the mine was fallow, it was haunted.

Duff walked over to the wall and held up the lantern. Something in the wall glittered back in the light.

"I'm going to pick here for a while and see what turns up," Duff said.

Sitting the lantern down, Duff began using the pickax on the wall. Each time he struck, large chunks of shale would tumble down from the wall. As he continued to strike at the wall the tailings piled up on the floor of the mine and Falcon got on his knees to sift through them, looking for any sign of color.

"Have you found anything?" Duff asked.

"No, not yet. Wait, there might be something here . . ."

Duff turned to look at Falcon, and when he did, he saw a frightening apparition behind him. A two-legged creature covered with hair, and with wild eyes, was holding a large rock in both hands, about to bring it crashing down on Falcon's head.

"Look out!" Duff yelled and, reacting quickly, Falcon leaped to one side as, with a loud scream, the creature brought the rock down.

Thanks to Duff's warning the rock had missed Falcon, but the creature lifted it over his head again, and with gleaming red eyes, came toward Duff. Duff used the head of the pickax to knock the rock out of the creature's hands. With another bloodcurdling scream, the creature turned and ran, disappearing into the dark tunnel of the mine as if able to see in the dark.

"Are you all right?" Duff asked.

"Yes," Falcon said, standing up and brushing himself off.

"What on earth was that?" Duff asked.

"I don't know. Maybe Mr. Guthrie's ghost?" Falcon replied.

"'Twas no ghost, for it was something physical."

"A bear, maybe?"

"I don't know about American bears, but I've never seen a bear in Europe that could use his hands like this one did."

"Are you going to continue to look for gold?"

"Sure'n you aren't thinking I'm going to be frightened off by a ghost, are you? Especially since it isn't a ghost."

* * *

The mine was neither fallow nor haunted, and Duff chuckled as he recalled the memory.

"Truth to tell, Elmer, first time I saw you I wasn't even sure you were human."

"Yes, sir, well, I'm human enough now, and if you think all the widder women in town ain't goin' to be happy to see me, why, you just got yourself another think comin'."

"All the widows, Elmer? Or would you be talking about one in particular? Mrs. Winslow, I believe?"

"Well, you got to admit, Duff, Vi Winslow is a handsome enough woman," Elmer said.

"Aye, she is at that," Duff replied. With a last minute adjustment to his hat, he started toward the door. "Come, Elmer. We don't want to keep the ladies waiting, do we?"

Elmer laughed. "No, sir, not at all. Why, it just wouldn't be right for a couple of handsome galoots like us to keep the ladies waiting."

The dance was being held in the ballroom of the Dunn Hotel. The hotel was on the corner of Bowie Avenue and First Street, and the ladies of the town had spent the entire day decorating it for the dance. Red, white, and blue bunting hung from the walls, and potted plants and bouquets of flowers were in the corners and on the tables that were placed around the outer corners of the floor, thus allowing enough space for the dance.

The ladies had been preparing food as well, and cakes, pies, cookies, doughnuts, divinity, and fudge were in crystal bowls around the floor. There was also a very large punch bowl filled with Roman punch made from lemonade, champagne, rum, orange juice, and egg whites.

The fire brigade had hired a band from Cheyenne, and when they had arrived earlier that same afternoon, several of the citizens of the town saw them step down from the stagecoach while gingerly handling their instruments. Soon word passed through the entire town that the band was here and the level of excitement increased throughout the town, for this was the social event of the year.

Back in her apartment over the Ladies' Emporium, Meghan lay three dresses out for her examination, and looked at them as she made up her mind which one to choose for the ball tonight. She had made all three: one white and demure, one blue and regal, and one red and daring. With a degree of boldness she didn't really feel, she chose the red one. With its low neckline, no sleeves, and tight bodice, it was a dress that would show off her figure to perfection. She picked it up, then held it in front of her as she looked in the mirror. She smiled at her image.

"Mr. Duff Tavish MacCallister, are you ready for Meghan, because she's ready for you," she said. Laying the dress down, she went back to fill the tub for her bath.

* * *

By dusk, the excitement that had been growing for the entire day was full blown. The sound of the practicing musicians could be heard all up and down Bowie Avenue as well as First Street. Children looked through the glowing yellow windows on the ground floor of the barn. As soon as the doors were opened, they rushed inside, then scrambled up the stairs to the balcony overlook in order to have the best view of all the proceedings.

Horses and buckboards began arriving and soon every hitching rail within two blocks of the Dunn Hotel was filled. Men and women streamed along the boardwalks toward the barn, the women in colorful dresses, the men in suits or clean, blue denims and brightly decorated vests.

A sign on the door and behind the bar of Fiddler's Green said that the establishment would be closed at six o'clock that evening. Most had already cleared out of the saloon except for Biff, who was behind the bar, young Lonnie Mathers, who was earning a little extra money by sweeping the floor, a couple of older gentlemen seated together in the back of the room, and three young cowboys: Al Woodward, Case Martin and Brax Walker.

As it so happened, these were the same three men that Biff had run out of his saloon at the point of a gun a few weeks earlier when they had gotten too surly with the piano player. They had returned the next day, contrite and repentant, asking politely to be allowed to visit the saloon again. Biff had granted them permission, and so far they had done nothing to violate his generosity.

"How come you're closin' at six?" Woodward asked.

"I'm closing at six because of the dance," Biff answered. "I promised my wife we would go. Besides, with most of the town being there, I doubt that I will have many customers."

"What dance?" Martin asked.

"You know what dance, Case," Brax Walker said. "Hell, they got the whole town plastered with banners and posters about it."

"Oh, yeah. I seen 'em."

"We ought to go," Brax said.

"Why? We ain't got no women to go with," Martin replied.

"That don't mean nothin'. Hell, they'll have women there. What do you say, Al? Think we should go to the dance?"

"Yeah, why not? Woodward answered. "We may as well. There ain't nothin' happenin' in this place now."

"You men," Biff called to the three as they left. "Stay out of trouble. A lot of people in town look forward to these dances, and I wouldn't want to see their time there upset by a bunch of men acting like fools."

"Yeah, yeah," Woodward replied with an impatient wave of his hand as he left. "Don't worry about it, old man."

* * *

Meghan arrived before Duff and, after receiving oohs and ahhs from all the other women about her dress, she walked over to one side so she could keep an eye on the door without being too obvious. As she was standing there, Sue Stearns came up to her to show off her dress, a dress Meghan had made for her.

"Oh, Meghan, I am getting so many compliments on this dress, you did such a wonderful job," Sue said.

"They aren't complimenting the dress, Sue, they are complimenting you. You look beautiful in it."

"Why, thank you," Sue said, blushing. Sue turned to leave, then she gasped. "Oh, my, look over there," she said.

Looking in the direction Sue had indicated, Meghan saw Duff standing just inside the front door. He was perusing the room, and he was in his kilts. For most men, in fact, for just about any other man Meghan knew, it would have been a farcical entry. But Duff towered over every other man there, not only in his height but in his raw power, broad shoulders, powerful arms, and muscular legs, shown off by what he was wearing. Duff was also carrying his bagpipes, having been asked by Biff Johnson to bring them. Biff's wife was Scottish, and had a fondness for the pipes.

Duff and Meghan saw each other at about the same time, and, with a big smile, Duff came toward her.

"My, don't you look beautiful tonight," Duff said.

"So do you," Meghan replied.

Duff laughed. "Sure 'n don't let Elmer hear you

say that. Methinks he is havin' a bit of a problem with m' wearin' o' the kilts as it is. And I suppose it is a bit pretentious of me."

"Nonsense, you look devilishly handsome," Meghan said.

"Ladies and gents!" someone shouted, and looking toward the sound they saw Fred Matthews standing up on the band platform. Fred was the city fire commissioner, and as such, was in charge of the Firemen's Benefit Ball.

"Ladies and gents, may I have your attention, please?" Fred said, holding his hands up.

The laughter stopped and the myriad conversations ended as everyone looked toward Fred.

"I want to thank you folks for coming tonight. And I thought you might like to know that the money we raised by selling tickets to this event is enough to buy a new pumper!"

Everyone cheered and applauded.

"And now, what do you say we have some fun?" he shouted, and there were more cheers and applause.

The caller stepped up to the front of the platform then. "Ladies and gents, form your squares!" he shouted, and the men and women rushed to the floor to form the squares. Elmer and Mrs. Violet Winslow, the attractive widow who owned Vi's Pies, joined the same square as Duff and Meghan.

The music began then, and the caller started to shout. As he did so, he clapped his hands and danced around bowing and spinning as if he had a girl and was in one of the squares himself. The floor became a kaleidoscope of color as the dancers moved and swirled to the caller's commands—the butterfly-bright dresses with skirts whirling out, the jewels in their hair, at their necks or on the bodices, sparkling in the light.

> *Ladies do and the gents you know,*
> *It's right by right and wrong you go,*
> *And you can't go to heaven while you carry on so,*
> *And it's home little gal and do-si-do,*

He was quiet for a moment, and the fiddle player stepped front so that the high skirling sound carried throughout the barn as the dancers moved in and out and whirled about.

The fiddler stepped back and the caller became king again.

> *Now it may be the last time, but I don't know,*
> *And oh by gosh and oh by Joe.*
> *Circle eight and you get straight,*
> *And we'll all go east on a westbound freight.*

Once more the fiddler held sway as the dancers continued. The fiddler worked the bow up and down the fiddle, bending over, kicking out one leg then the other as he played, his movements as entertaining as the music itself. Then, when his riff was over, the caller stepped up again.

> *Round we go and do si do*
> *Pass by Bill, say hello to Joe*
> *Knock down Sal and pick up Kate,*
> *And we'll all join hands and circle eight.*

Around the dance floor sat those without partners. As there were many more men than women, the only ones who were not dancing were the men. Every woman, regardless of her comeliness, or lack thereof, was engaged in one of the squares. Overhead, young boys and young girls lay on their stomachs at the edge of the balcony, the better able to look down on the dancing below.

Chapter Fifteen

Because there were so many more men than there were women, Duff agreed to sit several of the dances out in order that Meghan could dance with some of the unattached cowboys. Duff walked over to the punch bowl and poured himself a drink, but nearly choked, because over the course of the evening, cowboys had added so much whiskey to the punch that it was nearly pure whiskey by now.

"What's the matter, Miss? Is the punch a little too strong for you?"

The question asked was obviously a mocking reference to the kilts Duff was wearing. The questioner was a cowboy, nearly as big as Duff, and there were two more with him. The questioner and the two who were with him laughed at the sarcastic question.

Duff didn't know their names, but he had seen all three before. It took but a moment for him to recall that they were the three cowboys Biff had kicked out of the saloon a while back.

"Aye, 'tis a wee bit too strong and that is a fact," Duff replied. He didn't take the bait, so the cowboy tried again.

"Me 'n my buddies was lookin' at all the purty dresses the women folk is wearin' tonight, and what we was tryin' to do is figure out who was wearin' the purtiest dress. And damn me, if we didn't choose you."

"Aye, the kilt of the Black Watch is quite a handsome getup, I agree," Duff said.

"Come on, Al, hell, he either ain't got enough smarts or enough sand to get riled by us. Let's find us some women," one of the other cowboys said.

Duff watched them walk away, fighting back the quick flash of anger that had built up inside him. He didn't react to the baiting, because he had no wish to cause any trouble.

The music stopped, and Fred came over to talk to Duff.

"Any trouble with those galoots?"

"No trouble," Duff answered.

"They're the same ones caused a little trouble down at Fiddler's Green a while back, if you remember."

"Yes, I thought I recognized them. I don't know them, though."

"The big one is Al Woodward. The other two are Case Martin and Brax Walker. They hang around Woodward like gnats buzzin' around a dog's pecker. They can't hold a job more than a few months anywhere they've ever been, 'cause they are always getting into trouble."

"They did seem to be a bit quarrelsome," Duff agreed.

"Oh, the reason I come over here is that some of the folks were hoping you would play the pipes now," Fred asked.

"What about the band?"

"The caller says he needs a break, and the band is all for it. And you did bring your pipes with you."

"Aye, I brought them."

"What are you going to play? I'll announce it," Fred said.

"'The Skye Boat Song,'" Duff said.

Fred nodded, then he stepped up to the band platform. Because the music had stopped, it was easy to get everyone's attention.

"Ladies and gents, we are in for a treat tonight, and I mean a real treat. I have prevailed upon Mr. Duff MacCallister to play a tune for us on his bagpipes."

"Is he goin' to curtsey, and whirl around a bit in that little dress he's a' wearin'?" Al Woodward shouted. Walker and Martin laughed loudly at Woodward's taunt, but no one else did. On the contrary, the others stared at him in annoyance.

"If you—gentlemen—would kindly be quiet so the rest of us can enjoy this treat, I will go on," Fred said, separating the word "gentlemen" from the rest of his sentence.

"Yeah, go ahead, don't let us stop you!" Woodward shouted.

"You ain't stoppin' us, sonny," Elmer said. "But if you don't shut up, a few of us are likely to stop you."

There were enough grunts of agreement with

Elmer's thinly veiled threat that Woodward and the others shut up.

"The song Mr. MacCallister has chosen is a song of Scotland, called 'The Skye Boat Song.' Duff, the platform is yours," Fred said.

There was a scattering of applause as Duff moved up onto the platform. He inflated his bag, and there was a tone from the drone and chanter as Duff began to play. What he had not told Fred, and what he had not told anyone, ever, was that Skye McGregor had been named after this song.

After he finished, several came up to thank him for playing. Meghan, especially, was moved.

"That song means something to you, doesn't it, Duff?"

"Aye, 'tis a song of Scotland, and 'tis Scotland-born I am."

"No," Meghan said. "It's more than that. I have seen and heard you play before. But there is something very special about this song. I could see it in your face."

"You are a very astute lass, Meghan."

"It's Skye, isn't it? Yes, that's it. I believe Mr. Matthews said this was called the 'Skye Boat Song.' You were thinking of her when you were playing it."

Duff bowed his head slightly, and Meghan reached out to put her hand on his arm.

"Don't be embarrassed or self-conscious about it, please, Duff," she said. "You've no idea how wonderful I think you are for being able to sustain that kind of love. Skye was such a lucky woman."

"I should have chosen another song," Duff said. "I've no wish to bring such melancholy."

"I'm glad you chose it," Meagan said. She smiled. "And my dance card is free again."

"Ladies and gents, form your squares!" the caller shouted.

Over by the punch table, Woodward, Martin, and Walker, the three cowboys who had accosted Duff, were getting drunk on the heavily spiked punch.

"I got me an idea," Woodward said. "Martin, let's me 'n you join one o' them squares."

"We can't, we ain't got no women to dance with us."

"That don't matter none," Woodward said. "Once we start the dancin' and the do si do'n and all that, why, we'll be swingin' around with all the other women in the square."

"Yeah, Martin said. "That's right, ain't it?"

"No, it ain't right," Walker said.

"What are talkin' about? What do you mean, it ain't right?" Woodward asked.

"Well, think about it. Whichever one of you takes the woman's part will be do si do'n with all the other men when you get to swingin' around."

"Yeah, I hadn't thought about that," Martin said.

"Hell, that ain't nothin' to be worryin' about," Woodward said. "Next dance, why, we'll just switch around. Martin, you can be the woman on the first dance, then I'll set the next one out, and Walker you can come in and let Martin be the man. Then on the third dance, why, I'll come back in and be the woman. That way, all three of us can do si do with the other women."

"All right," Martin said. "But let's pick us a dance with some good-lookin' women in it."

When the next set of squares was formed, Woodward and Martin joined the same square as Duff and Meagan.

"Well, lookie here, Martin," Woodward said, pointing toward Duff. "Looks like you won't have to do si do with all men. You'll get a man in a dress. That ought to count for somethin'."

Martin laughed just as the music started.

As the couples broke apart to swing with the others, Martin made a round with the men, including Duff. But on the next round, he rebelled. Pushing one of the men aside, he started swinging around with all the women until he got to Meghan. That was when Duff stepped out into the middle of the square and grabbed him by the arm.

"Get out of my way, girlie," Martin said. He reached for Meghan, but as he did so Duff, with his thumb and forefinger, squeezed the spot where Martin's neck joined his shoulder. The squeeze was so painful that Martin sunk to his knees with his face screwed up in agony. The other squares, seeing what was happening in this one, interrupted their dancing. Then the caller stopped, as did the band, the music breaking off in discordant chords.

"If you gentlemen are going to dance in our square, you'll be for doing it correctly," Duff said, talking quietly to the man, who was on his knees in pain.

"Missy, you done started somethin' you can't finish," Woodward said. Woodward was the other interloper cowboy, and he swung a powerful right fist toward Duff.

As gracefully as if he were performing a dance

move, Duff bent back at his waist and allowed Woodward's fist to fly harmlessly by his chin. Duff counterpunched with one blow to Woodward's jaw, and he went down to join Martin, who was still on the floor.

Suddenly a gunshot erupted, and men shouted and women screamed.

"Ow!" one of the young boys cried out from the balcony above. "I got shot!"

Looking toward the sound of the gunshot, Duff saw the third of the three cowboys he had encountered earlier. This was Walker, and he leveled his pistol at Duff.

"No!" Meghan shouted.

Duff reacted before anyone else did. Pulling the *sgian dubh*, or ceremonial knife, from its position in the right kilt stocking, he threw it in a quick underhanded snap toward Walker. As he had intended, the knife rotated in the air and the butt, not the blade, hit Walker right between the eyes, doing so with sufficient force to knock him down.

One of the men close to Walker reached down quickly and grabbed his pistol.

Marshal Ferrell and his deputy took charge then, escorting all three of the troublemakers out of the dance hall and down to the jail.

In the meantime Dr. Pinkstaff had gone up the stairs to the balcony to check on the boy who was hit.

"It's all right, folks," he called back down. "He wasn't hit with a bullet, just with a splinter of wood."

"But it hurt anyway," the boy said, and the crowd laughed, more from relief than anything else.

"Ladies and gents, form your squares!" the caller shouted, and the dance resumed.

Elmer and Vi Winslow were sitting this dance out.

"Don't they make a good-looking couple?" Vi asked.

"Oh, handsome enough, I reckon," Elmer said. He smiled. "But iffen you was to ask me, why I'd say we make a right handsome couple our ownselves."

Vi laughed and waved her hand at Elmer. "Hush, Elmer. You've got me blushing like a young girl."

"Why hell, Vi, you are a young girl," Elmer said. "Purty as one, anyhow. And you make the best pies I ever et."

"Elmer!" Vi said, hitting him playfully. "Now I don't know if it is me or my pies you are interested in."

"Both," Elmer said.

"Well, after the dance, you'll have to stop by the restaurant for a piece of pie."

"Say, that sounds like a good idea. We'll get Duff and Miss Parker, too."

"No."

"Why not?"

"Meghan and I discussed it," Vi said. "This will give them a chance to be alone."

"Oh?"

"And us too."

"Oh."

* * *

After the dance Duff walked Meghan home, and she invited him up to her apartment.

"Would you like a cup of coffee to help keep you awake for your drive back out to the ranch?" Meghan asked.

"I'd like to, but Elmer and I came into town together, and he . . ."

Meghan smiled at Duff and put her finger on his lips. "Worry not about Elmer. Vi will keep him busy for a while."

"How do you know?"

"Would you believe me if I said we arranged it?" Meghan asked.

Duff chuckled. "Who would have thought that women could be so devious?"

"Oh, devious?" Meghan said, and she hit him, but her response was ameliorated with a laugh. "Not devious, cooperative," she said.

"Cooperative," Duff agreed.

Meghan stepped over to the cooking stove that already had wood and kindling laid in. She lit the fire, which caught quickly, and within a few minutes her apartment was permeated by the rich aroma of coffee at the boil.

They spoke of the dance and laughed at some of the events of the evening as they drank their coffee.

"I got a letter from the Kansas City Cattle Exchange today," Duff said. "So I expect I will be leaving Monday morning to go to Kansas City."

"Will you write to me while you are gone?"

Duff smiled. "Aye, if you think the scribbling of a Scotsman would be of interest."

"Oh, I think it would be of great interest,"

Meghan said. "And I also want you to do something else for me, if you would."

"And what would that be?"

Meghan walked over to a cabinet and opened a drawer. Reaching in, she pulled out a piece of yellow ribbon.

"I've sewn a lock of my hair into this ribbon," she said. "And I've added a few drops of my favorite perfume. It's foolish, I know. But if you would, I would like you to carry it with you."

"Meghan, I . . ." Duff started, but Meghan held up her hand to interrupt him.

"Worry not about any implied meaning," she said. "It is for luck, and for luck only. It will comfort me to know that you have it with you."

"I wasn't about to protest," he said. "I was about to tell you that I would be most happy to carry it with me." He lowered the ribbon from his nose to his lips. "The French call this a *jeton d'affection.*"

"Oh, what lovely sounding words," Meghan said. "What does that mean?"

"It means a token of affection."

Meghan smiled. "Really?" she said.

Duff raised the ribbon to his nose, inhaled the perfume, then kissed it.

"You can be satisfied with kissing the ribbon," Meghan said. "Or . . ."

"Or?"

"This," Meghan said, standing on her tiptoes and lifting her lips to his to kiss him. The kiss was quick and chaste, but when Meghan pulled away from him, her face was flushed with embarrassment.

"I hope you do not think ill of me for doing such a thing," she said.

"Meghan Parker, I could never think ill of you," Duff said. "And I promise you that this"—he held up the yellow ribbon—"and your kiss," he put his finger on Meghan's lips, "will be with me for m' whole journey."

Chapter Sixteen

Duff and Elmer had not ridden into town, but had driven a buckboard. They were talking animatedly about the events of the night as they drove back home, but about two miles from Sky Meadow, they saw an orange glow in the dark sky ahead.

"What's that?" Elmer asked.

"It looks like a fire at home," Duff replied.

"Hyah!" Elmer shouted, snapping the reins and urging the team into a gallop.

As they got closer to the ranch they could see flames in the sky, and closer still, they saw that the barn was on fire.

"Sure 'n what would make the barn catch fire?" Duff asked. "We left no lanterns or such."

The team ran all-out for the last two miles, and Elmer applied the brake and pulled them to a halt as they slid to a stop in the front yard. By now, the barn was totally involved, the fire was leaping high into the air, and they could feel the heat.

It was too late to do anything about the fire or

even to help the animals, the two milk cows, and Sky. Fortunately, Elmer's horse, Rebel, was one of the two that were pulling the buckboard.

There was no sound except for the pop, snap, and roar of the fire.

"Sky," Duff said, shaking his head.

They heard a horse whinny, and looking around, saw Sky standing near the house, his eyes shining in the light of the fire.

"Sky!" Duff said, leaping down from the buckboard and running to him. Sky lowered his head and let Duff pet him. "I thought I had lost you."

Sky pulled away from Duff and trotted over to the fence, then he turned back toward Duff, whinnied again, and began bobbing his head.

"What do you think he's found over there?" Elmer asked, climbing down from the buckboard. He and Duff started toward Sky but saw, even before they got there, what Sky was trying to show them. There was the body of a man lying on the ground. The man's fingers were clutched around the handle of a kerosene can.

"I'll be damned," Elmer said. "This must be the son of a bitch who burned the barn. What's he doing here?"

"Look at the side of his head," Duff said. "I think Sky must have killed him."

"Well good for you, Sky," Elmer said. He leaned down for a closer look. "Wait a minute. I know this galoot."

"You do? Who is it?"

"His name is Clete Wilson. You heard the story

they told about the fella that braced me in Fiddler's Green?"

"Yes."

Elmer pointed to the body. "This is him. He must've found out that I lived out here and figured burnin' your barn would get him even with me. I'm sorry, Duff. Looks like I brought this one to you."

"Nothing for you to be sorry about," Duff said. "You had nothing to do with it."

"What do you want me to do with him?"

"Take him into town tomorrow, I suppose. Take him to Constable Ferrell's office, I expect he will know what to do next."

"All right," Elmer said.

"Poor Tillie and Sable," Duff said, speaking of the two milk cows. "They were such gentle creatures. It's a shame they had to die like this."

By the next morning, there was nothing left of the barn but a pile of blackened boards and rubble. Fortunately, the tack house was separate from the barn, so the saddles and tack were unharmed by the fire. Duff had also withdrawn the money earlier, and it was safe in an attaché case in the house.

Duff and Elmer poked around in the residue of the barn to see if anything could be salvaged. They found the charred remains of the two milk cows, and though there wasn't much left to bury, they buried them over in the corner of the corral where they liked to stand and look out toward Bear Creek.

It was late morning by the time Duff was ready to leave for Cheyenne. Elmer had loaded Wilson's body onto the back of the buckboard and covered it with a tarpaulin. After an exchange of good-byes, the two men left at the same time, going in opposite directions.

Because Duff got away from Sky Meadow late, he didn't reach Cheyenne until it was already past normal business hours at the J.C. Abney Livery Stable. Only the night crew was there, two teenage boys, neither of whom Duff knew. One was white and one was an Indian. Both of them came out front to meet him.

"Wantin' to board your horse, Mister?" the white boy asked.

"Aye. And for some time, at least a week. Maybe longer. Where's Donnie?"

"He don't work nights. You know Donnie?"

"I do, I've boarded here before."

"Then you know that it'll be fifty cents a night, and that Mr. Abney, he likes to have the money in advance."

"Suppose I pay you for four weeks. That would be fourteen dollars."

"What if you come back before that?"

"I would imagine you are going to write me a receipt," Duff said. "I'll simply show the receipt and get the money back."

"Yeah, I didn't think of that. Hawk, you want to take the man's horse and put it up?"

Duff reached up to remove the suitcase and briefcase he had attached to the horse as the Indian led the animal away.

"What's your name?" the boy who was making out the receipt asked.

"Duff MacCallister."

The boy looked up in awe. "Wait a minute! You the one that made that shot here a while back, ain't you? The one what kilt Tyler Camden. Folks is still talkin' about that."

"I suppose I am," Duff said.

"Well, sir, it's a good thing you done it, 'cause iffen you hadn't done it, one day I would've."

"Really?"

"Yes, sir. Camden was a no-account," the boy said. "My sister, she, uh, works, down at the Eagle Saloon. She don't do the kind of work that most folks would consider decent, if you know what I mean, but that don't give nobody the right to beat her up, and that's just what Camden done. And my sister, she wan't the only one he beat up. He beat up a lot of girls for no reason at all."

The boy finished the receipt and gave it to Duff.

"I'm just real proud to have met you, Mr. MacCallister. And don't you worry none about your horse. Me 'n Hawk and Donnie, why, we'll just take real good care of it."

After taking care of his horse, Duff walked back to the Inter Ocean Hotel to check in, and to leave his suitcase while he went to dinner. He thought about leaving his briefcase as well, but decided against it. After all, there was almost sixteen thousand dollars in his briefcase, not a sum of money to be taken lightly.

Because he was carrying the briefcase with him, he decided to have dinner in the Cheyenne Club, believing it to be more secure than a restaurant. He ordered a steak and baked potato, and was just finishing his meal when Warren and Converse came in, already in the midst of some conversation. Seeing him, they walked over to his table.

"Hello, Duff. Do you mind if we join you?"

"Not at all," Duff said, standing and shaking hands with each of them as they joined him.

"What are you doing back in Cheyenne so soon?" Warren asked.

"I'm taking the train to Kansas City to pick up my cattle," Duff said.

"You mean they won't ship them to you?" Converse asked.

"In the letter, they said no."

"That doesn't sound like they want your business all that much," Warren said. "In fact, it doesn't sound like the KCCE at all. I bought my first Herefords from them, and they shipped them right to me, made all the arrangements themselves."

"Well, you forget Francis, Duff is getting Black Angus. Maybe they are afraid some buffalo will get into the herd and take care of the bulls' business," Converse said.

Warren, and even Duff, laughed.

"Say, Duff, you haven't run into a fella by the name of Gilbert Patten since you got into town, have you?" Converse asked.

"No, I can't say as I have," Duff replied, shaking his head. "Who is he?"

"He's a man that wants to do for you, what Colonel

Prentiss Ingraham has done for your cousin, Falcon," Converse said. "He wants to write about you in one of his novels and make you famous."

"He has read about your exploits, the events up in Chugwater last year, the more recent shows here, and on the road back to Chugwater," Warren added.

"He's here in the club, right now," Converse said. "We can introduce you to him, if you would like."

Duff shook his head. "No, thank you, I would rather not meet him."

Warren chuckled, then held his hand out toward Converse, palm up. "What did I tell you?" he said. "You owe me fifty dollars."

"Yeah, yeah, you were right, don't rub it in," Converse said. He removed five ten-dollar bills and counted them out into Warren's hand.

"In case you are wondering what this is about, I bet Converse that you wouldn't want anything to do with Patten," he said.

"And I was sure you would," Converse said.

"What made you think such a thing?" Duff asked.

"Why, everyone would like to be famous, wouldn't they?"

"I don't know about everyone else. But as for me, I will pass on that cup, thank you," Duff said.

"Then, if you really don't want to meet him, you'd best leave by the back door," Warren said. "He's sittin' out front in the lobby right now, and sure as a gun is iron, if you walk through there, someone is goin' to point you out to him."

"Thanks," Duff said and, gathering his briefcase, he stepped out through the back door.

It was dark now, and he was in the alley between

the buildings, holding a briefcase that contained almost sixteen thousand dollars in cash. Such a thing would be intimidating for most people, but Duff didn't give it a second thought as he walked toward the hotel.

A few minutes later, Duff was standing at the window of his room on the third floor of the Inter-Ocean Hotel, looking out at the traffic, both foot and carriage, on Sixteenth and Capitol below. There was no greater demonstration of the difference between Cheyenne and Chugwater than this, for by this time of evening in Chugwater the streets and sidewalks were totally empty, with the restaurant and Fiddler's Green showing the only signs of life. Here, though it was past eight o'clock, the streets were teeming.

Duff held up the little piece of yellow ribbon Meghan had given him and, as he let the hair brush against the tip of his nose and inhaled the perfume, he thought of her. Could Meghan take the place of Skye McGregor?

No. Nobody could ever take Skye's place.

But, could Meghan find her own place in Duff's heart, a place that was at least equal to Skye's?

It was too early for Duff to make that appraisal, but he was already willing to admit that the idea wasn't beyond possibility.

Then, even as he considered it, he thought of what happened to Skye. He had been the one they were shooting at, not Skye, but Skye was the one they had killed. And, already here, he had shown a proclivity for finding himself in dangerous situations. He had been attacked on the trail going back home last week. If Meghan had been with him then, she could have been killed.

Then there was the burning of his barn, last night. Yes, Elmer said they were after him, but it didn't matter. He had lost two cows in the fire, and it could just as easily have been his house that was burned. If Meghan had been in his house, she could have been killed. If another young woman died just because she loved him and he loved her, he didn't know if he could live with it. Was he really willing to take that chance with Meghan?

Turning, he put the ribbon away, then turned off the lamp and crawled into bed. Before going to sleep, he thought about the trip tomorrow, and the arrangements he would have to make to bring his cattle back home. And at twenty-five cows per car, he would have to lease twenty cars, but he had already been in contact with both railroads and was assured that it would not be difficult to make such arrangements.

He also thought about Meghan. Would she want to give up her dress shop and come out to the ranch to live? Was he premature in even thinking such a thing? In fact, he had no idea what Meghan really thought of him.

Even though he was thinking about arrangements for shipping his cattle, and wondering where his relationship was going with Meghan, when he finally drifted off to sleep, he dreamed of Skye.

"Skye, would you step outside with me for a moment?" Duff asked.

"*Ian, best you keep an eye on them,*" one of the other customers said. "*Else they'll be outside sparking.*"

Skye blushed prettily as the others laughed at the jibe. Duff took her hand in his and walked outside with her.

"*Only four more weeks until we are wed,*" Skye said when they were outside. "*I can hardly wait.*"

"*No need to wait. We can go into Glasgow and be married on the morrow,*" Duff suggested.

"*Duff MacCallister, sure and m' mother has waited my whole life to give me a fine church wedding now, and you would deny that to her?*"

Duff chuckled. "*Don't worry, Skye. There is no way in the world I would start my married life by getting on the bad side of my mother-in-law. If you want to wait, then I will wait with you.*"

"*What do you mean you will wait with me?*" Skye asked. "*And what else would you be doing, Duff MacCallister? Would you be finding a willing young lass to wait with you?*"

"*I don't know such a willing lass,*" Duff replied. "*Do you? For truly, it would be an interesting experiment.*"

"*Oh, you!*" Skye said, hitting Duff on the shoulder. It was the same shoulder Alexander had hit in the fight and he winced.

"*Oh!*" she said. "*I'm sorry. You just made me mad talking about a willing lass.*"

Duff laughed, then pulled Skye to him. "*You are the only willing lass I want,*" he said.

"*I should hope so.*"

Duff bent down to kiss her waiting lips.

"*I told you, Ian! Here they are, sparking in the dark!*" a customer shouted and, with a good natured laugh, Duff *and Skye parted. With a final wave to those who had come outside to "see the sparking," Duff started home.*

Duff had to get Skye out of his mind. Not out of his heart; he would always have a place for her in his heart, but he had to get her out of his mind or the grieving would never stop.

He inhaled the perfume of the little yellow ribbon again and thought of Meghan. He knew that she could help him get Skye out of his mind, but would it be fair to Meghan? Would he just be using her as a means of getting over the grief, once and for all?

Duff was an astute man; he knew what Meghan was feeling for him. And if he was honest with himself, he would admit that he appreciated it. More than that, he believed that he reciprocated it.

He took another sniff of the ribbon, then he got ready for bed.

Chapter Seventeen

Fremont, Nebraska

When Crack Kingsley arrived in Fremont, he told people that his name was Carl Butler, that he worked for the Kansas City Cattle Exchange, and was there to check out the local ranchers and farmers to ascertain for his employer whether or not they had any cattle for sale. He let it be known that he would be hanging out in the OK Saloon and would be willing to talk to any rancher or farmer who cared to come see him.

He was "interviewing" now.

"So, let me get this straight," Lloyd Evans was saying. "The Kansas City Cattle Exchange will buy ever'one of my cows, pay top dollar for 'em, an' all I got to do is drive 'em in here to the railroad? They do the shippin'?"

"That's right," Kingsley said.

"Well, hell yes, I'd be willin' to do that. What

you're sayin' is I'll be savin' money on the shippin' cost. Sign me up."

Kingsley laughed and held out his hands. "Don't be so quick. All I'm doin' now is what is called makin' a survey. The company wants to see if there will be enough people interested to actually make it worthwhile."

"Well, you can definitely sign me up for bein' interested," Evans said. "I don't know how anybody wouldn't be."

"Good, I'll put your name down."

"Where?"

"What?"

"Where at are you goin' to put my name down? You ain't got no book nor paper nor nothin' like that with you."

"Oh, I meant before I leave to go back to Kansas City," Kingsley said.

In the last two days he had interviewed four farmers and two ranchers, promising all of them that the Kansas City Cattle Exchange would not only buy their stock at top dollar per head, but would also arrange and pay for all shipping. While he was waiting for the train on which his target would be riding to arrive, he decided that it might be good to have someone with him, just as a bit of insurance. During his two days, he'd watched the saloon customers as they came and went. On the evening of his first day in Fremont, he had also witnessed an exchange between the deputy town marshal, and a man named Clem Crocker.

"Crocker, where were you last night at about

eight o'clock?" the deputy, whose name was Archer, asked.

"Why is it any business of your'n where I was?" Crocker replied.

"Because someone broke into Larry Thrower's Grocery store and stole twenty-seven dollars."

"What makes you think it was me?"

"You done it once before, that's why I think it was you."

"Iffen I was goin' to break into another store, do you think I'd be dumb enough to break into the same one twicet? It wasn't me. I was right here last night, from six o'clock 'til nigh midnight. An' you can ask anyone here."

"That's right Deputy," the bartender said. "Crocker was here the whole time."

"Yeah, well," Archer said. He pointed an accusing finger at Crocker. "You just keep yourself on the straight 'n narrow, Crocker, 'cause I'm goin' to be keepin' an eye on you."

"I ain't done nothin', so you can just quit jawin' on me," Crocker replied.

Archer hitched up his gun belt, then looked around at the others in the saloon to see if anyone would dispute the story told by Crocker and the bartender, then he turned and left.

Kingsley had done nothing then, but this afternoon, seeing Crocker sitting at a table alone, he took a bottle of whiskey and his glass over to Crocker's table, then sat down to join him. He refilled Crocker's glass.

"What's this for?" Crocker asked. "You're wastin'

your time with me, Mr. Butler. I ain't got no cows to sell."

Kingsley smiled. "That's all right. My name's not Butler, it's Kingsley. Crack Kingsley. And I'm not here to buy any cows."

"What do you mean? Ain't that what you been doin' here these past two days? Talkin' to folks about buyin' their hogs 'n cows?"

"Yeah, that's what I been doin', but only because that's what I'm wantin' folks to think."

"Then what are you doin'?"

Kingsley pulled out a Long-Nine cigar, though he did not offer one to Crocker. "I'm gettin' set to make some money," Kingsley said, as he struck the match. He took several puffs before he continued. "You can too, if you're interested."

"What do I have to do?"

"Nothing you ain't never done before, if the deputy was right yesterday," Kingsley said, squinting at Crocker through the tobacco smoke.

Crocker held up his hand, palm out, and he shook his head. "I didn't break into Thrower's store the other night."

"Not the other night, but you did do it before, didn't you?"

"Yeah. But I done served six months in jail for that."

"How much money did you get?"

"Twelve dollars."

"Was it worth serving six months for twelve dollars?"

"No. I've learned my lesson."

"Have you now? Tell me, Crocker, what lesson

have you learned? Not to steal again? Or just not to steal such a small amount of money?"

Crocker drank his whiskey before he spoke again. "What are you gettin' at?"

"Suppose you was to get a hundred dollars?"

Crocker shook his head. "Ain't no store in town keeps that much money overnight, except the bank. And I ain't about to try an' hold up the bank. Hell, I couldn't get away with it anyway. Ever'one in town knows me."

"The job I'm talking about has nothing to do with a local store. Or anyone local, for that matter. And you won't have to be breaking in. In fact, the only thing you are going to have to do is spot my target, and be my lookout."

"How am I supposed to spot your target, if it ain't someone local? Like as not, I won't have no idea who it is."

"I'll tell you how to spot him," Crocker said.

"And I'll get a hundred dollars for that? Just for spottin' the man you're goin' to rob, and bein' a lookout for you?"

Kingsley shook his head. "Yes."

"All right. You got yourself a deal."

Chapter Eighteen

The Union Pacific Depot in Cheyenne was located at the south end of Capital Street just catty-corner from the Inter Ocean Hotel. The depot was the biggest building in town, two stories high and a block long. It also had a tower in the middle, which was the highest structure in the city, and from which many photographs of the town had been taken.

Sixteenth and Main were two of the busiest streets in town, and Duff, who was carrying a suitcase in one hand and a briefcase in the other, had to wait for three wagons, a stagecoach, and an omnibus to pass before he could cross the road.

There were at least seven hacks, one fine carriage, and a few buckboards parked in front of the depot. Some were standing empty with the teams secured by hitching posts, but others had drivers waiting for fares. A few of the drivers were reading books or the newspaper, while a couple more had their heads lolled forward, napping. Reaching the road where all the vehicles were parked, Duff, with his suitcase in one hand and briefcase in the other, picked his way through.

The inside of the depot seemed much larger than one would suppose a town the size of Cheyenne would be able to support. It rivaled depots in the much larger cities of Denver, St. Louis, and Chicago. But such was the confidence in the growth of the town that Union Pacific had spared no expense in the building. Its defenders pointed out, though, that the large depot was justified by the fact that Cheyenne was an important stop for passengers who were traveling through from coast to coast. As many passengers came through Cheyenne in one week as there were citizens in the entire town.

Just inside the depot, there was a big chalkboard with the schedules of east- and westbound trains. One column had the name of the train; the next, whether it was west- or eastbound; the next the time it was due; and the final column was labeled "Latest telegraphic intelligence on train schedule."

Next to the blackboard with the train schedules was another, smaller one, with information on stagecoaches.

The train Duff would be taking was the "Western Glory," and according to the "latest telegraphic intelligence on train schedule," it was on time.

There was also a stagecoach schedule there and, in the corner, a booth for stagecoach ticket sales. This might seem contradictory, as the two transportation systems were competitive; but in another real way, as recognized by the stagecoach ticket booth in the railroad depot, they were also symbiotic.

Duff stepped up to the railroad ticket window.

"Yes, sir, where to?"

"Kansas City, Missouri."

"Would that be one way? Or round trip?"

"Round trip."

The ticket agent got out a long string of connected tickets, then began writing on them. After that he picked up a stamp, pushed it down into an ink pad, then affixed the stamp to the four tickets.

"These two are the ones you will use going out," he explained. "You will change trains in Fremont, Nebraska, and you'll need this one. When you come back, you'll change trains there again, and you'll need this one when you board in Kansas City and this one when you change in Fremont."

"Thanks."

"Will you be wanting a roomette on the train?"

"What time will I get to Fremont?"

"About eleven-thirty tonight. And the train from Fremont to Kansas City will leave at one o'clock tomorrow afternoon."

"No, I don't need a roomette. But a sleeper berth would be nice."

"Very good, sir," the ticket agent said. "That will be five dollars extra for the berth."

"Is there a dining car?"

"Yes, sir, you will need lunch and dinner, that will be seventy-five cents."

Duff paid the fare.

"Will you be checking your luggage through?"

"Just the suitcase," Duff said. "I have some work in my satchel that I shall need to attend to."

Duff had no intention of letting the briefcase get out of his hand.

"I need to send a telegram," Duff said.

"Yes, sir, the telegrapher's window is at the end," the ticket agent said.

Duff stepped up to the Western Union window, then filled out the telegraph form.

MR. JAY MONTGOMERY, KANSAS CITY CATTLE EXCHANGE

DEPARTING KANSAS CITY AT 8:30 A.M. ON THIS DAY. WILL ARRIVE IN KANSAS CITY AT 9:30 P.M. TOMORROW. WILL COME TO YOUR OFFICE ON THE DAY FOLLOWING.

DUFF MACCALLISTER

With his tickets in one hand and his briefcase in the other, Duff walked through the cavernous waiting room, his footfalls echoing back from the marble floor and the arched ceiling until he was out on the depot platform.

There was a snake-oil salesman standing out on the platform of the depot, pitching his wares to a captive audience.

"Yes, sir, this here extract of buchu can be used in treating any disease known to man. Men, do you suffer from catarrh, or problems too delicate to be mentioned in public company? Women, are you afflicted with bearing down feelings, or private problems? Then extract of buchu is for you. It will cure cancer, consumption, and dropsy. But don't go askin' any doctor for it, 'cause you ain't goin' to get no doctor to give it to you."

"Why is that?" someone from the gathering crowd asked.

"Why, Mister, I can answer that question for you in a heartbeat," the medicine salesman said. "There ain't no doctor goin' to give this to you 'cause if he did, and if word got around as to how wonderful this here miracle drug is, why, doctors would just naturally be out of business."

Duff smiled at the spiel as he walked over and sat on a bench to await the arrival of the next east-bound train.

"Oh, Mama! Here comes the train!" a young girl said excitedly, and the crowd on the platform moved expectantly toward the track. Even from his position on the waiting bench just outside the depot, Duff could hear the approaching train, first the whistle, then the sounds of puffing steam. As the train moved into the station, two more sounds were added: that of a clanging bell, and the squeak of brakes being applied. The train rushed by with steam pouring from the actuating cylinder as the operating rod moved back and forth, powering the driver wheels. The train was so heavy that as it passed by, Duff could feel it in his stomach.

Finally, the train came to a halt and the conductor stepped down from one of the cars, then stood there as the arriving passengers disembarked. In the year Duff had been in America, he had gone twice, by train, back to New York. He had learned from such trips that the composition of the passengers was different, depending on which way you were going.

Most of the westbound passengers were embarking upon new adventures, and they were high of spirits and eager with anticipation to see what their new lives would present. The passengers going east consisted of two groups: those who had succeeded in their ventures and were now going back in triumph, and the much larger group who were returning dispirited and frustrated by their lack of success.

When all the arriving passengers had disembarked, the conductor looked at his watch importantly; then, just as importantly, called out his order.

"All aboard!"

Duff waited as all the other passengers stepped aboard, then he boarded as well. He chose a seat facing forward; and just across from him, facing to the rear of the train was an elderly gentlemen with white hair, a beard, and wearing a three-piece suit. He introduced himself.

"Henry Pollard is the name, sir," he said, holding his hand out.

"Duff MacCallister."

'I'm going back to Boston," Pollard said. "I spent most of my adult life away from the place, and now that I am retired, I intend to go back to Boston to live out the rest of my days in the city of my youth."

"I hope you have a pleasant trip," Duff said.

"I intend to, sir, I intend to, thank you very much."

Duff kept his answers pleasant, but did nothing to initiate any further conversation. He much preferred to make the trip alone, with his own thoughts.

Pollard obliged Duff until lunch, at which time they found themselves seated at the same table in the dining car.

The tables were already set, and little flashes of light bounced off the shining silverware, the sparkling china, and the softly gleaming stemware. Here, Pollard resumed his conversation.

"Mr. MacCallister, have you ever stopped to consider what a marvelous time we live in? I mean, think of all those people who came west by wagon train. The trip was arduous, dangerous, and months long. Today, one can go by train from coast to coast in but a week's time, enjoying the luxury of a railroad car that protects them from rain, snow, beating sun, or bitter cold. They can dine sumptuously on meals served in dining salons that rival the world's finest restaurants. They can view the passing scenery, while relaxing in an easy chair, and they can pass the nights in a comfortable bed with clean sheets.

"And not only that, we enjoy electric lights, and in all of the cities in the East, and an increasing number of cities in the West, one can use the telephone to talk to a friend or a relative in some distant location. Yes, sir, the times are marvelous."

"They are, indeed," Duff said.

"Mama, how fast are we going?" a little girl sitting at the table across the aisle from them asked.

"One moment, young lady, and I will tell you,"

Pollard said. He pulled out his pocket watch, opened it, and stared at it for a short while. "We are doing eighteen miles to the hour," he said.

Duff chuckled. "That sounds about right," he said. "But how can you say with such certainty?"

"It's quite easy," Pollard said. "One need only count the clicks made as the train passes over the rail joints. The number of clicks you can count in twenty seconds, represents the speed in miles per hour."

"How do you know that?"

"It was my business, young man," Pollard said. "Until last month, when I was retired because of my age, I was a railroad engineer for Northern Pacific."

Kansas City

When Denman got the telegram from Duff saying that he was on his way, he checked the rail schedule so he would know when MacCallister would arrive in Fremont. Then, in accordance with a pre-arranged code, he sent a telegram to Kingsley, letting him know when MacCallister would be arriving. After that, he returned to his desk, then began contemplating what he would do with all the money he would be getting. Even after Kingsley's share, he would still have enough money to pay off all his debts and save his father-in-law's property.

But more and more, another thought began entering his mind. He could pay off his debts and save his father-in-law's property, that was true. But, he would also have the money to leave Kansas City, leaving his debts, father-in-law, and wife behind him. He could start new, somewhere else. He could change his name, get a job in a bank somewhere, and live comfortably.

It was certainly something worth considering.

Fremont

Because it would be the middle of the night when Duff left the train, he had purposely not taken a Pullman parlor car. He did take a sleeper car, and though the porter came through to make up all the beds when it got dark, he waved the porter off, instead sitting in his seat looking out into the dark as the train raced across the prairie. His seat companion, who had chosen the top bunk "because up there, there is no window to distract me," bade Duff good night and went to bed.

Nearly everyone else in the car went to bed as well, leaving Duff and the porter, who sat in a chair at the front of the car, as the only two people who weren't in bed. And, because the porter was napping in his chair, Duff was the only one in the car who was still awake.

Once, he thought of the little yellow ribbon Meghan had given him, and he stuck his hand into his jacket pocket and pulled it out. He had a small electric reading light between the windows, and he turned it on to look at the ribbon. He ran his fingers over the little lock of hair, then he lifted it to his nose to smell the perfume.

About half an hour later, the porter came back to his seat. "You want me to make your bed now, sir?" he asked.

"Thank you, no. I will be getting off just before midnight, so I won't be going to bed."

"Very good, sir," the porter said. He walked away and Duff began looking through the window. It was a cloudless night, and the moon was full and high. Because of that, he could see more of the scenery outside than one might expect, though nighttime had robbed the world of all color except for silver and black.

A few minutes later, the porter returned.

"Seein' as you ain't sleepin' like all the others, I went up to the dinin' car and brung you back a cup of coffee. Hope you likes it black, 'cause I didn't put nothin' in it."

"Aye, black is just fine, thank you," Duff said. He reached into his pocket and pulled out half a dollar.

"Oh, no, sir, no need for you to be tippin' me none just for doin' a good deed," the porter said, waving the money away. "I just thought you might want some coffee."

"I'm much obliged to you," Duff said.

"You ain't from here, are you?"

"No, I'm from Scotland."

"I ain't never been to Scotland, don't even know where that is. I don't think we have any trains that go through there."

Duff chuckled. "There are trains in Scotland," he said. "But not the Union Pacific."

"You said you wasn't goin' all the way through. Where you gettin' off?"

"I'll be changing trains at Fremont."

"Fremont, is it? Well, you don't have much longer

to be on the train. We'll be pullin' in to Fremont in just about an hour."

"Thanks."

The porter walked on to the back of the car and Duff killed the light, then sipped his coffee as he continued to look out into the blackness beyond the window.

When he left the train in Fremont an hour later, it was nearly midnight, a great dark emptiness, quiet under a panoply of very bright stars. From Fremont, he would leave the Union Pacific Railroad and take the Missouri Pacific Railroad to Kansas City.

He reached for the attaché case on the seat beside him and thought of the money in it, and how lucky he was to have it. He knew that he would not have it, had it not been for the mine he and Elmer, and to be honest, mostly Elmer, had been working for the last year.

Chapter Nineteen

As he had every day since he arrived in town, Crack Kingsley went to the Western Union Office to see if there was a telegram for Carl Butler. When he walked in today, a smiling telegrapher handed it to him.

"Here you go, Mr. Butler. You must be a happy man today."

Crack read the telegram.

BABY BOY BORN THIS MORNING. MOTHER IS DOING WELL.

That was the agreed-upon code, and it meant that MacCallister would be coming through Fremont tonight.

"It's tonight," Kingsley told Clem Crocker when he met him at the OK Saloon.

"Let me get this straight," Crocker said. "All I have to do is spot him, then come back and tell you. Right?"

"That's all you have to do."

"And I get a hundred dollars for it?"

"You'll get a hundred dollars for it," Kingsley said. "Meet me back here tonight at eleven o'clock."

Despite the coffee the porter had brought him earlier, Duff had drifted off to sleep while sitting up in his seat, his head resting against the window.

He was sitting on the front porch of his house at Sky Meadow. In front of him he could see cattle: Black Angus for as far as the eye could see.

"They are beautiful. You were right to insist upon Black Angus. We do have the finest ranch in all of Wyoming."

Duff reached across the gap between them and took Skye's hand in his. Standing, she bent over him.

"I love you, Duff Tavish MacCallister," she said.

As she leaned over to kiss him, Duff looked up and saw not Skye McGregor, but Meghan Parker!

"Sir! Sir," the porter said, shaking his shoulder gently. "We're comin' in to Fremont."

Duff sat up and looked around. He wasn't on the front porch of his house; he was on a train. And neither Meghan nor Skye was with him. No, that isn't true. They were both with him now, so much a part of him that they peopled his dreams. And that just made everything even more confusing for him.

"Thank you, Porter," he said, yawning and stretching before getting out of his seat, then walking to the back of the car to step out onto the platform.

Only six more people left the train: a preacher in liturgical dress, a man, his wife, and their three sleepy children.

Duff, with his attaché case in hand, went into the depot.

"Yes, sir, can I help you?" the night agent asked.

"I'm going on through to Kansas City; I just want to make certain that my luggage goes through as well."

"You can go out and stand by the baggage car to make certain it gets off," the depot agent said.

"Good idea."

Duff stood by as the baggage was taken off the train and loaded onto a large pushcart. He saw his suitcase, and saw that it was transferred over to another cart marked "Missouri Pacific." Satisfied that his luggage was accounted for, Duff inquired as to the location of a hotel and, given directions, left the depot with briefcase in hand.

Clem Crocker had been told to look for a man carrying a small satchel, and he saw a man getting off the train carrying one. That really didn't matter, though. Only three men had stepped down from the train: one was a preacher, and the other was a father and family man, so this had to be him.

As the man made arrangements for his luggage, Crocker hurried on up South Union Street to Dodge Street. The hotel was on Dodge between Clarkson and Irving, and Kingsley was waiting there in the space between Watkins' Mercantile and Freeman's Hardware store.

At least, he was supposed to be waiting there, but when Crocker got there, he didn't see him.

"Kingsley?" he called. "Kingsley, you here?"

"Shut up, you fool," Kingsley called from the dark

shadows between the two buildings. "Don't be shoutin' my name out like that."

"I seen 'im. He'll be comin' along in a few minutes."

"Is he carryin' a satchel?"

"Yep, just like you said."

"Go across the street and wait. When you see him comin', step back in between them buildin's so's he can't see you, then light a match. Whenever I see the match, I'll know he's near here."

"What are you goin' to do?"

"What difference does it make to you, as long as you get your hundred dollars?"

"You're right. It don't make no difference to me at all," Crocker said.

Crocker hurried back across the street, stepped in between White's Drugstore, and Wong's Laundry, then looked back toward Union. It was dark here, and he had to urinate, so he did. He was just finishing when he saw the man he was looking for turn off Union onto Dodge, then pass under the street lamp.

"Damn, I'm glad I seen him," Crocker said to himself. "If I had'a missed him while I was takin' a leak, that would have been one expensive pee." He giggled at the thought.

Crocker moved back toward the street and watched until the man with the satchel got closer. Then, when he thought he was close enough, he stepped farther back in between the two buildings, and lit a match.

* * *

Kingsley saw the flare of the match, then stepped up to the corner of the building and pulled his gun from its holster. Turning it around, he grabbed the barrel of his pistol and waited.

He heard the sound of footfalls on the boardwalk, gauging by the sound how close Duff was coming. When he knew he was just about there, he raised his pistol and, as MacCallister passed by, he brought the butt of the pistol down on his head. MacCallister dropped to the boardwalk and didn't move.

Quickly, Kingsley grabbed the briefcase and opened it, just as Crocker came running across the street.

"Did you kill 'im?" Crocker asked.

"I don't know," Kingsley said. He pulled out a little packet of bills, then closed the attaché case before Crocker got there. He counted off five twenties and handed them to Crocker.

"How much money is there?" Crocker asked.

"What does it matter to you? I promised you a hundred dollars, here it is. And all you had to do was tell me when he was comin'."

"Yeah, I guess you are right," Crocker said.

"Ain't no guessin' to it," Kingsley said. "Here's your money."

With the briefcase firmly in his grasp, Kingsley hurried on down Dodge Street. Crocker watched until he disappeared in the darkness.

"Damn, I better get out of here my ownself," Crocker said aloud. Just as he started to leave, he saw a piece of yellow ribbon lying on the sidewalk, some feet away from the man Kingsley had hit.

Thinking it may have been dropped as someone was leaving Sheinberg's Mercantile, he walked over to pick it up. When he did so, he noticed that it had a lock of hair attached to it. He could also smell perfume on it.

"Well, now, lookie here," he said. "I wonder what woman dropped this."

"Get up. Get up and get on out of here. I don't need some drunk lyin' up agin' the front of my store. You'll be runnin' off my customers."

Duff MacCallister opened his eyes and saw that he was, indeed, lying on the boardwalk. It was daylight, and he had no idea why he was lying here. The last thing he could remember was walking from the depot toward the hotel.

"Get up, I tell you," the man said with an angry voice. He hit at Duff with the straw end of his broom. "Get up before I sweep you off this walk with the rest of the trash."

Duff sat up, and when he did, he was so dizzy that when he tried to stand, he lost his balance and sat back down, hard.

"Look at you. You're still drunk."

Duff stood up, bracing himself against the wall of the store as he did so. What was he doing lying on the boardwalk? He put his hand around to the back of his head, then winced when he touched a knot. When he brought his hand back around, there was blood on his fingers.

"My money!" he said. Looking around for his briefcase, he saw that it was gone. "I've been robbed."

"Mister, you mean you weren't drunk last night?" the storekeeper asked.

"No," Duff said. "I came in on the train and I was going to the hotel. I don't remember anything after that. I must have been hit over the head, and whoever did it took my money."

Duff reached around to his back pocket and felt his wallet. Taking it out he opened it and saw that the money there was untouched.

"Don't look to me like they took your money," the storekeeper said.

"Not this money," Duff said. "The money I had in my briefcase. Where is the constable?"

"I beg your pardon?"

"The police, or town marshal, or whatever law you have."

"We have a town marshal. His office is right over there," the store owner said, pointing across the street.

"Thank you."

Duff started across the street, but again a wave of dizziness overtook him and he had to grab hold of the post that supported the overhanging roof.

"Are you going to be all right? Do you need help walking?" The tone of the storekeeper's voice had changed from one of irritation to consideration.

"Thank you, I'll be all right," Duff said. He stood for just a moment until the dizziness passed, then he crossed the street and went into the marshal's office. There were two men inside, both drinking coffee. One was sitting behind the desk with his feet on the desk, the other was sitting in a chair that was tipped back against the wall. Evidently, one of them had said something funny, because both men were laughing when Duff stepped inside.

"Yes, sir, can I help you?" the man behind the desk asked. He didn't take his feet down.

"Aye, or at least 'tis hoping I am, that you can be of help," Duff answered. "I was robbed last night."

"Where?"

Duff looked through the window toward the store where he had been when he regained consciousness. The storekeeper was still sweeping the porch and walk. He read the sign on the store.

"Watkins' Mercantile," he said.

"Wait a minute, you say you were robbed at Watkins' Mercantile store last night? What time?"

"Just before midnight."

"Mister, what were you doing in his store at midnight? I know for a fact that Billy closes his place at seven o'clock."

"I did not say I was *in* the store. It was *at* the store, I was. I left the train at half-past eleven, and was walking to the hotel. I woke up but a moment ago, lying on the boardwalk in front of the store."

"Hey, that's right, Marshal Bivens, I was goin' to say somethin' about that only I forgot," the man in the tipped chair said. "I seen him lyin' over there this mornin' when I come in to work, but I just figured he was drunk. I was goin' to give him a chance to wake up on his own, only if he didn't, I was goin' to go over and wake him up myself and put him in jail. So, you're sayin' that was you I seen lyin' drunk on the walk in front of Sheinberg's?"

"Aye, 'twas me you saw, but I was not drunk." He bent his head down to show them the lump.

"Look at this, Deputy Archer. He took quite a lick," Bivens said.

"It's no wonder you lay there 'til dawn," Archer said. "In fact, it's a wonder you wasn't kilt."

"Like as not, it was somebody that got drunk in the OK Saloon last night," Marshal Bivens said. "Prob'ly got drunk and lost some money playin' cards, so he figured to make it up by stealing a few bucks off someone that just got off the train. I'll do some checkin' around. How much money did he get?"

"Fifteen thousand, eight hundred and twelve dollars," Duff said.

Archer's chair came down with a bang on the floor at the same time Bivens swept his feet down off the desk. Both peace officers looked at Duff in openmouthed shock.

"Wait a minute. How much money did you say he got?" Bivens asked.

"Fifteen thousand, eight hundred and twelve dollars," Duff repeated.

"Mister, uh, what is your name?"

"MacCallister. Duff Tavish MacCallister."

"Mr. MacCallister, excuse me for askin', but just what in hell were you a' doin' carryin' so damn much money? Do you always carry that much with you?"

"I am a rancher in Chugwater, Wyoming. I was on my way to Kansas City to buy five hundred head of cattle. That's why I was carrying so much money."

"I see. Well, whoever stole it hit the jackpot, didn't they? I mean, here they figured to get maybe twenty or thirty dollars and they got over fifteen thousand," Bivens said. They got lucky."

Duff shook his head. "No, 'twas not luck, I'm thinking. Not at all. Whoever did it knew I would have the money, and they knew I would be here in the middle of the night last night, to change trains today to complete the trip to Kansas City."

"You don't say," Bivens said. "Now would you like to tell me just how in the Sam Hill you come up with that idea?"

Duff pulled his wallet from his pocket and opened it to show to the marshal. "I have two hundred thirty-seven dollars in my wallet. That's exactly how much I had in my wallet when I stepped down from the train. If someone just happened to rob me, he would have gone directly to my wallet, and probably wouldn't even have looked in the briefcase I was carrying."

Marshal Bivens stroked his chin. "I don't know," he said. "You may have a point there. But how would anyone in Fremont know that? You don't know anyone in town, do you?"

"I don't know a soul. And I doubt that the person, or persons, who robbed me even live here."

"All right, if what you say is true, if someone was lyin' in wait for you here, how did they know about you?"

"That's what I'm going to have to find out," Duff said.

"How do you plan to do that?"

"I don't know," Duff admitted. "I've got the *what*

I need to do all figured out. What I don't have figured out is *how* I'm going to do it."

"I'll give you what help I can," Marshal Bivens said. "But you got to understand that if the fella that done this is outside the town limits, there really ain't nothin' I can do."

"I know," Duff said. "I need to get myself a hotel room, and I also need to send a couple of telegrams."

"The telegraph office is in the depot," Marshal Bivens said.

"Thank you."

There was a train just pulling into the station when Duff stepped into the depot. The train was going west, and for a moment, Duff considered getting back on it. But only for a moment. He stood back against the depot with his arms folded across his chest, watching as the arriving passengers disembarked and the departing passengers boarded. A man and his wife got on the train. So did an attractive young woman, after a tearful good-bye to her parents. Duff overheard enough of their preboarding conversation to know that she was going farther west to teach school, and Duff thought of Meghan and how it must have been for her when she left her home to come west.

A young man, who had no one to see him off, got on the train. Duff watched him board, wondering if, perhaps, he might be the one who had robbed him last night.

Why couldn't he remember anything? He had no

memory at all between the time he left the train, and when he awoke this morning.

He wanted to go grab the young man before he boarded and search him to see if he had his money, but he knew that he couldn't do that.

He felt a queasiness in his stomach, and it wasn't all from the blow on his head. He had lost a lot of money, a year's work in the mine, and perhaps the future of his ranch.

The engineer blew the whistle for two long blasts, signaling the conductor that the brakes had been released and he was about to proceed. The actuating cylinder puffed loudly, then there was a series of very quick hisses as the great driver wheels spun in place a couple of times before gaining traction. Then the train, with noisy, steady gushes of steam, moved forward, pulling out all the slack between the cars with a succession of rattles. Gradually, the train began increasing speed as it hurried out of the station.

Duff went inside and, locating the telegraph office, walked over to it.

"I would be for sending a telegram if you don't mind."

"Yes, sir, there's the form," the telegrapher said.

MR. JAY MONTGOMERY, KANSAS CITY CATTLE EXCHANGE

HAVE ENCOUNTERED UNEXPECTED DIFFICULTY. WILL BE DELAYED.

DUFF MACCALLISTER.

The second telegram he sent back to Chugwater to Elmer Gleason.

ELMER. HAVE RUN INTO A BIT OF A PROBLEM.
PUT SKY ON THE TRAIN, SEND HIM TO ME IN
FREMONT, NEBRASKA. DUFF.

Duff considered sending another one to Meghan, but knew that Elmer would tell, not only Meghan, but Biff and Fred as well.

"That will be sixty-six cents," the telegrapher said.

Duff paid the fee, then, getting his luggage, went outside and hired a buckboard to take him and his luggage to the hotel. There he secured a room where he washed the wound on his head. It wasn't until then, that he realized he had lost the yellow ribbon Meghan had given him. Compared to the loss of all his money, losing the ribbon was an insignificant thing, but he found it upsetting, nevertheless.

Chapter Twenty

After taking his lunch in the hotel restaurant, Duff walked down to the OK Saloon.

"What'll it be?" the bartender asked, coming down to stand in front of Duff. He took a towel from his shoulder, wiped the bar, then flipped the towel back over his shoulder.

"Would you be for havin' Scotch whiskey?" Duff asked.

"Beer and Old Overholt."

"I'll have a beer," Duff said, putting a nickel on the bar.

The bartender drew a mug of beer from the barrel behind the bar, then set it in front of him.

"I've not seen you before. Just get off the train, did you?"

"Aye, last night," Duff said. Picking up the beer, Duff turned his back to the bar and looked out over the customers. There was a game of cards going on at one of the tables and one man seemed to be the big winner. The winner let out a whoop as he raked in the pot.

"Whooee, boys, that's the third hand I've won today!"

"What's got into you, Crocker? You ain't never won three hands in one game."

"He ain't winnin' these. He's buyin' 'em," one of the players around the table said.

"Yeah, and what I want to know is, where did he get the money to buy the hands? Hell, most of the time the son of a bitch is here beggin' for drinks. Yesterday he didn't have two pennies to rub together."

"I got the money from beating people like you in poker," Crocker replied, arrogantly. "Yes, sir, I'm ridin' a lucky streak now." Crocker picked up a yellow ribbon and held it to his nose. "And this is my lucky charm."

Before Crocker could even put the ribbon back down on the table, Duff closed the distance between them. He grabbed the front of Crocker's shirt with both hands and lifted him from his chair, knocking the chair over in the process as he literally carried a protesting Crocker over to the bar.

"Here! What's goin' on here?" one of the other players shouted in alarm. All the other players leaped up from the table.

Paying no attention to the shouts of surprise and alarm, Duff slammed Crocker back against the bar. Then, reaching over to grab a whiskey bottle, he broke it on the bar with a spray of whiskey, shattered pieces of glass flying from the point of impact. What he had remaining in his hand was the neck of the bottle and several wicked shards. He placed those shards against Crocker's neck, then pushed the bottle hard enough to break the skin.

"Where did you get it?" Duff asked.

"Where did I get what? What are you talking about?" Crocker cried out in alarm.

Duff shoved the sharp edges of the bottle just a little deeper into Crocker's neck, enough to be painful, and to start bleeding—though not enough to really harm him.

"Oww!" Crocker called out. He started to raise his hands in protest.

"Don't be for movin' now, you lowlife scoundrel, or so help me God, I'll open up your throat like I'm gutting a swine," Duff said. "Now, I'll ask you again. Where did you get that yellow ribbon?"

"I found it."

"Where did you find it?"

"Mr. MacCallister, you want to pull that bottle out of Crocker's neck?"

Duff recognized Deputy Archer's voice, so he pulled the bottle out, then stepped back, still glaring at Crocker.

Crocker put his hands to his throat. There was some blood, but not much.

"MacCallister? You are MacCallister?" Crocker asked.

"Aye. And how is it that you know my name?" Duff replied.

"I don't know—I," Crocker started, then he stopped in mid-sentence. "I just now heard the deputy call you that."

"You are lying. You spoke the name as if you had

heard it before. Where have you heard it? How did you know I was carrying the money?"

"What is all this about, MacCallister?" Deputy Archer asked.

Duff walked over to the card table. Meghan's yellow ribbon was lying there by the pile of money in front of where Crocker had been sitting. He picked it up, then showed it to the deputy.

"Whoever robbed me last night took this from me," he said.

"I didn't take it offen you. It was was just layin' there on the porch," Crocker said.

"It was laying by me?"

"Yeah, it was just . . ." Crocker started, then he put his hand over his mouth. "I mean, no, I didn't say it was layin' by you, all I said was it was just layin' there on the porch."

"Where did you get the money?"

"What money?"

"I heard one of the players say that yesterday you didn't have two pennies to rub together. Today you seem to be flush. Where did you get the money?"

"Yeah, Crocker, that's a good question," Deputy Archer said. "Where did you get the money?"

"I earned it."

"How?"

"I just earned it, that's all."

"You're lying," Duff said again. Duff stepped up to Crocker, pulled his pistol, and stuck the barrel into Crocker's mouth. He pulled the hammer back.

Crocker tried to protest, but with the pistol in his mouth, he couldn't say one word.

"Take your gun out of his mouth, MacCallister,"

the deputy said. "He can't talk as long as you have that pistol shoved halfway down his throat."

Duff pulled his pistol out, and Crocker gagged and coughed, coughing up blood from where the gunsight had bloodied the top of his mouth.

"I'm tired of dealing with you," Duff said. Again cocking his pistol, he held it up to Crocker's forehead. "If you aren't going help me, I'll just kill you here and now and go on my way."

"No, no!" Crocker said. "I didn't have nothin' to do with takin' your satchel!"

Duff let the hammer down and put the pistol back in his holster. "Satchel? Who said anything about a satchel?"

"I don't know what made me say that."

"So far, you haven't made me angry," Duff said. "But I believe I'm about to be angry."

"Son of a bitch!" one of the other card players said. "If he ain't been angry so far, I wonder what he's like when he really gets angry!"

"You're about to find out," Duff said. Again he pulled his pistol. "I'm going to shoot your fingers off, one at a time, until you tell me what I want to know."

Duff pointed the pistol directly at Crocker's crotch. "After I shoot off your pecker," he said.

"No! Wait! Wait! His name was Kingsley. Crack Kingsley!"

"Crack Kingsley was here?" Deputy Archer said.

"Do you know this man Kingsley?" Duff asked the deputy.

Archer shook his head. "I've never seen him, but we have some paper on him. He's wanted for murder. Are you saying Crack Kingsley was in town?"

"He was here," Crocker said. "Only he was tellin' ever'one that his name was Carl Butler."

"Carl Butler? You mean the fella that was buying livestock for the Kansas City Cattle Exchange?" the bartender asked.

"Yeah," Crocker said. "Only he wasn't buyin' no livestock. He was just sayin' that so he could stay in town 'til MacCallister come through with his money."

"How did he know I would be here?" Duff asked.

"I don't know, he never told me that."

"Where is he now?"

"I don't know that, either. I just know he give me a hundred dollars to give him a signal when I seen you comin' up the street."

"How did you recognize me? We've never met."

"It was easy. He said you would probably be the only one carryin' a satchel."

Kingsley sat on his horse on top of a ridge and looked down on the little ranch before him. The house, barn, and smokehouse looked well cared for, evidence that the ranch was well run. That also meant that there would be meat in the smokehouse and probably an ample supply of flour, coffee, and beans, everything he would need for an extended stay on the trail. He planned to stay on the trail because he had no intention of going back to Kansas City to share the money with Denman.

Kingsley rode down to the ranch house where he

saw a young girl, no more than twelve or thirteen, drawing water from the well. So intent was she upon her task that she didn't see Kingsley until the pail of water was sitting on the rim of the well; she picked it up to transfer it into the empty water bucket she had brought outside.

"Oh! Sir! I did not see you!" the girl said.

"Where's your pa, girl?" Kingsley asked.

"He has gone into town, and he won't be back until late this afternoon," the girl said. "You'll have to come back then."

"Will I, now?" Kingsley said, smiling as he dismounted.

"Ellie Mae, come into the house," an older woman called from the back porch.

"Yes, mama," Ellie Mae said and, holding the water pail with both hands, she started back toward the house.

"Here," Kingsley said. "Let me get that for you."

Before Ellie Mae could protest, Kingsley took the pail from her, then walked quickly toward the house.

"You don't have to do that, Mister," Ellie Mae's mother said. "She is quite capable of carrying the water herself."

"Here, now, I'm just tryin' to be nice," Kingsley said. "I'm in need of some supplies. I thought maybe I could get them here. Bacon, flour, coffee, sugar, beans. I'd be glad to pay you top price for them."

"There is a store in town, no more than five miles from here," the woman said. "I'm sure they'll have everything you might want. Don't come any closer. You can put the water down there and go on, now."

Ellie Mae stepped up onto the porch and stood alongside her mother.

"Is that any way to treat a guest?" Kingsley asked. "Like I told you, I'm willin' to pay for anythin' that I take."

Kingsley took another step closer, then was shocked when he saw the woman pull her hand out of the folds of her dress. She was holding a pistol.

"I told you to go on," she said. "Go on, I don't want any trouble."

"Could I at least fill my canteen with water?"

"All right. But go back to the well to do it."

"I'll just get my canteen off my horse," Kingsley said.

Kingsley walked back to his horse, then stepped around behind it as he made a big show of getting his canteen. Then, suddenly, his hand appeared over the top of the saddle, and he was holding a pistol.

"Mama!" Ellie Mae shouted, but her warning was too late.

When Todd Raymond came back home from town late that afternoon, he had a big bag hanging from the pommel of his saddle.

"Julie! Ellie Mae! Harley!" he called. "How come none of you came to meet me? Wait until you see what I bought for all of you!"

Todd dismounted, removed the bag from the saddlehorn, and started toward the house. That was when he saw them. Julie was lying on her back on the porch, and Ellie Mae was on her stomach on the ground.

"God!" Todd shouted. "God! No! No! No!"

At eleven-thirty that same night, Duff MacCallister was standing on the depot platform waiting for the train to come in. He had checked the blackboard frequently for the latest information on the train, which was updated by telegraph as the train passed each of the stations en route. The most recent intelligence indicated that the train was running about fifteen minutes late.

During the day, he had learned as much information as he could about Crack Kingsley. As Deputy Archer had said, the marshal's office had received Wanted posters on him that not only provided a detailed description of his appearance, but also listed all the crimes for which he was wanted, including train robbery, stagecoach robbery, bank robbery, and murder.

Crack Kingsley rode with Doc Jennison and the Jayhawkers in the Missouri-Kansas border war prior to, and during the Civil War. He took part in several depravities during that time. He is known to have a fondness for the cigars known as Long-Nines. He is seldom to be seen without one.

*It is his habit to smoke no more than one half of
the cigar before he discards it.*

When the train arrived, Duff waited until it
stopped, then he moved forward to the stock car to
watch as the animals were offloaded.

"I brought Rebel, too," a familiar voice said and
turning toward the voice, Duff saw Elmer.

"Elmer, what are you doing here?"

"You did say you ran into a bit of a problem,
didn't you?"

"Aye, you might say that."

"Then I figured I would come along too. Anytime
someone is havin' a problem, it's always good to
have help in gettin' it took care of. So that's what I
aim to do. I aim to help you get this problem, whatever it is, took care of."

"You're a good man, Elmer Gleason," Duff said.

"There's Rebel," Elmer said.

Rebel came down the ramp first, followed by Sky.
Neither horse was saddled, though the saddles were
on the train, having been sent as baggage.

Half an hour later, the two men had their horses
boarded and their saddles stowed.

"I'm staying at a hotel just up the street here,"
Duff said. "I'm sure there is another room on the
same floor."

"A bed would feel good," Elmer said. "The trip
was long."

The two men walked quietly up the street for another moment before Elmer spoke again.

"Well, are you goin' to tell me?"

"Tell you what?" Duff asked.

"What this bit of trouble is that you got yourself into."

"Oh, that."

"Yes, that."

"I was robbed," Duff said.

"Robbed?"

"Aye."

"Well, how much did they get?"

"Fifteen thousand, eight hundred and twelve dollars and fifty cents," Duff said.

"Whew," Elmer said. "Yeah, I would say you are right in saying that you had a bit of trouble. Who did it? Or do you know?"

"It was a man named Crack Kingsley."

"Crack Kingsley? Are you sure it was Crack Kingsley?"

"Yes. Why, have you heard of him?"

"Oh, yes, I know the son of a bitch. He rode with Doc Jennison during the war."

"Yes, I read that in the report at the marshal's office that he rode with Doc Jennison. I wasn't sure what that meant."

"Crack Kingsley and I both grew up in Clay County, Missouri."

"So, you were friends?"

"We know'd each other, but I'd hardly call the son of a bitch a friend. When the war started, we had boys from the county who joined the South and some who joined the North, in some cases brother against brother. Those men we could understand. But what Kingsley done was even worse. He went over into Kansas and started ridin' with the Jayhawkers. They would raid into Missouri taking everything, robbing the houses of bed and clothing, taking all the horses, cattle, sheep, oxen, and wagons they could find. They killed every man between the ages of fifteen and seventy-five, then they tore the clothing off the women and raped them." Elmer was quiet for a moment. "One day, Kingsley led a group of men into Clay County. They hit a farmhouse . . . the Dumey place. They killed Mr. and Mrs. Dumey, then they raped and killed a young woman named Alma. We were to have been married.

"I went after the bastards, and I'm happy to say that I caught up with most of them and I killed them. But not Kingsley. Kingsley got away."

"Then I would be accurate in saying that you have your own reasons for pursuing him," Duff said.

"Yeah, my own reasons," Elmer said.

"In that case, Elmer, I shall welcome your company."

Duff and Elmer were having their breakfast in the hotel dining room the next morning when Deputy Archer came in. Archer stood in the doorway for a moment, looking around the room until he spotted Duff. Seeing him, Archer strode purposefully toward his table.

"Good morning, Deputy," Duff said. "This is my friend, Elmer Gleason. Won't you join me for breakfast? Perhaps a cup of coffee?"

"No, thank you, I don't have time, and I don't reckon you will either, after you hear what I have to say."

"What is it?"

"We've got a report on Kingsley, the fella you are looking for. There is someone over at the marshal's office I think you might want to talk to."

Duff had just about finished his breakfast, so the tossed down the last of his coffee, then stopped at the counter to pay for it before he and Elmer followed Archer out of the hotel and down the street to the marshal's office. There were four people in the marshal's office: Marshal Bivens, a man wearing the liturgical garb of a minister, another man, and a boy. The man looked to be about forty, the boy about ten. Though the boy was not crying out loud, a steady stream of tears was running down his cheeks. The man had as sad a face as Duff had ever seen.

"Hello, Mr. MacCallister," Marshal Bivens said when Duff and the deputy stepped into the office. "This is Todd Raymond and his boy Harley. When Mr. Raymond got back home yesterday afternoon, he found his wife and his young daughter, both of them shot to death. The boy saw it all, and had sense enough to stay hidden until the killer left."

"I am so sorry, Mr. Raymond," Duff said.

Raymond nodded, but said nothing.

"Now, here is why I sent for you," Bivens said. "The boy gave us an excellent description of the killer. The description is a perfect match for the man we knew as Carl Butler, but who we now know is Crack Kingsley."

"Lad, if it not be a trouble to you, would you be for describing him to me?" Duff asked.

The boy looked at his father.

"It's all right, Harley. Tell him what you saw."

"He looks like a haint," Harley said. "He is tall, but he is very skinny. His face, it is narrow here," he put his hands on either side of his mouth, "but it is wide here. He has a cut, a big, ugly cut, that starts on this eye." He put his finger just outside his right eye, then paused for a moment. "No, that is because I was looking at him. He has a cut that starts at this eye," he put his hand to his left eye, "and it runs down to here where it turns back up. It looks like a fishhook."

"A cut? You mean a scar?"

"Yes, a scar."

"That is the man who stayed here in town for a few days," Bivens said. "As I say, we knew him as Butler, but according to Crocker, his real name is Crack Kingsley."

"Go on, son, you are doing very well," Duff said.

"I was in the kitchen when mama told the man to go away. The man went back to his horse and I thought he was going to go away, like Mama told him to, but when he got to his horse, he pulled out his gun and he shot both Mama and Ellie Mae. I . . ." the boy stopped, and before he could speak again, he started crying, so that he was sobbing the last few words.

"I wanted to go out and help Mama and Ellie Mae, but I was too afraid. I am a coward!"

"No, son, you are far from being a coward," Duff said. "There is nothing you could have done then, and if you had tried, you would have gotten yourself killed. You did the right thing. You looked very closely so you could describe him, and now we know who did it."

"Mr. MacCallister is right," Marshal Bivens said. "You did exactly what you were supposed to have done. Todd, you should be very proud of your boy."

Todd put his arm around his son and drew him closer to him. "I am proud of him, Marshal. I am prouder than I can say."

"I hope they catch him," Harley said. "I hope they catch him and I hope they hang him. And when they do hang him, I want to be there to watch."

"Oh, I will catch him," Duff said.'

"You will catch him?" Harley asked.

"Yes, sir, I will catch him. You can count on that."

"Good," Harley said.

"Mr. Raymond, if you don't mind, when you go back to your ranch, I would like to go back with you and have a look around," Duff said.

"I don't mind at all," Todd Raymond replied.

Chapter Twenty-one

"He rode off this way," Elmer said, pointing south as he and Duff examined the signs at the Raymond farm.

Leaving the Raymond place, Duff and Elmer started south. After about fifteen minutes, Duff spotted something on the trail ahead of them and hurrying toward it, he dismounted to examine it more closely. It was a half-smoked cigar.

Elmer dismounted as well, and holding the cigar to his nose, he sniffed a couple of times.

"Half a day old," he said.

Remounting, they continued to track Kingsley. He wasn't moving very fast, evidently confident that he had gotten away cleanly. At nightfall they camped out on the trail, thinking that would be better than to continue on and lose his trail in the darkness.

They followed the trail for another day and night; then the next morning, they came across a railroad track that was running south. It quickly became obvious that Kingsley was following the track.

"If he gets into Lincoln, he could catch a train to just about any place in the country," Elmer said.

"Then we need to step up the pace a bit so we can catch up to him before he gets on the train," Duff suggested.

"Since we know where he's a-goin', there ain't no real need to be trailin' him no more," Elmer said. "So I don't see no reason why we can't just go on 'bout as fast as the horses will let us go," Elmer said.

When Kingsley was about a mile away from Lincoln, he dismounted, took down the briefcase, then slapped the horse on its rump and sent it running. If anyone was following him, that might throw them off the track. It had been his experience that men on the run were often identified by the horses they were riding. Besides, this was a stolen horse, and though he thought time and distance probably made it improbable that he would be picked up for riding a stolen horse, it was foolish to take the chance, especially since he was carrying as much money as he was.

Just before Kingsley got to Lincoln, he saw an old abandoned house, and he stepped inside. The house, which was constructed of unfinished, rip-sawed lumber, was fading badly. It consisted of one room, the floor covered with about an inch of dirt. At one time the walls had been papered, but what paper there was now hung in long, ragged, colorless strips. There was no furniture. Upon examining the place, Kingsley found a loose board in the wall and, pulling it out, was able to slip the briefcase behind it, after first removing one thousand dollars.

After hiding the briefcase, Kingsley walked the rest of the way into town. Because he was hungry, he stopped at the first restaurant he saw, a place called Kirby's Café. Inside, he took a small table next to the wall, then lit a cigar as he waited.

"Yes, sir, what can I get for you?" a waitress asked.

Kingsley enjoyed a meal of roast beef, mashed potatoes and gravy. Then, grounding out his cigar butt, left the café and walked across the street to the Cow Lot Saloon.

Loomis Byrd was in the back of the Cow Lot Saloon when he saw a familiar figure come in through the front door. It took him only a moment to recall who it was and, getting up from the table, he walked up to the bar just as Kingsley got there.

"It's been a long time, Kingsley," Byrd said.

Startled at hearing his name called, Kingsley turned to man who had spoken to him. The expression on his face indicated a lack of recognition.

"Damn, don't you 'member me? After all the ridin' we did together?"

"What ridin' would that be?"

"Ridin' with the best cavalry in the whole Union army. I'm talking about the Jayhawkers."

Kingsley smiled. "That what you're callin' it now? Cavalry?"

"What you doin' in this part of the world, Kingsley? I thought you would be back in Missouri. That is where you're from, ain't it?"

"Yeah. That's where I'm from, but the folks there don't take too highly to me yet. You're Byrd, ain't you? Loomis Byrd?"

Byrd smiled upon being recognized. "Yeah, that's me all right. What you been doin' with yourself?"

Kingsley bought a bottle of whiskey and the two men retired to the back of the saloon where they found a table and began catching each other up on old times.

"You know what I miss?" Byrd said. "I mean, what I miss the most? It's the ridin' with a bunch of men like the ones we was ridin' with then. You know, we went where we wanted to go, took what we wanted to take, and there wasn't nobody with gumption enough to stand up agin' us."

"Yeah, them was good days, all right," Kingsley agreed.

"There's two more of 'em that rode with us that live here, you know, them bein' Curtiss and Rawlins. And not more'n twenty miles from here is Jones and Wales. That would be six of us, countin' you and me," Byrd said.

"Six of us for what?"

"I don't know. I reckon we'd let you figure it out. But if you had an outfit of six good and experienced men, I'm sure we could come up with somethin' we could do."

"Like what?"

Byrd looked around the room before he spoke

again. "Look, I heard tell you was on the dodge. To me, that means you're ridin' the outlaw trail. All I'm suggestin' is, as long as you're goin' to be ridin' that trail, you may as well do it with company. All these men has rid the trail before, and what's more, they have rode the trail with you."

"You still ain't said what we could do."

"Well, hell, with an outfit like that, there ain't nothin' we couldn't do. We could rob banks, trains, stagecoaches, just like in the old days. Only this time it would all be for us."

Kingsley drummed his fingers on the table as he considered it. He had fifteen thousand dollars now, more money than he had ever had in his life. It had been incredibly easy to get. On the other hand there was something to what Byrd was saying. An outfit of experienced men could do just about anything it wanted to do. And it would take more than a sheriff and a temporary posse to stop them.

"What do you think?" Byrd asked.

"I think I want to get me a whore and think about it for a while."

"Elmer, look over there," Duff said.

Looking in the direction where Duff was pointing, Elmer saw a horse without a rider coming toward them. They urged their own horses into a trot until the caught up with it. The horse was saddled, but there was no sign of a rider anywhere.

Elmer got down and examined all four of the horse's hooves before nodding and making his pronouncement.

"This is the horse we've been following, all right," he said. "The question is what is he doing out here without a rider?"

"And where is the rider?" Duff added.

"Could be that he was throwed," Elmer suggested.

"Or, it could be that he let the horse go, just to throw us off."

"Yeah, that, too."

"We're no more'n five or six miles from town. This horse came from that same direction. I'm sure that when he decided to abandon the horse and walk the rest of the way into Lincoln, he was probably no more than a mile away," Duff suggested.

"Which means he is probably there now," Elmer said.

"Let's hurry it up. I'd like to catch up with him before he gets a train," Duff said.

"What about this horse?" Elmer asked.

"I have a feeling it is a stolen horse, and I also have a feeling that he knows where he is going. I'd say let him go."

"Good idea."

Clouds had been building up all day, and by late afternoon the rain had started. There was nothing Duff and Elmer could do but break out their slickers and hunker down in the saddle. They were soaked thoroughly when they reached the outskirts of Lincoln, and the thought of getting out of the rain was quite an incentive. There was a banner spread across the street as they entered town.

COUNTY FAIR, AUG 4, 5, 6.
RACES, WRESTLING, PATRIOTIC SPEECHES.

One corner of the banner had come loose, and the banner was furled like a flume, so that a solid gush of water poured from the end.

The first thing they did was go to the livery to get their horses out of the weather. After that, they walked over to the railroad station.

"No, sir, there ain't been nobody like that bought a ticket today, or in the last two or three days," the ticket agent said.

"Thank you, 'tis appreciative I am for the information," Duff said. He turned to Elmer.

"I'm bettin' he's still here," Elmer said.

"Aye, 'tis a good bet I'm reckoning. He's got money and it does a man no good to have money if he can't spend it, and the only place he can spend it is in town."

Elmer chuckled. "You got that right," he said. "Speaking of which, what do you say me 'n you spend a little money now and get us somethin' to eat?"

"Sounds good to me," Duff replied.

Duff and Elmer picked their way across the muddy, horse-apple-strewn street, and headed toward the café.

Kingsley crawled out of the whore's bed and walked over to relieve himself in the chamber pot by the window. As he stood there, he glanced out the window and got a start from the two men he saw picking their way through the rain and across a muddy street.

"Son of a bitch!" he said.

"What is it, honey?" the whore asked. "You ain't got the burns, have you? 'Cause I'm clean, and if you got the burns you didn't get it from me. And if

you got it, and you give it to me, that's goin' to cost
me some money, 'cause don't nobody want to bed
with a woman if she's got the disease."

"Oh, shut up," Kingsley said. "I ain't talkin' about
nothin' like that."

The two men went into Kirby's Café, just across
the street from the Cow Lot Saloon. Kingsley was a
little surprised to see MacCallister; he thought he
had hit him hard enough to have killed him. But
what really surprised him was the other rider he saw
with him. Was that Elmer Gleason? No, it couldn't
have been. Gleason was dead. Kingsley was sure he
had heard that. Still, it looked an awful lot like him.

Dressing quickly, Kingsley went back downstairs.
He saw Byrd sitting at a table with a couple of other
men and started to call Byrd over to him, then he
thought he recognized them. They were much
older, but he was sure they were men he had ridden
with during the war. Byrd had said their names were
Curtis and Rawlins, though he had no idea which
was which.

When Kingsley walked over to the table, the three
men stood up and Curtis and Rawlins stuck out
their hands.

"Do you remember us?" one of them asked.

"I remember you," Kingsley said. "You're Curtis
and Rawlins. Don't remember which of you is
which, though."

"I'm Curtis," one of them said. He was bald,
which would make it easy to remember.

"Byrd was tellin' us you'd like to start a gang,"
Rawlins said. "If you do, me 'n Curtis want to be
in it."

"I haven't actually said that I was goin' to," Kingsley said. He thought about MacCallister and Gleason being in town. He had no idea how it was that they were together, but he was pretty sure why they were here. They had come after him. Maybe putting a gang together, if for no other reason than protection, might not be a bad idea.

"You said you was goin' to think about it, though," Byrd said.

"Yeah, I did say that, didn't I? All right, I've thought about it. Are you willin' to do what I ask you to do?"

"Yeah, hell, a gang has got to have a leader," Rawlins said.

Kingsley nodded. "I'm glad you see it my way." Kingsley reached inside his shirt and took out a packet of money, the one thousand dollars he had taken from the satchel.

"I don't want anyone who works for me to think I'm cheap," he said. He counted out one hundred dollars apiece for the three men, then he put the rest of the money back inside his shirt.

"What's this for?" Rawlins asked.

"There are a couple of men in town who are lookin' for me," Kingsley said.

"What do they want with you?" Curtis asked.

"They want to kill me. And they will, unless we kill them first."

"We?" Rawlins asked.

"Yes, we," Byrd said. "We just took his money, which in my book means we just signed on with him. So if someone is after him, that means they are after us as well."

"Rawlins, when you think about it, Byrd is right," Curtis said. "If we took the money, that means we are all together."

Rawlins thought for a moment, then he smiled. "Yeah, well, the way I see it, we're four against their two. And they prob'ly don't know that Kingsley has took on any partners."

"You got that right," Kingsley said. "There don't nobody know about you three at all."

"All right, who are they?"

"Like I say, there's two of 'em. The young one is as big as a tree. His name is MacCallister. The old one with him is Gleason. Elmer Gleason."

"And you say they are in town now?"

"Yes."

"Where are they?"

"Right now, they're in the café across the street. I reckon they'll be comin' in here pretty soon."

"How do you know they'll come in here?"

"Because they are lookin' for me," Kingsley said. "And when you are lookin' for someone, the best place to start is a saloon."

"I got me an idea," Byrd said.

"What's that?"

"We'll split up, one of us sittin' in each corner of the saloon. Soon as they come in, why, you can give us the signal. We'll have 'em surrounded, an' they won't have no idea that they are in danger."

"Sounds like a good idea to me," Rawlins said. "What about you, Kingsley? What do you think?"

"Yeah. I say we can give it a try," Kingsley said.

Across the street in Kirby's Café, Duff and Elmer were just having their dinner. Outside, the rain had stopped, but it was still dark because of the heavy cloud cover.

"Elmer, look at that table over there, in the ash tray," Duff said.

The table Duff pointed out was one of the smaller tables that were set up against the wall with only two chairs. In the ashtray was half of a cigar. A waitress was walking by then, and Duff got her attention.

"Yes, sir, something else for you?" she asked with a practiced smile.

"Could you be for tellin' me, lass, about the man who left the cigar in the ash tray there?"

"Oh," she said. "How awful. Who would want to eat there with a smelly cigar butt in front of them? Thank you for calling it to my attention."

"Yes, ma'am, but 'tis more interested I am in the man who left it there. Was he tall and gaunt? And did he have a scar, here?" Duff traced his face where young Harley had said there was a scar.

"Yes, oh, quite a frightening thing he was, what with the scar. And his eyes. I've never seen eyes like his. They were like the eyes of a snake." She shivered as she explained them.

"Thank you, lass, you have been most helpful."

"Did you see where he went when he left the café?" Elmer asked.

The waitress shook her head. "No, I'm sorry. I didn't notice."

"He went over to the Cow Lot," one of the others in the café said.

"The Cow Lot?"

"That's the saloon just across the street."

Chapter Twenty-two

Behind the bar of the Cow Lot Saloon there was a sign that read: "We insist upon honest gambling. Please report any cheating to the management."

Just above the sign was a life-size painting of a reclining nude woman. Some marksman had already added his own improvement to the painting by putting three holes through the woman in all the appropriate places, though one shot had missed the target slightly, giving her left breast two nipples.

To either side of the painting, there was a long glass shelf upon which stood several bottles of various kinds of liquor, their number doubled by the reflection in the mirror behind. There were also several large jars of pickled pigs' feet on the bar.

The saloon had an upstairs section at the back, with a stairway that led up to the second floor. A heavily painted saloon girl was taking a cowboy up the stairs with her.

The upstairs area didn't extend all the way to the front of the building. The main room of the saloon was big, with exposed rafters below the high ceiling. There were several tables in the saloon, nearly all filled with men who were drinking and talking, some of whom were playing cards.

The piano player wore a small, round derby hat and kept his sleeves up with garter belts. He was pounding on the keyboard, though the music was practically lost amidst the ambient noise of the saloon.

Duff and Elmer stepped up to the bar.

"You men look pretty wet," the bartender said. "Is it still raining outside?"

"Not at the moment," Duff said. "Would you have any Scotch?"

"A Scotch man, are you? Well, I'm a rye man myself, but I do have Scotch for them that fancies it. And you, sir?" he asked Elmer.

"Sonny, I've drunk ever'thing from coal oil to champagne. Whatever you put in front of me will be just fine," Elmer said.

The bartender chuckled. "Since I have the Scotch bottle out, that's what you'll get."

Suddenly a shot rang out and the bottle of Scotch exploded in the bartender's hand. Passing through the bottle, the bullet slammed into the mirror behind the bar, sending cracks all through it. The women in the saloon screamed, and several of the men shouted out in alarm. Many of the men ran, though a few dove to the floor. A second shot hit the bar between Duff and Elmer, erasing any doubt, if there had been any, as to who the targets were.

"Go that way!" Duff shouted, pushing Elmer

toward one end of the bar to get him out of the line of fire. Duff ran toward the other end of the bar, pulling his pistol as he did so. Now two rounds were fired at the same time, but, as before, the bullets missed.

When Duff reached the end of the bar, he stepped around the end of it, then squatted down. He saw one of the shooters, a man standing in the corner and holding a smoking gun in his hand. For the moment, it was as if the man was confused and was trying to make up his mind whether to shoot at Duff or Elmer. Duff took one shot and the man fell back into the corner, then slid down to the floor.

Elmer fired, and from the corner of his eye, Duff saw another man go down.

"Kingsley!" someone yelled. "This is your fight. Don't you run from this, you cowardly bastard!"

Duff looked toward the back door just as Kingsley slipped through it. He started toward him, but was interrupted by a shot from the man who had yelled at Kingsley. Duff had to retreat momentarily to the relative safety of the corner of the bar.

There was another exchange of shots. Duff's adversary missed. Duff didn't.

For a long moment after Duff's final shot, there was total silence in the saloon. Men, and the few women who were there, stayed absolutely still. Duff ran to the back door and looked out, but saw nothing. By the time he turned back toward the saloon, the patrons, those who had run and those who had dove to the floor, were beginning to be animated.

"Duff, are you all right?" Elmer called.

"Aye, I'm fine. And you?"

"I wasn't hit."

"How about you, bartender?" Duff called, and the bartender, who had dove for cover after the opening volley, was now standing up, examining himself carefully.

"I'm all right," the bartender said, tentatively. Then, when he realized for sure that he was unhurt, he repeated it, much louder and with more enthusiasm. "Yes, sir, I'm all right! I ain't hurt at all!"

"That there is Loomis Byrd," one of the saloon customers said, pointing to Byrd's body.

"This here is Lou Rawlins."

"And this one over in this corner is Gordon Curtis."

"What the hell! Why are they all scattered out like that? They was all sittin' together when I come in here a while ago. I mean, they was all good friends, you purt nigh always seen 'em sittin' at the same table. But lookie here, they's one of 'em in ever' corner."

"I'll tell you why," someone said. "They was all spread out 'cause they was set up special to bushwhack them two fellers that just come in to the saloon."

Now the attention turned to Duff and Elmer.

"Who are you fellers, and why was they shootin' at you?" the bartender asked.

Before they could answer, two officers from the Lincoln police came into the saloon. Both had their guns drawn, but seeing that the shooting was over and relative peace had been restored, they holstered their pistols.

"What happened in here?" one of the policemen asked.

A dozen men started talking at once, trying to tell what happened. It took a while for the police to get the story all sorted out, but when they did, they were convinced that Duff and Elmer had acted in self-defense.

"Do you know any of these men?" the police sergeant asked.

"I've never seen any of them before," Duff said.

Elmer went over to look at all of them before he replied. "I don't know any of them either," he said.

"Their names are Byrd, Curtis, and Rawlins," the sergeant said. "They are locals, and all of them have been in trouble at one time or another. But as far as I know, they've never shot anyone. Why do you suppose they tried to shoot you two?"

"I expect it had something to do with Crack Kingsley," Duff said.

"Crack Kingsley? Who is that?"

"If you will check your files, you will see that Kingsley is wanted for murder. He is also the man who stole a great deal of money from me."

"What did he have to do with the shooting?"

"He was here, but he ran out the back door when the shooting started."

"That's right, Sergeant," the bartender said. "I seen him go out myself."

"You know this man, Kingsley?" the police sergeant asked the bartender.

"No. But Loomis Byrd yelled at him, called him by name. Called him a coward too, for running way. And now that I think about, he yelled, 'this is your fight.'"

"You're sure that's what he yelled? 'This is your fight'?"

"That's what he yelled all right, Sergeant, I heard it too," one of the saloon patrons said.

"Yeah, I heard it, too."

"Are either of you men wanted?" the police sergeant asked.

"There ain't no paper out on neither one of us," Elmer said.

"Of course that is what you would say. What are your names?"

"My name is Duff MacCallister."

"I'm Elmer Gleason."

"Where are you from, Mr. MacCallister?"

"We're both from Chugwater, Wyoming. The constable there is a man named Jerry Ferrell. You could telegraph him, he can tell you about us."

"We will do that. I don't suppose you would mind coming to the police station with us while we take care of that?"

"We won't mind at all," Duff said.

It took less than half an hour for the exchange of telegrams. When Duff's story was verified, the police let the two of them go.

"I'm sorry about the rough welcome you received from some of our citizens," the chief said. "And I apologize for detaining you."

"No apology necessary," Duff said. "We understand that you were just doing your job."

As they left the police office, Elmer spoke up.

"I didn't want to say nothin' before, but the fella named Byrd? I have run across him before."

"Where?" Duff asked.

"Mind that I told you that I caught up with the ones that kilt Alma and her family, and that I kilt 'em all 'cept for Kingsley? Well, that ain't quite true. There was another'n who rode with Kingsley, and that was Loomis Byrd. I'm not sure I would have recognized him, if that police feller hadn't a' spoke his name."

"Aye, it all makes sense now," Duff said.

"What makes sense?"

"How three strangers would suddenly start shooting at us. They were strangers to us, but not to Kingsley. I'm sure he recruited them for this, though how he did so I don't know."

"You said he stole all the money from you. More'n likely he paid them," Elmer said.

"Aye, that would be my belief. The question now is where did he go?"

"That's a good question, all right," Elmer said. "And the problem is with all this rain, it ain't goin' to be that easy to track him."

The first thing Kingsley did after running from the saloon was return to the abandoned house where he had hidden the money. His first thought was to get on the next train leaving Lincoln, but he was certain that MacCallister and Gleason would be checking the depot. He wished now that he hadn't let his horse go. He could steal another one, but in

order to do that, he would have to go back into
town, and he didn't particularly want to do that. On
the other hand, if he was walking and they were
both mounted, they would overtake him in no time
at all.

Then, even as it seemed as if he had nowhere to
turn, he saw someone riding up the road headed
for town. He stood on the side of the road and held
up his hand to stop the rider.

"Yes, sir, what can I do for you?" the rider asked.

"I want to buy your horse," Kingsley said.

"Well, Mister, I couldn't sell you this horse even
if I wanted to," the rider replied. "This here horse
belongs to Mr. Barkley, who owns Crossback Ranch.
He just lets those of us that work for him use the
horses."

"I'll give you three hundred fifty dollars."

"I told you, it ain't my horse to sell."

"Five hundred dollars," Kingsley said, growing
more desperate.

"If you need a horse that bad, hell, you ain't
more'n a quarter of a mile from town. They sell 'em
at the livery and prob'ly half a dozen other places
too."

"I'll give you seven hundred dollars for your
horse."

"Seven hundred dollars? Mister, are you loco?
That's three times what this horse is worth!"

"Are you going to take the offer or not?"

"Well, yeah, I'll take it. I can pay Mr. Barkley what
the horse is worth and keep some for myself."

The cowboy dismounted, then, with a big smile

on his face, held out his hand. "Where's the money?"
he asked.

The smile left the cowboy's face when he saw a
pistol pointed toward him.

"Hold on, here! What's this about?"

"You didn't really think I would give you seven
hundred dollars for that horse, did you?" Kingsley
asked.

Kingsley pulled the trigger and the cowboy went
down.

Fifteen minutes later as Duff and Elmer were
about to leave Lincoln, they saw a man walking
toward them, holding his stomach, weaving about
stumbling, barely staying on his feet. They hurried
to him and saw a lot of blood on his right thigh.

"Here! What happened?" Duff asked.

"Some son of a bitch shot me and stole my horse,"
the cowboy replied.

"Elmer, help me get him up on Sky," Duff said.
"We'll get him to a doctor."

The doctor washed his hands, then looked over
at Duff and Elmer. "I've got the bullet out and the
bleeding stopped."

"Is he going to make it?" Elmer asked.

"I don't know. Caine has lost a lot of blood."

"You know him?" Duff asked.

"Yes. He rides for the Crossback Ranch. I know
most of Mr. Barkley's riders."

"You say he has lost a lot of blood. I have read about
replacing blood. Is that a possibility?" Duff asked.

"I know about blood transfusions," the doctor

said. "Sometimes they are successful, and sometimes they seem to make the situation worse. Nobody knows why. I think if he rests, he'll build his own blood back up. That is certainly safer than trying to replace his blood."

"Is he conscious?" Duff asked.

"Yes. He is weak, but he is conscious."

"I would like to talk to him, if you don't mind."

"Go ahead, talk to him."

Duff walked over to the bed where the cowboy lay, shirtless and with a fresh bandage around his lower abdomen. His eyes were closed.

"Mr. Caine?"

The cowboy opened his eyes. Looking up at Duff, he smiled. "You're the feller that brung me in, ain't you?"

"Aye," Duff answered. "I was wondering if you could tell me about the man who shot you."

Caine shook his head. "Don't know him. I never seen him before."

"Was he a thin man, dark eyes, and with a scar on his face?"

Caine became more animated. "Yeah! Yeah, that was him, all right. Do you know him?"

"I certainly know of him," Duff said. "His name is Kingsley. Crack Kingsley."

"Tell me about the horse," Elmer said.

"He's a pinto. Answers to the name of Lucky."

"Will he give Kingsley any trouble?" Elmer asked. "I mean, being as he's a stranger and all."

"No, Lucky's a good horse, he ain't never met no stranger," Caine said.

"All right, thank you, Mr. Caine. We'll let you get some rest now," Duff said.

Duff and Elmer started to turn away when Caine called out to them.

"One thing might help, that is, if you're plannin' on trackin' Lucky."

"What's that?" Duff asked.

"His rear shoes. The ends of both of 'em points way in."

"Thank you, Caine. That will be a big help," Elmer said.

Chapter Twenty-three

The Kansas City Cattle Exchange was busy this morning, with telephones ringing, the ticker-tape machine clacking, and a man reading the latest quotes, then calling them out loudly to another who was posting them on the blackboard.

Hodge Denman took a telegram from his desk drawer and looked at it again. It was dated six days ago.

HAVE ENCOUNTERED UNEXPECTED DIFFICULTY.
WILL BE DELAYED. DUFF MACCALLISTER.

Denman knew exactly what the difficulty was. He had been robbed.

Just as they had worked out a code for Denman to let Kingsley know what day to expect MacCallister to arrive in Fremont, they had also worked out a code whereby Kingsley could let Denman know when the job was done.

Denman had heard nothing from Kingsley, but he had intercepted MacCallister's telegram to Jay Montgomery; therefore, he knew that Kingsley had stolen the money.

That was six days ago. Kingsley had plenty of time to get back to Kansas City and make the split. If he was going to. But so far, Kingsley had not even let Denman know that he had succeeded. And Denman was now convinced that Kingsley had no intention of ever coming back to split the money. All his plans for getting out of debt, or of having enough money to run away and start over, were for naught. The entire thing was about to come down on his head.

On the other side of the banister that separated the bull pen from the rest of the Cattle Exchange office, Jay Montgomery was perusing all the latest transactions. He saw that he was still holding and feeding five hundred head of Black Angus cattle that were consigned to Mr. Duff MacCallister of Wyoming Territory. He saw, also, that Hodge Denman was in charge of that operation, so he stepped into the pandemonium of the bull pen and walked over to Denman's desk.

"Mr. Montgomery?" Denman said, surprised to see his boss standing right in front of him.

Montgomery dropped some papers onto Denman's desk. "What do you know about this transaction?" he asked.

Seeing MacCallister's name at the head of the page, Denman knew immediately what Montgomery was talking about.

"Yes, I've been putting off talking to you about this," Denman said.

"Putting it off? Why?"

"Well, sir, it is beginning to look to me like Mac-Callister isn't going to show up."

"Show up? What do you mean, show up? Had we not agreed to ship his cattle to him upon receipt of a bank draft for the necessary amount?"

Denman hesitated for a moment. He had been the one who changed the details of the sale, insisting that MacCallister show up with cash in hand and make his own arrangements to take the cattle back. He nearly let it slip with Montgomery that he had changed things.

"Uh, yes, sir, that was the arrangement. He was to send the bank draft. But as of this morning's mail, no bank draft, nor have we heard a word from him," Denman lied. "I am beginning to think that the whole thing may have been a ruse of some sort."

"A ruse? What do you mean, a ruse? Why would he do something like that? What would be in it for him?"

"Who knows why people do such things?" Denman replied. "Perhaps he just wanted to make himself feel important. I'm sure he is nothing but a cowboy somewhere with grandiose ideas."

"No," Montgomery replied. "He is legitimate, all right. I received a letter from Mr. Woodson of the American Aberdeen Angus Association about Mac-Callister. Woodson did some research on him and said that he owns a great deal of improved land, is very well respected, and very serious about introducing Black Angus into Wyoming."

"Good," Denman said. "I would hate to think we had been duped by someone. But we still have the problem of him not having claimed or paid for the cattle, and it is costing us every day we keep and feed them."

Montgomery stroked his chin. "Yes, that is true. They are not only costing us to feed them, they are occupying pen space that we could use for other cattle. This is most distressing."

"Would you like for me to redistribute the herd and sell the cattle as best I can?"

"Where is your business sense?" Montgomery asked.

"I beg your pardon, sir?"

"As of today's market, the price of Angus is down two dollars per head. That means the MacCallister contract is worth one thousand dollars more than we could get by unloading the herd today. It is to our advantage to hold the cattle for him. That is, if he actually goes through with the contract. On the other hand, if we don't hear from him within two weeks, then the cost of keeping them will eat up the difference in market price and we will be forced to sell."

"Yes, sir."

Montgomery started toward the railing that separated the two areas, then turned back toward Denman.

"But you let me know the moment we hear from him."

"The moment we hear from him, I will, Mr. Montgomery," Denman said.

Two more weeks, Denman thought. Interesting

that he would say two more weeks. Two more weeks was just about how long he had before the rest of the world would come crashing down on him.

Chugwater

There were no customers in the Ladies' Emporium at the moment, so Meghan was using the time to unpack the three boxes of material that had come in on special order this morning. She had just taken the last bolt of gingham out when the telegrapher, Mr. Murchison, stepped into her store.

"Yes, Mr. Murchison, what can I do for you?" she asked, greeting him with a smile. But when she saw he was holding a telegram in his hand, she gasped in fear.

"Oh! What is it?" she asked, her voice breaking.

Murchison, seeing that he had frightened her, held his hand out. "I don't know, it may be nothing," he said quickly. "But, it's something I thought you might want to know."

"What? What is it?"

"I'm not supposed to do this, but I'm going to share a couple of telegrams with you, seeing as I think you might have a special interest," Murchison said. "This first one was from Duff to Elmer Gleason. It came in last week." He handed the telegram to Meghan.

ELMER. HAVE RUN INTO A BIT OF A PROBLEM.
PUT SKY ON THE TRAIN, SEND HIM TO ME IN
FREMONT, NEBRASKA. DUFF.

"Well, sir, Elmer didn't just put Sky on the train; he took him."

"Have you heard anything else from either of them?" Meghan asked.

"Not from either of them, but I did get this telegram today from a Mr. Jay Montgomery of the Kansas City Cattle Exchange. Only thing is, it was sent to Duff, but Duff isn't here." He showed the second telegram to Meghan.

MR. MACCALLISTER. AS PER YOUR INSTRUCTIONS, I HAVE ASSEMBLED A HERD OF FOUR HUNDRED EIGHTY HEIFERS AND TWENTY BULLS OF THE BLACK ANGUS BREED. WE EXPECTED YOU HERE ONE WEEK PREVIOUS. IF YOU ARE NOT HERE TO TAKE DELIVERY OF THE CATTLE WITHIN TWO WEEKS, I WILL BE FORCED TO SELL OFF THE HERD AS BEST I CAN. THE AMOUNT NOW OWED IS THE ORIGINAL FIFTEEN THOUSAND, EIGHT HUNDRED TWELVE DOLLARS AND FIFTY CENTS, PLUS TWO HUNDRED DOLLARS PER WEEK FOR FEEDING AND HANDLING. PLEASE REPLY AS SOON AS POSSIBLE. JAY MONTGOMERY.

"I'm not sure what to do, Miss Parker. I mean, he wants a reply, but Duff isn't here."

"Don't do anything for the moment," Meghan said. "I mean, since you can't deliver the telegram to him, there's nothing you can do, is there?"

"No ma'am, I don't reckon there is. But I know you and Mr. MacCallister are friends, so I thought you might like to know."

"You were right, it is something I would like to

know. And, Mr. Murchison, I thank you very much for bringing this to my attention."

"You're welcome. I should probably get back to my office now."

Meghan thought about the two telegrams for the rest of the day and far into the night. Around midnight, she got an idea. It took her another couple of hours to decide whether the idea was good or bad. She also had to consider whether or Duff would agree with the idea.

She finally decided that Duff wasn't here to offer any agreement or disagreement. She was going to have to make up her own mind, and that is exactly what she did. Then, the next morning, she left the little CLOSED sign on the window of her front door, and instead of opening her shop, walked down the street to speak to Fred Matthews.

"Miss Parker," Matthews said, surprised to see her. "What brings you here?"

"Mr. Matthews, I need to raise some money," Meghan said.

"Well, Miss Parker, you have a very good business going, I'm sure the bank will lend you some money on it. Do you owe anything on your building?"

"No."

"Then you shouldn't have any trouble raising money. How much do you need?"

"I need sixteen thousand dollars."

"Sixteen thousand?" Matthews gasped. "Miss Parker, there is no way you are going to be able to borrow that much money on your store."

"I know. That's why I have come up with an idea that involves you, Mr. Guthrie, and Mr. Johnson. If

I could get four thousand dollars from each of you, that would be twelve thousand, and I can come up with four thousand on my own."

"What do you want the money for?"

Meghan showed Matthews the telegram that had been meant for Duff.

Matthews read it, then looked up.

"Where is Duff? Why didn't he show up?"

Meghan showed him the telegram that Duff had sent to Elmer.

"I don't know what the 'bit of a problem' is, but I can't let Duff lose that herd. He has worked all year to get things ready. I can't let him lose it."

"Meghan, and if we are talking this kind of money between us I think I should be able to call you by your given name, do you realize what you are asking? You are asking me—and I suppose you will be asking R.W. and Biff—to loan you four thousand dollars when you have no collateral you can pledge, and you won't even tell us what it is for?"

"But you will have collateral," Meghan said. "The herd will be collateral."

Matthews drummed his fingers on his desk for a moment, then he laughed. "I'll give you this. Nobody can say that you don't have brass. All right, I've known you for a while. And I know you to be not only a smart businessperson, but a good one as well. I'll lend you the money."

"Thank you," Meghan said. "Now I have another request of you."

Matthews shook his head in disbelief and smiled. "You've just hit me up for four thousand dollars and you have another request? All right, let's hear it."

"I want you to go with me when I talk to Mr. Guthrie and Mr. Johnson," Meghan said. "I want you to help me talk them into going along with this."

"Why not?" Matthews said. "They say that a fool likes company."

One hour later Meghan walked down to the bank.

"Hello, Miss Parker," the teller greeted. "Here to make a deposit? Or a withdrawal?"

"Neither," Meghan said. "I would like to speak with Mr. Dempster if I could."

"Certainly, he is back in his office. Just knock on the door," the teller said.

Scott Dempster welcomed Meghan with a smile, then invited her to have a seat across from his desk.

"Now, Miss Parker, what can I do for you?"

"I need sixteen thousand dollars," she said.

Dempster reacted in surprise. "Did you say sixteen thousand dollars?"

"Yes. Actually, I will probably need seventeen thousand dollars."

"Miss Parker, I—I don't know what to say. You are a very good customer and your store is very profitable. But there is no way I can lend you seventeen thousand dollars."

"I didn't say I wanted to borrow seventeen thousand. I said I needed seventeen thousand. I have three thousand dollars in the bank, and I want to borrow two thousand dollars against my store."

"Oh, my," Dempster said. "Well, yes, I suppose I can lend you two thousand against your store, but with that and what you have in the bank, you will still be short twelve thousand dollars."

Meghan slid three bank drafts across Dempster's desk, each one for four thousand dollars.

"This will make up the difference," she said.

Dempster examined the bank drafts: one from Fred Matthews, one from R.W. Guthrie, and one from Biff Johnson.

"You convinced these men to loan you this money?"

"Yes. I take it that their bank drafts are good?"

"Oh, absolutely, all three of these gentlemen are more than good for their drafts. It's just that . . ." he let the sentence hang.

"It's just that what?"

"Well, Miss Parker, this entire thing is extremely unusual," Dempster said. "I mean, the fact that you have convinced three of our finest citizens to advance you so much money, and that you are contributing even more of your own funds. May I ask what this is for? It isn't necessary that you tell me, you understand. It's just a matter of curiosity."

"I am helping a friend," Meghan said, without any further explanation.

"She must be some friend."

"He is," Meghan said.

That evening Meghan worked late in her shop. It was quite a task, but she sewed one hundred and seventy one-hundred-dollar bills inside two petticoats.

The next morning, wearing the two petticoats, she bought a stagecoach ticket to Cheyenne.

Fred Matthews, R.W. Guthrie, and Biff Johnson

came down to the stage depot to see her off. They were sitting in the far corner of the depot, away from the rest of the passengers, so they could talk without being overheard.

"Do you have the money?" Matthews asked.

"Yes."

"Where?"

Meghan smiled. "I'm a seamstress, remember?"

"I don't understand."

Meghan looked over toward the others in the depot, and then when she was sure she couldn't be seen, she lifted the hem of her skirt, to show her petticoats. "In here," she said.

Matthews laughed out loud. "What a marvelous way of hiding it," he said.

The others laughed as well.

"Is the message he sent to Elmer, asking him to send his horse to him, the only thing anyone has heard from him?" Guthrie asked.

"Yes, as far as I know. Only, from what I understand, Elmer didn't send Sky to him. Elmer took Sky to him."

"I wonder what kind of trouble Duff ran into?" Matthews asked.

"I don't know," Biff said. "But you men know Duff as well as I do. And you know damn well that he can handle just about any trouble he runs into."

"Yes, but if he can handle 'just about' any trouble he runs into, that means that from time to time there will be trouble he *can't* handle," Guthrie said.

"Damn, R.W., do you have to look at the negative side of everything?" Biff asked.

"I'm just trying to be practical, is all," Guthrie replied.

"What do you think, Meghan? You haven't spoken much," Biff asked.

"I tend to agree with you, that there isn't much that Duff can't handle. But I know how badly he wants that herd, and if the telegram from the cattle exchange was sent to him here, that means they haven't heard from him and they don't know how to get ahold of him."

"I hate to agree with R.W., but something like this can make a person worry and wonder," Matthews said.

"All right, folks!" the depot manager called. "The stagecoach for Cheyenne is about to leave. If you're plannin' on goin', you need to get onboard now."

The coach was drawn up in front of the depot. It was a Concord coach, green with yellow wheels, black window trim, and red letters:

WYOMING OVERLAND COACH AND MAIL

The six horses, now in harness, stood patiently, waiting for the command to begin their toil.

"John, you and Willie got your slickers?" Guthrie called up to the driver and shotgun guard, who were already sitting up on the driver's box. "Looks like it's goin' to rain."

"Yeah, it does look like it, don't it?" the driver called back down. "But we got 'em."

Matthews helped Meghan climb into the coach. Once inside, she looked back out through the open window.

"Thank you again," she said. "All of you."

"If you find out anything, or you need anything, send us a telegram," Biff said.

"I will," Meghan promised.

"Hyah!" the driver shouted. He snapped the whip over the heads of the team, and it popped like a pistol shot. The team started at a brisk trot and the coach lurched ahead.

Meghan stuck her head out through the window and yelled back at the three men who had come to see her off.

"'Bye!" she called. "I'll send you a telegram to let you know how things are working out!"

"'Bye," Matthews called. "Be careful!"

The three men watched as the coach moved rapidly up Bowie Avenue until the avenue turned into the road leading to Cheyenne.

"What do you think?" Guthrie asked. "Have we just told our money good-bye?"

"I don't think so," Matthews said.

"Well, yeah, you would say that. You helped her raise it."

"If Fred hadn't helped her, I would have," Biff said. "Besides, what's the worst that could happen? We'll all be part owners of a herd of Black Angus cattle."

Chapter Twenty-four

Jefferson County, Nebraska

"Look," Duff said, pointing to something on the trail in front of them.

"Yeah, I see it. It's a cigar butt," Elmer said.

"I know not whether 'tis ignorance or arrogance, but 'twould appear that our quarry is leading us to him like Hansel and Gretel."

"Like who?"

"You've never heard of Hansel and Gretel? It's a fairy tale," Duff said. "It is a children's story about a family that is starving, so the parents lead their children into the middle of the forest, then leave them there."

"They leave 'em there? What the hell did they do that for?"

"Because they are very short of food, and it is their hope that the children will not be able to find their way back so that the parents will not have to share what little food they have with their children."

"Now them must have been some kind of parents," Elmer said.

"Yes, but the children left a trail of crumbs of bread so they could find their way back."

"They left a trail of crumbs of bread? What kept the animals from eating it?"

"Nothing. That is exactly what happened. The birds ate the bread, so the children remained lost until they were found by a witch who wanted to eat them."

Elmer laughed. "Duff, now I must that is one hell of a story. And it is supposed to be for children you say?"

"Aye. And you are right. It does make one wonder why such a tale would be told to children. But the point is, Kingsley is doing that with his cigar butts. He is leading us directly to him."

"Yeah, well, I got to say that I do like the part about the witch eatin' 'em," Elmer said. "Because when we find Kingsley, I might just consider that."

Duff chuckled.

"I'm serious."

"What do you mean, you are serious?"

"You ever heard tell of a fella by the name of Liver Eatin' Johnson?" Elmer asked.

"Liver Eatin' Johnson? I can't say that I have. 'Tis a most unusual name, I must say. Is there really such a person?"

"Oh, yeah, he's real all right. He's a friend of mine. At one time or another he has been a sailor, scout, soldier, gold seeker, hunter, trapper, whiskey peddler, wagon train captain, and a deputy sheriff.

But he got his name from when he went on a personal warpath against the Crow Injuns. Seems they kilt his Injun wife, so he commenced killin' them. He kilt about twenty of 'em, and he cut the liver out of ever'one he kilt, then he cooked it up, and he et it. Turns out that was big medicine to the Crow, and they finally decided to make peace with him."

"You wouldn't really do such a thing, would you, Elmer? I mean, eat Kingsley's liver?"

"I might," Elmer said.

Duff didn't know if Elmer was serious or not, so he decided not to press the issue any further.

"Look at the tracks there," Elmer said. "See them rear hooves? The shoes are curved inward, just like that young cowboy said."

Elmer dismounted and picked up the cigar butt. "And this cigar butt hasn't dried out yet," he added. "It can't be more than a couple of hours old."

"It looks like we are catching up with him," Duff said.

"Yeah. But for me, it is twenty-five years too late," Elmer said.

"Aye, m' friend, but as they say, revenge is a dish best served cold."

"Not cold," Elmer said. "If I eat the son of a bitch's liver, I plan to fry it up first."

Kansas City

Hodge Denman was at the supper table with his wife, Mary, when Mr. Terrance Cooper came into the house. Cooper was Denman's father-in-law.

"Hello, Mr. Cooper," Denman said. "Won't you join us for supper?"

Cooper's face was contorted in anger.

"What have you done?" Cooper shouted, yelling so loud that spittle was flying from his mouth.

"Father, what is it?" Mary asked. "Why are you so angry?"

"Your mother and I are about to lose everything," Cooper said. "That's what it is. And it is your husband's fault!"

"Hodge, what is father talking about?"

"I can explain," Denman said weakly.

"Explain? Explain? I am losing my farm, my house, everything I have worked for, for my entire life, and you can explain?"

"I had no choice," Denman said. "I needed the money. The people I was in debt to are very bad people. If I did not pay them, they would have killed me."

"So you gave them my house?"

"Hodge, what are you talking about? Why did you borrow from such people? Why did you need money so badly?" Mary asked.

"I didn't borrow from them. I borrowed from the bank to pay the people that I owed. It's the bank who has the mortgages not only on your father's house, but ours as well," Denman said.

"If you didn't borrow from those men, how is it that you owed them so much money? I don't understand."

"They were gambling debts," Denman said.

"Gambling? You gambled away my house?" Cooper said.

"I had no choice."

Mary began crying. "Hodge, how *could* you?" she asked. She turned to her father. "Oh, father, I am so sorry. I knew nothing about this. Nothing."

"I know you didn't, darlin'," Cooper said. "It is all the fault of this no-count bastard you married."

"I won't be married to him any longer," she said. "In fact, I don't intend to spend one minute longer with him. Please, Father, I know I have no right to ask. But take me with you."

Cooper opened his arms, and his daughter came to him.

"Denman," Cooper started, but Denman interrupted him.

"I'm sorry," Denman said. "If there is any way I can make it up to you, I will."

"The only way you can make it up to me, you miserable son of a bitch, is to die," Cooper said.

"Mary, please," Denman said. "Give me another chance."

"You got into trouble like this once before by gambling," Mary said. "You told me then that you quit, remember? But you didn't quit. And now this is worse than anything you have ever done."

"Come, Mary. Let's get out of here."

"I need to pack a bag," Mary said, starting for the bedroom.

When Mary left the room, only Denman and Cooper remained.

"I had a plan to get us out of all this," Denman started. "And it still might work, if you'll just give me a little more time."

"I will get myself out of it," Cooper said. "I've already talked to the bank, and they have agreed to rewrite the loan. As far as I'm concerned, you have no time left."

"Please try to understand," Denman begged. "I was terrified. I had no choice!"

"You had a choice," Cooper said. "You could have faced it like a man, instead of the whimpering coward you are." Cooper called to the bedroom. "Mary, are you about ready? I can't stand to be in the company of this son of a bitch for a moment longer!"

Denman walked into the living room, then opened the drawer to the hall coat tree. Reaching inside, he removed a Colt .44 pistol; then, holding it down by his side, he returned to the dining room just as Mary came out of the bedroom carrying her suitcase.

"I didn't get everything," she said. "I'll come back for the rest when you are gone."

"No need," Denman said.

"What do you mean, no need?"

"You won't be needing them," Denman said. Raising his hand, he pointed the pistol toward Cooper.

"Hodge! What are you doing?" Mary screamed.

"You son of a . . . !" Cooper shouted, but that was as far as he got before Denman pulled the trigger.

The sound of the gunshot was ear-piercing inside the house.

Mary screamed as Cooper went down.

Denman turned the pistol toward Mary. He smiled at her, a crooked, mirthless, smile, then he raised the pistol to his own head and pulled the trigger.

Mary watched in horror as blood, brain, and bone detritus burst from the wound.

She continued screaming as she looked down at the two men, her father and her husband, both lying dead on the dining room floor.

Cheyenne

It was a six-hour trip to Cheyenne by stagecoach, and Meghan was familiar with it because she had made the trip many times before. There were seven people on the coach, including the driver and the shotgun guard. It had started raining shortly after they'd left Chugwater, and Meghan couldn't help but feel sorry for the driver and guard, who were sitting outside in the downpour. Both were wearing yellow rubber ponchos, but she knew the ponchos were doing little to keep them dry.

Meghan had heard them talking before they left, commenting that as they were not carrying any money, they were unlikely to be stopped. That meant that the guard's only purpose would be to give the driver someone to speak to. She wondered what they would think if they knew she had seventeen thousand dollars in cash sewn into her petticoat. As for the passengers, the jolting of the heavy vehicle over the roughening road made conversation difficult. The drummer sitting across from Meghan was asleep with his arm passed through the swaying strap and his head resting upon it. Mrs. Petre, who was traveling to Cheyenne in order to take the cars to San Francisco to see her daughter, was also asleep, unconscious of her appearance now, a disarray of ribbons, veils, and shawls.

Because there was no conversation, there was no sound but the rattling of wheels and the drumming of rain upon the roof. Pulling the isinglass curtains across the windows managed to keep out the rain, but it also made the interior of the coach very close and unpleasant. She was glad when they finally reached Cheyenne.

Thankfully, the rain had stopped by the time the coach rolled into Cheyenne. The coach stopped at the train depot, by arrangement, and because most of their passengers were departing or arriving on trains, the stage depot was in the train depot.

When Meghan bought a train ticket to Fremont, she was told it would not depart until the next day. She then walked across the road to the Inter Ocean Hotel, where she took a room to spend the night. As she waited in her hotel room that night, a room that had the luxury of electric lights, she took a piece of the hotel stationery and drew a line down the middle. On one side of the line she put all the positives about what she was about to do with the money. On the other side she put all the negatives. She was as frank and candid as she could be, putting down even the most remote positives and negatives, just to make certain that everything was covered.

When she was finished, she put it to one side, intending to free her mind of it for the time being. She walked over to the window of the hotel and looked out on Cheyenne at night. The electric street lamps, as well as the many lights in all the buildings, commercial and residential, made the city quite beautiful, sparkling like a jewel. She contrasted this with the gloomy nights in Chugwater, and wondered when Chugwater would get electricity, or indeed, if it ever would.

Finally, after giving it some time without thinking about it, she returned to the table and picked up the paper. Then, without bothering to assign weight to her entries, she counted them down either side of the paper.

There were two more positives than there were negatives.

"Yes!" she said aloud.

Smiling, she wadded the paper into a ball, threw it in the trash can, then went to bed.

Kansas City

When Hodge Denman didn't come in to work the next morning, Jay Montgomery asked some of the other clerks who worked in the bull pen if they had any idea why he was absent.

"Was he acting sick or anything yesterday?" he asked.

"No, sir," Ernie Tobias said. Tobias occupied the desk next to Denman's desk. "We were talking yesterday about putting together a contract to sell the Angus herd. He didn't give any idea that he wouldn't be back today."

"He didn't say anything to me, either," Montgomery said.

"I'll say this," Tobias said. "He has been acting mighty peculiar lately."

"Peculiar in what way?"

"I don't know, just sort of peculiar."

"That's Mr. Montgomery over there," someone said and, looking toward the speaker, Montgomery saw two men wearing badges, standing just inside the door. He walked over to them.

"I'm Jay Montgomery. May I help you gentlemen?"

"I'm Deputy Pease, this is Deputy Anderson, we are from the sheriff's department. Was Hodge Denman one of your employees?"

"Yes, he is." Montgomery paused, and a curious expression crossed his face. "What do you mean, was?"

"He's dead," Deputy Pease said. "According to his wife, he killed his father-in-law, then committed suicide."

"Denman did such a thing?" Montgomery said. "That is hard to believe."

"Yes, sir, well, we do have two bodies and Mrs. Denman's testimony," Deputy Pease said. "I wonder if we could look through his desk. We can get a warrant if necessary."

"No, that won't be necessary," Montgomery said. "Please, come this way. I'll show you his desk."

With Montgomery watching, the deputies went through Denman's desk. Then, not finding anything that was of interest to them, they thanked Montgomery for his cooperation and left.

The deputies didn't find anything that interested them, but Montgomery did. He saw the carbon copy of a letter over his signature. It was a letter he had not authorized or even read before this moment.

Dear Mr. MacCallister:

This is to inform you that we have received your request for five hundred Black Angus cattle. We are now in the process of making the arrangements for you. However, it will be necessary for you to come, in person, to take delivery of your cattle. The amount of money due upon your receipt of the herd is fifteen thousand, eight hundred twelve dollars and fifty cents. This sum will cover all costs attendant to this transaction, to include the price of the cattle and our handling fees.

Too often, bank drafts drawn upon small banks in remote areas of the country have been nonprocessed due to the failure of the banks in question. Therefore, it is the policy of the Kansas City Cattle Exchange that all transactions must be conducted in cash, so we ask you to bring the money with you. We apologize in advance for any difficulty this may cause the buyer.

Please advise us by telegraph, when you expect to arrive in Kansas City. Thank you for choosing to do business with us.

> *Sincerely,*
> *Jay Montgomery, President,*
> *Kansas City Cattle Exchange*

This had not been part of their agreement. Montgomery had not demanded that he bring cash, and he wondered why Denman would have sent such a letter.

Then he saw two telegrams from MacCallister.

MR. JAY MONTGOMERY, KANSAS CITY CATTLE
EXCHANGE

DEPARTING KANSAS CITY AT 8:30 A.M. ON THIS DAY.
WILL ARRIVE IN KANSAS CITY AT 9:30 P.M.
TOMORROW. WILL COME TO YOUR OFFICE ON
THE DAY FOLLOWING.

DUFF MACCALLISTER

And another:

MR. JAY MONTGOMERY, KANSAS CITY CATTLE
EXCHANGE

HAVE ENCOUNTERED UNEXPECTED DIFFICULTY.
WILL BE DELAYED.

DUFF MACCALLISTER.

Montgomery had not seen either of these telegrams before, either. In fact, Denman had specifically told him that they had heard nothing from
MacCallister.

Why had Denman lied to him? What was
going on?

Chapter Twenty-five

Fremont

When Meghan arrived in Fremont, it was nearly midnight. Hiring a cab, more for the escort than the need for a ride, she had him drive her to a hotel where she took a room.

The next morning after breakfast she called upon the city marshal. The marshal and his deputy were playing a two-hand game of poker, but both of them stood when Meghan stepped into the office.

"Can we help you, ma'am?"

"I hope so, Marshal . . . ?"

"Bivens, ma'am. And this is my deputy, Archer."

Deputy Archer touched the brim of his hat and nodded at her.

"Marshal Bivens, I am concerned about a friend of mine. The last word any of us had from him was from here in Fremont, when he sent a telegram saying that he had, as he put it, 'run into a bit of a problem.'"

"Who is it?" Bivens asked. "And did he say what the problem was?"

"No, he didn't say what the problem was. I was hoping you could help me with that," Meghan replied. "His name is Duff MacCallister."

"Duff MacCallister. A Scotsman, is he?"

Despite her nervousness, Meghan smiled. "Very much the Scotsman," she said.

"Then that was him, Marshal," Archer said quickly. "The same feller she's talkin' about."

"*Was* him?" Meghan asked, her voice cracked with worry. "What do you mean 'was' him? Please, God, has something happened to him?"

"No, no, didn't mean to worry you none," Deputy Archer said quickly. "I mean, yes, something has happened to him, but he hasn't been hurt, or anything like that."

"What happened to him?" Meghan asked, nervously.

"He was robbed," Bivens said.

"Robbed? No, that doesn't seem possible. Duff MacCallister is an extremely capable man. He is more than able to take care of himself."

"Yes, ma'm, I think he probably is. But apparently the brigand who robbed him stepped out of the alley in the middle of the night and struck him from behind."

"And here is the thing," Deputy Archer threw in. "They must have known he was carrying as much money as he was, because they took only the briefcase—they didn't take his wallet."

"I see. Where is he now?"

"He found out who it was that robbed him—a

murderin' scoundrel by the name of Crack Kingsley. And he and another fella, an older man, raw-boned, gray hair and a gray beard."

"Yes, that would be his friend, Elmer Gleason," Meghan said.

"Yes, ma'am, I believe Gleason was his name. Anyhow, Mr. MacCallister and Mr. Gleason went after Kingsley."

"Have you heard from them since they left?"

"Not exactly, but we have certainly heard about them," Marshal Bivens said.

"What do you mean, you have heard about them?"

"Like you said, ma'am. It would appear that this fella MacCallister can take care of himself. According to the police in Lincoln, Kingsley and three other men tried to bushwhack your friends MacCallister and Gleason. Jumped them in a saloon, it was. There was a shoot-out, and three of the four men who attacked MacCallister were killed."

"And Duff?" Meghan asked anxiously.

"He wasn't hurt none at all," the marshal said. "And neither was Gleason."

"You said the police informed you of this. Are Duff and Mr. Gleason in any kind of trouble?"

"No ma'am. There were enough witnesses there to tell the police exactly what happened, so there ain't no charges or anything against them."

"Do you know if Duff is still in Lincoln?"

"I doubt it. Kingsley, the man MacCallister is after, got away. Not knowin' MacCallister any better than I do I would still be willin' to make a bet that he left town after Kingsley."

"Yes, I'm sure he did," Meghan said.

"Will you be goin' on to Lincoln to try and find him?" Marshal Bivens asked.

"No," Meghan said. "I have some business in Kansas City that I must take care of."

"I don't expect him to be comin' back this way," Marshal Bivens said. "But just in case he does, do you have a message for him?"

"Yes, tell him that I . . ." Meghan stopped in the middle of the sentence. What message would she have for him? That she loved him? Did she? She wasn't sure, but whether she did or didn't, it wasn't a message to be conveyed by a marshal who was a stranger to both of them.

"Tell him what, ma'am?" Marshal Bivens asked.

"Just that his friends back in Chugwater are anxious about him."

"Yes, ma'am," Marshal Bivens said. "If he comes back through here, I'll be sure and tell him that."

Plymouth, Nebraska

The little town that rose in front of Kingsley was no more than a scattering of buildings, some of wood, some of sod. It had one street, Main, that ran through the middle of town, then a cross street, Columbus, which formed the letter X. The only buildings that were constructed of lumber were the commercial buildings, and they were all on Main Street. All the houses were constructed of sod, and they lined both sides of Columbus.

Kingsley hoped the town would have a saloon, and he was gratified to see a crudely painted sign in front of one of the buildings that read: BROWN DIRT SALOON.

He rode up to the saloon and dismounted in front, just as two cowboys came out. One of them had just said something funny, and they were both laughing.

One of them noticed Kingsley's horse.

"That's a nice-looking horse, Mister," the cowboy said. "Where did you get him?"

"I bought him."

"Oh? Where did you buy him? And when?"

"Sometime back, don't remember exactly. Why are you asking?"

The two cowboys checked out the brand.

"Sum' bitch, Jed, look at this. You see this here brand?"

"What's your name, Mister?" the cowboy called Jed asked.

"It's Carl Butler, if it's any of your business. What is all this about?"

"The Brand is CB. Could be Carl Butler, I guess."

"Sure looks like Crawlback's brand though."

"If you boys is questionin' whether or not I stole this horse, why don't you come right out and ask it, and let's get this settled once and for all. I've got the paper says I own this horse, and I'll show it to you if you want to see it. Then, like as not, I'll kill you for questioning me."

Kingsley was bluffing. He had no paper. But he figured that if he came down hard enough, and aggrieved enough, that he could run his bluff.

"Here, now, Mister, no need in gettin' all upset over nothin'. We was just commentin' on how much your brand looks like the brand for Crawlback is all," Jed said.

"There ain't nothin' fancy about it," Kingsley said. "And one CB is goin' to look pretty much like another CB."

"I reckon that's true," Jed said. "Come on, Arnie, let's go."

Kingsley watched them mount their own horses, then ride off. Not until they reached the end of the street, then urged their horses into a gallop, did he go inside.

He was pretty sure that MacCallister and Gleason were following him, but he hoped that the rain that had been falling off and on for the last two days had washed out enough of his tracks to cause them to lose the trail. And whether they were trailing him or not, he was hungry. He also wanted a drink. No, he needed a drink.

"Beans, bacon, biscuits," the bartender answered Kingsley's question about food.

"That'll do fine. I'll take the bottle," he said, putting a twenty-dollar bill down on the bar.

"You got 'nything smaller than this?" the bartender asked. "This'll just about take ever' bit of the change I got in the cash register."

"Keep the change," Kingsley said.

"What? Mister, are you sure?"

"I'm hungry, and I want a drink," Kingsley said. "And I want to be left alone. Will this twenty get all that for me?"

"Yes, sir!"

"I'll be over there in the corner," Kingsley said as,

with bottle in hand, he started across the saloon floor.

He was just pouring himself a glass of whiskey when someone walked up to his table.

"Hello, Crack. It's been a long time," the man said.

Looking up, Kingsley saw the man who had been his cell mate at the Nebraska State Penitentiary at Lincoln a few years earlier.

"Scooter Margolis. I thought you was serving life," Kingsley said.

Margolis smiled. "Yeah, that's what Warden Wyman thought too. Only I had other ideas. And by the way, I'm callin' myself Donovan now. Pat Donovan."

"What are you doin' in this little burg?"

"Workin' down at the stable. What are you doin' here?"

"I'm just passin' through," Kingsley said.

"You got somethin' goin', do you?" Margolis asked.

"What do you mean?"

"I know you, Kingsley. You've always got somethin' goin'."

"What if I do?"

"I want in on it."

"It ain't like you think."

"Don't matter to me what it is. I'm so tired of shovelin' horse shit, I'm willin' to do anything. What have you got goin'?"

Kingsley's food was brought to the table so he said nothing until the server left.

"I might have somethin' goin'," Kingsley said.

Margolis smiled broadly. "I knew it! The moment I seen you come into this place, I knew you was up to somethin'. What is it?"

"It don't really matter what it is," Kingsley said. "Because the truth is, I got a couple of people doggin' my trail, and until I get rid of them, I can't do nothin' else."

"Who you got after you?"

"Bounty hunters. There's a lot of paper out on me. You too, I reckon."

"Yeah, last I heard there was five thousand dollars out for me. Son of a bitch, I hate bounty hunters."

"Yeah, well, here's the thing. They are after me right now, but to them, one is as good as another. If they was to get wind that you was here, hell, they might even forget about me and go after you. Especially since you are worth more than I am."

"Who are they?" Margolis asked. "Do you know their names?"

"I don't know their names," Kingsley said. "But I know what they look like. If you'll help me take care of 'em, why, I could see lettin' you come in on me for my next job."

"You ain't told me yet what your next job is goin' to be," Margolis said.

Kingsley shook his head.

"No, I ain't. And I ain't goin' to, 'til after we take care of the two bounty hunters. Are you in, or not?"

"I don't know. I could just leave, I reckon. I mean, if they are trailin' you, chances are they don't even know that I am here."

"You could do that," Kingsley said. He put his hand inside his shirt pocket and pulled out a bound packet of twenty-dollar bills, from which a few had already been taken. "Or, you could take this four hundred dollars and help me take care of the problem."

"What?" Margolis said. "Where the hell did you come up with this much money?"

"There's plenty more where that came from," Kingsley said. "Once the bounty hunters are out of the way."

Margolis reached for the packet of money, but before he could touch it, Kingsley pulled it back.

"Are you in or out?" he asked.

"I'm in!" Margolis said. "Hell yes, I'm in!"

Kingsley pushed the money across the table to him. "Good," he said. "Now, as soon as I finish eating, we'll go set up a welcome for them."

Two miles out of town the road crossed a stream known as Little Blue Creek. The stream could be forded, but it was a deep enough ford to slow the horses down. Also, the stream was running very quickly, so that the horses had to fight to stay on their feet. Just beyond the stream, the road made a turn to the right. On the left side of the road, just as it made its turn, was a low-lying ridge crowned by oversized flat rocks. That created a perfect observation post from which to monitor the approaching road. It was here that Kingsley set up his ambush.

Crack Kingsley lay on top of one of the flat rocks, looking back along the trail.

"How do you know they'll be comin' this way?" Margolis asked.

"They're comin'. I fixed it so they would."

"How did you fix it?"

"Don't matter none how I did it. I did it. You just be ready."

"I'm ready," Margolis said.

"There's two of 'em now," Elmer said. "I wonder where he picked up a friend. Hell, more than that, what kind of man would be his friend in the first place?"

"He has fifteen thousand dollars in cash," Duff said. "It matters little how evil a person is. With that much money, he can buy friends."

"You got that right," Elmer said. "There's another cigar butt."

"Odd," Duff said. "That's the third butt we've seen in the last mile." Duff dismounted, picked up the cigar butt, examined it, then held it to his nose and smelled it.

"It's just what I thought," he said.

"What?" Elmer asked.

"This cigar hasn't even been smoked. I thought it was strange to find three of them so close together."

"Damn, he's leading us on, ain't he?" Elmer asked. "He's wanting us to find him."

"Aye."

"You know what that means, don't you? That means he's plannin' to set up an ambush."

"So it would appear."

"Well hell, we ain't goin' to just ride into it, are we?"

"We are," Duff said. "But remember, forewarned is forearmed."

"Yeah," Elmer said. "That sounds pretty good. I just wish I knew what the hell it meant."

"It means that when he springs his ambush, we shall be ready for him."

"Margolis, there they are," Kingsley said. "Get ready. As soon as they get into the stream, start shooting. Their horses won't be able to react fast enough, and we'll have 'em dead in our sights."

"What if they don't come across the creek?" Margolis asked.

"They'll come. They want me too bad to hold back. Get ready."

Both Kingsley and Margolis cocked their rifles and waited.

"Now!" Duff shouted, and both men leaped down from their horses, just as they approached the edge of the creek.

The road exploded with the sound of gunfire as Kingsley and Margolis opened up on what they thought would be easy targets. Instead, their bullets whizzed harmlessly over the empty saddles of the riderless horses, then whined off into empty space.

Duff and Elmer had chosen their position perfectly, for after they leaped down from their horses, they separated, Duff getting behind a rock on the left side of the road, while Elmer found one on the right.

"What the hell?" someone shouted. "Kingsley! Do you see 'em? Where did they go?"

Duff fired toward the sound of the voice, and the man behind the voice fired back. There was silence for several seconds, and then came the bark of Elmer's rifle. Immediately after Elmer fired, Duff heard a grunt of pain, and then he saw a rifle come sliding down the rock and splash into the water. A second or two later a man followed the rifle, sliding belly up, down the rock, winding up, as did the rifle, in the water.

It wasn't Kingsley.

Nobody moved for several moments; then, carefully, first Duff, then Elmer, came out. Not being fired upon, they ran across the creek, then, gradually, worked their way up to the top of the rock where the shooting had been coming from.

They found a few empty cartridges, ejected from the rifles, but there was no one there.

Kingsley had gotten away.

Chapter Twenty-six

Kansas City

In the hotel the night before, Meghan had very carefully removed all the money from her petticoat. Now, with the money in an attaché case, she arrived at the Kansas City Cattle Exchange in the back of a hansom cab.

"Do you wish me to wait, ma'am?" the cab driver asked as she stepped out of the conveyance in front of the KCCE office building.

"Thank you, but I don't believe that will be necessary. I am certain that someone here will arrange for my transportation." Meghan paid the driver, including a tip; he touched the brim of his hat then drove off.

Seeing any woman inside the Cattle Exchange office was a rarity. Seeing one as beautiful as Meghan caught everyone's attention. No fewer than three men came to assist her.

"I would like to speak with Mr. Jay Montgomery, please," Meghan said.

"I'm Jay Montgomery," a tall, thin, dignified-looking gray-haired man said. "May I help you?"

"I hope so," Meghan said. "I want to buy some Black Angus cattle."

"Black Angus, you say?" Montgomery replied. "Well, what a happy coincidence this is. It just so happens that we have quite a few Black Angus on hand. How many do you want?"

"I want four hundred and eighty heifers and twenty bulls," she said.

Montgomery looked surprised. "This isn't just a coincidence, is it?"

"Not at all," Meghan said. She opened her attaché case and began counting out money. "I trust you will be able to arrange transportation for me and the cattle back to Cheyenne?"

"Yes, ma'am. We will take of everything for you."

That night, just before Meghan boarded the special car that had been attached to the train taking the cattle back to Cheyenne, she sent a telegram to Fred Matthews.

HAVE TAKEN POSSESSION OF THE CATTLE. PLEASE
HAVE DROVERS MEET ME IN CHEYENNE TO DRIVE
THE HERD UP TO SKY MEADOW. MEGHAN PARKER

Corning, Kansas

"This is the horse," Elmer said, examining the rear hooves of the pinto. "Hello, Lucky," he said.

The pinto, upon hearing his name, bobbed his head up and down several times.

The horse was tied in front of the Union Saloon.

Having learned from his cousin Falcon MacCallister how to enter a saloon, Duff checked the place out as soon as he and Elmer stepped inside. He did not see Kingsley, nor anyone else who represented a danger to him. Glancing over toward Elmer, he saw that he was doing the same thing, and satisfied that the room was clear, they stepped up to the bar.

The bartender stood behind the bar. In front of him were two glasses with whiskey remaining in them, and he poured the whiskey back into a bottle, corked it, and put the bottle on the shelf behind the bar. He wiped the glasses out with his stained apron, then set them among the unused glasses. Seeing Duff and Elmer step up to the bar, the bartender moved down toward them.

"Scotch, if you have it," Duff said.

The barman reached for the bottle he had just poured the whiskey back into, but Duff shook his head.

"Never mind. Beer will do."

"Me too," Elmer added.

Shrugging, the saloonkeeper pulled the handle on the beer barrel, filling two mugs and putting a head on both.

"Could you be for helping us out?" Duff said. "We're looking for someone."

"This here ain't the lost person's bureau," the bartender replied.

"The pinto tied up out front is the horse he rode in on," Duff said. "I say the horse he rode in on, rather than his horse, for 'tis a stolen steed."

"I can't help you, Mister. What I do is pour drinks. Other than that, I mind my own business."

"He is a murdering scum," Duff said. "He killed a young woman and her daughter."

"And that ain't the only women he kilt. He kilt another woman, too, only this here 'n he kilt, he raped before he kilt her," Elmer added.

"Are you men the law?" the bartender asked.

"No."

"Bounty hunters then? I don't have much truck with bounty hunters."

"Bounty hunters?" Duff asked, looking toward Elmer for clarification.

"No," Elmer said. "We ain't bounty hunters."

"Then, what are you after this fella for?"

"Didn't we give you enough justification? He murders women," Duff said.

"People like that you ought to let the law handle."

"I don't have time to wait for the law."

"Is there a reward?"

"I'm sure there is. But that 'tis no business of mine," Duff said. "This is personal."

"What does this fella look like?"

"He is about medium height, gaunt of face, with a purple scar that runs from his eye down to the corner of his mouth, thusly." Duff ran his finger down his face, illustrating the scar.

The barkeeper didn't say anything, but Duff noticed a slight reaction to his description.

"He is here right now, isn't he?" Duff asked.

The saloon owner said nothing, but he raised his head and looked toward the stairs at the back of the room.

"Thanks," Duff said.

"I didn't tell you nothin'," the bartender said.

At the back of the saloon, a flight of wooden stairs led up to an enclosed loft. Duff started up the stairs, pulling his gun as he did so.

The few men in the saloon had been talking and laughing among themselves. When they saw Duff pull his gun, their conversation died, and they watched him walk quietly up the steps.

Duff tried to open the first door, but it was locked. He knocked on it.

"Go 'way," a man's voice called from the other side of the door. "Get your own woman."

Duff raised his foot, then kicked it hard. The door flew open with a crash and the woman inside the room screamed.

"What the hell?" the man shouted. He stood up quickly, and Duff saw that it wasn't the man he was looking for.

"You son of a bitch! Get the hell out of here!"

"I'm sorry," Duff said, holding up his hand. "Wrong room."

Duff heard a crash of glass from the next room and he ran to it, then kicked that door open as well.

He saw the window broken, and a breeze lifting the curtain out over the floor.

"Who are you?" the woman shouted. "Get out! Get out!"

Duff ran to the window and looked down, but he saw nothing.

Suddenly, out of the corner of his eye, he saw Kingsley holding out a knife.

It had been a trick! Kingsley had broken the window to make it appear as if he had jumped outside. Now Kingsley was coming toward him, making a slashing motion with the knife. He managed to cut Duff's hand, forcing him to drop his pistol. Kingsley made another slash and Duff jumped back, barely avoiding being disemboweled.

"I'm going to gut you like a fish," Kingsley said, swinging again.

Again Duff managed to avoid him, this time by going down on one knee. He felt around on the floor, searching desperately for the pistol he had dropped, but he couldn't find it. What he did find was a long, jagged shard of window glass. Duff picked it up, and thrust upward into Kingsley's belly. The shard was turned sideways, and it slipped easily in between Kingsley's ribs. Duff pushed it all the way in, and he felt hot blood spilling across his hand. Kingsley's eyes opened wide, and he dropped to his knees, with his hands clasped over his wound.

"You—you kilt me," he gurgled.

"Aye," Duff said calmly. "It seemed to be the thing to do."

By the time Kingsley fell to the floor, Elmer was in the room.

"Hold it, woman!" Elmer shouted. "Put the gun down!"

Duff had forgotten all about the woman and, looking toward her, he saw that she had pulled Kingsley's pistol from his holster and was pointing it at Duff. She lowered the gun, and Duff stepped over to take it from her.

"Don't kill me, don't kill me," the woman pleaded.

"You don't need to worry none about that, Miss," Elmer said. "The only one in here that ever kilt a woman is the son of a bitch that's lyin' dead on the floor."

Kansas City

"No, sir, I'm sorry, Mr. Montgomery isn't here," the man in the Kansas City Cattle Exchange office said. "He has gone to St. Louis. My name is Stan Cornett. I am temporarily in charge. May I help you?"

"Aye, I hope so," Duff said. "I am here to take possession of my cattle."

Cornett got a confused look on his face. "Take possession of your cattle? And what cattle would that be?" he asked.

"Black Angus. I believe you are holding a herd of five hundred Black Angus for me. Four hundred eighty heifers, twenty bulls."

"Oh, yes. I wasn't here, but I think I did hear something about that. Would you be Mr. Mac-Callister?"

"Aye," Duff said, a broad smile spreading across his face. "Then you do have them?"

"No, I'm sorry," Cornett said. "Those cattle have been sold."

"Sold? Why? I sent a telegram explaining that I would be delayed."

"I'm afraid I am unable to give you all the facts about it," Cornett said. "As I said, Mr. Montgomery, who is our director, is gone. He is in St. Louis. And Mr. Denman, the man who was handling your account, is deceased. I don't have any of the specifics, other than the fact that the herd of Black Angus has been sold."

When Duff stepped back outside, Elmer was leaning up against the front of the building with his arms folded across his chest.

"Where's your cows?" Elmer asked.

"They're gone," Duff said.

"Gone? What do you mean, gone? Where did they go?"

"I don't know," Duff said. "Come on, Elmer. Let's go home."

The train ride back to Cheyenne was frustrating. Duff had encountered and overcome obstacle after obstacle, only to be denied the goal of acquiring a herd of Black Angus.

"You ain't give up, have you?" Elmer asked.

"I don't know. Maybe it would be easier to just raise Herefords. Or even Longhorns."

"You don't want to do that," Elmer said.

Duff chuckled. "Elmer, you are the one who said it was foolish for me to try and introduce Black Angus to Wyoming. You, and as matter of fact, just about everyone in Chugwater, said that I should raise Longhorns or Herefords."

"That was then, and this is now," Elmer said. "You've done been through too much to give up on 'em now. I say, soon as we get back home, you should wait until this Montgomery feller gets back into his office, then order you some more Black Angus. You got most of the money back from Kingsley. And this time when you go after 'em, I'll go with you."

"I appreciate it, but I'm tired of having a cattle ranch without cattle. I think I'll just stock it with whatever I can buy here. It's not like there aren't any cattle available."

"That ain't what you want though, is it?"

"It'll be all right."

"That ain't what you want, though, is it?" Elmer repeated.

Duff smiled, put his hand on his friend's shoulder, squeezed it, then leaned his head back on the seat to take a nap.

Two days later, after offloading their horses from the attached stock car, they rode back to Sky Meadow. After they passed the southern tip of the Laramie Mountain Range, just before they came to Bear Creek, they heard the sound of bawling cattle.

"What the hell?" Elmer said. "Duff, do you hear that?"

"Aye, I do hear it," Duff replied. "The question is what is it?"

"Sounds like cattle."

"Aye, it is cattle, but why are we hearing cattle? There shouldn't be any cattle here. I don't have any cattle, and I have the only ranch in this area."

The two men urged their horses into a trot; then, as they came over the last ridge, they had a panoramic view of Sky Meadow spread out below them. Gathered along the banks of both the Bear and Little Bear Creeks were large clusters of cattle.

They weren't just any cattle. They were Black Angus cattle.

"What is this?" Duff asked. He looked over at Elmer. "Where did these cattle come from? And look, the barn has been rebuilt! Elmer, do you know anything about this?"

"I swear to you, Duff, I don't know a thing about it," Elmer said. "This here has me as bamboozled as it does you."

"Well, let's find out, shall we?"

Slapping their legs against the sides of their horses, the two men galloped down toward the ranch. Seeing the two horses approach at a gallop, the cattle parted as they rode through. A rider came toward them from the bunkhouse. Duff recognized him as one of the three cowboys who had caused trouble at the dance.

"What are you doing here?" Duff asked. "It's

Woodward, isn't it? Didn't you and I have som
difficulty at the dance a while ago?"

"Yes, sir, the name is Al Woodward," the cowbo
said. "I didn't think you would remember me. An
I'm awful sorry 'bout what happened at the dance
I was just bein' stupid, is all."

"I remember you, all right. But I'll ask you again
what are you doing here?"

"Why, Mr. MacCallister, I'm keepin' an eye o
your cows," Woodward said. "Me 'n Case Martin an
Brax Walker. Them was the other two that was ther
that night, actin' just as stupid as I was. Right nov
they're both down at the other end of your propert
roundin' up some of the cows that wandered off
These here cows sure is pretty. I ain't never see
cows like these before."

"How did these cattle get here?" Duff asked, n
more enlightened than when he began the que:
tioning.

"Well, me 'n Case 'n Brax brung 'em down from
Cheyenne after they come in on the railroad. M
Matthews, he hired us. And, seein' as you ain't got n
other cowboys workin' for you, well, he hired us t
stay here 'n keep an eye on 'em 'til you come back
So that's what we done, an' the truth is, why, me '
the boys was kind of hopin' you'd hire us on fo
good."

"You want me to hire you?"

"Yes, sir, we do. I mean, seein' as we was ridin' yo
at the dance 'n all, we could understand if you don
want to hire us. But we'd make good hands for you
Mr. MacCallister, I promise you that we would. Be

des which, you got the nicest bunkhouse any of us
ave ever been in."

"Have you already been paid to bring the cattle
own?"

"Yes, sir, we was paid for that, and we done been
aid for the rest of the month, 'cause didn't nobody
now how long it would be before you come back."

As Duff and Elmer sat on their horses talking to
Voodward, two other riders came up from the west.

"Here comes Case 'n Brax now," Woodward said.

The riders pulled up. "We got all the cows back
ith the others," one of them said. Then, recogniz-
g Duff, he nodded.

"Mr. MacCallister, I'm Brax Walker. It's good to
ee you home, sir."

"Mr. MacCallister, I'm Case Martin," the other
der said.

"Who built the barn?" Duff asked.

"Well, sir, Mr. Guthrie, he brung out all the mate-
al, the lumber and such," Woodward said. "And
e three of us built it."

"And you want to work for me?"

"Yes, sir!" all three said together.

"All right, you are hired. This is Elmer Gleason.
e is the foreman, and you will answer to him. Have
u any problem with that?"

"No, sir, we ain't got no problem with that at all."

"You stay here, Elmer. I'm going into town to see
hat this is all about," Duff said.

"Okay."

Duff started to turn his horse, but before he did,
e looked back at Woodward and the others.

"And just for your information, gentlemen, wh
I was wearing that night is called kilts. And 'tis in th
colors of the Black Watch, as noble a military unit
ever served in Her Majesty's Armed Forces. I'll na
brook any more teasing."

"No, sir, you ain't never goin' to hear nothii
about that from us again, I can promise you that
Woodward said.

"No, sir, nor from us, either," Walker added, ar
Martin nodded his own head in agreement.

Elmer laughed out loud as Duff rode off.

Chugwater

When Duff called upon Fred Matthews to see wl
there were Black Angus cows on his ranc
Matthews said that this subject could best be di
cussed over coffee and pie at Vi's Pies.

Matthews nodded to one of his clerks, who le
the store without further instruction.

"I have to make a few entries in my book
Matthews said. "Give me a moment, and I'll be rigl
with you."

"What's going on, Fred?" Duff asked.

"It'll only be a moment longer," Matthews r
plied, without answering Duff's question.

Five minutes later the two men walked down
Vi's Pies. When they stepped inside, Duff saw R.\
Guthrie, Biff Johnson, and Meghan Parker sitting
a table. There were two empty chairs at the tabl
Seeing Matthews's clerk hurrying off, he knew th
he had been sent to set up this impromptu meetin

"Take a seat, gentlemen," Vi Winslow said. "Duff, I baked a fresh cherry pie this morning. I know that is your favorite."

"Aye, thank you," Duff said, still confused by everything.

His friends at the table were smiling at him as he sat down.

"Now," Duff said. "Is this going to be a secret forever? Or is someone going to tell me what is going on?"

"Fred, you be our spokesman," Biff suggested.

Matthews told Duff how they had gotten word that he had experienced a bit of difficulty, and how they had also heard from the Kansas City Cattle Exchange that they would be forced to sell off the herd if he did not show up in two weeks.

"It was all Meghan's idea," Matthews said. "She knew how badly you wanted those black cows, though I still haven't figured out why," he added with a chuckle. "So, she came to me, R.W. and Biff, then she put in her own money, and all of us together raised enough to buy the herd in order to prevent them from selling the cows out from under you. She took the money to Kansas City, bought the herd, and put them on the train back here. I hired three cowboys to meet the train, and drive the cows down to your ranch. I assume that you have seen the cows and met your cowboys."

"Aye. And I'm not sure which was the bigger surprise, seeing the cows, or those three hooligans," Duff said.

"They promised they would be on their best behavior," Matthews said.

"Duff," Meghan said, and there was a worried expression on her face. "I hope we weren't out of line in this. If we were, and if you are angry with anyone, please be angry with me and not with them. I am the one who talked them into going along with the idea."

"Upset?" Duff said. "How can I be upset? 'Tis wondering I am how a Scotsman like me, barely a year in this country, could have made as wonderful friends as the four of ye."

"Duff, you are an honest and good-hearted man," Biff said. "How hard is it to be friends with such a man?"

"The bit o' trouble I encountered was in being robbed," Duff said. "But I've recovered the money, and I'll be repaying all of you, with interest, and my thanks."

"No interest needed, your thanks are enough," Matthews said.

"That goes for me too," Biff said.

"And me," Guthrie added.

"Not for me," Meghan said.

"Meghan, you want interest on your loan?" Matthews asked, surprised by her response.

"No interest," Meghan said. "And no loan. I own one fourth of the herd, and I'm not selling."

"What?" Duff asked.

Meghan smiled and put her hand on his. "We're going to be partners, Duff MacCallister. One way or another," she said.

Duff registered no expression to Meghan's announcement. He took a bite of his cherry pie and chewed it thoughtfully as everyone stared at him, waiting for his response.

Then, to the relief of everyone, he placed his hand on Meghan's, and smiled.

"Aye," he said. "Partners."

In William W. Johnstone's bestselling
The Last Gunfighter, Frank Morgan is the last
of a breed—until he confronts a young gun who
shares his name, skill, and maybe even his blood . . .

LIKE FATHER. LIKE SON. LIKE HELL.

Morgan has one son he knows of—and Kid
Morgan, the Loner, has become famous in his
own right. But in Montana, Morgan comes
face-to-face with a young man with a deadly swagger
and a stunning claim: that he's Frank's son, too.
And his one and only goal is to kill his old man.
For Frank Morgan, the first thing to do is find out if
Brady Morgan is truly his own flesh and blood.
That means tracking down a woman he once loved,
and then untangling her lies, lust and a scheme to
steal prime Montana ranch land. Suddenly, Frank is
in the middle of a bloodbath of a range war—and
he's standing on the opposite side from young
Brady Morgan. In a clash of guns and greed,
two Morgans will face each other one last time:
to decide who will live and who will die . . .

Turn the page for an exciting preview of

THE LAST GUNFIGHTER: MONTANA
GUNDOWN

by William W. Johnstone
with J. A. Johnstone

On sale now wherever Pinnacle Books are sold.

Chapter One

It was nice to be home.

Of course, a man like him didn't have a home in the strictest sense of the word, like most folks did, Frank Morgan reflected as he and his friend, the old-timer named Salty Stevens, rode through a valley with majestic mountains looming over it.

There was a good reason Frank was known as The Drifter. Every time he had tried to put down roots in the past thirty years or so, something had happened to prevent it.

Often something tragic.

But despite that, he had grown to regard the entire American West as his home. Recently, he had spent time in Alaska and Canada, and while he had to admit that those places were spectacularly beautiful, it was nice to be back in the sort of frontier country where he felt most comfortable.

Cattle country, like the places where he had grown up in Texas, even though this particular valley was located in Montana. Frank saw stock grazing here and there on the lush grass. This was his kind of territory, and his kind of people lived here.

"Pretty, ain't it?" Salty asked, as if reading Frank's mind.

Frank nodded and said, "Yep."

"Well, don't get all carried away and start waxin' poetical about it."

Frank grinned. The expression softened the rugged lines of his face . . . a little.

He was a broad-shouldered, powerfully built man who had been wandering the West for more than thirty years since coming home to Texas as a youngster after the Civil War. It was not long after that when he discovered, through no fault of his own, how fast and deadly accurate with a gun he was.

Other people became aware of that natural talent of his. Some tried to use him to their advantage. Others just wanted to test their own skills against his in contests where the stakes were life and death.

And with each man that fell to his gun, Frank Morgan's reputation grew. He left his home in search of peace, but gun trouble followed him, and as years passed and men died, his reputation became more than that.

It became a legend.

He was tagged with the nickname The Drifter because of his habit of never staying in one place for very long, but some folks had started calling him The Last Gunfighter. In these days when the dawn of a new century was closing in fast, most people considered the Old West to be finished.

Hell, it had been more than twenty years since

ck McCall had put a bullet in the back of Wild
ill Hickok's head in the Number 10 Saloon in
eadwood. Wes Hardin was dead, too, also shot in
ne back of the head by a coward; Ben Thompson
ad gone under; Smoke Jensen was living the
eaceful life of a rancher in Colorado; and nobody
uite seemed to know what had happened to Matt
odine.

So it was understandable that people considered
rank Morgan to be the last of a dying breed, that
f the shootist and pistolero. In truth, he wasn't.
here were still quite a number of men in the West
ho were quick on the draw and deadly with their
uns. They just didn't get the notoriety such men
nce did. The newspaper and magazine writers
ked to write about how modern and civilized
verything was.

Only the dime novelists still cared about the fron-
er. They never got all the details right, but there
as some truth in the feelings they conveyed. Even
rank, who had been cast as the hero of a number
f those lurid, yellow-backed, totally fictional tales,
ad come to realize that.

Clad in worn range clothes, including a faded
lue bib-front shirt and a high-crowned gray Stet-
on, Frank rode easy in the saddle of a leggy golden
orrel stallion he had dubbed Goldy. He was lead-
ng the rangy gray known as Stormy, and a big, wolf-
ke cur called Dog trotted alongside the horses.
rank, Stormy, and Dog had been trail partners for
long time, and although Goldy was younger, he
ad fit in with them, too.

Salty, in a fringed buckskin vest over his flannel

shirt and with a battered old hat pushed down o
his thatch of white hair that matched his bristlin
beard, rode a pinto pony and led a sturdy pac
horse. The packs were full of supplies given to ther
by Bob Coburn, an old friend of Frank's and th
owner of the Circle C Ranch, where they had sper
the past few weeks.

Dog, Stormy, and Goldy had been watched ove
by a livery owner in Seattle for months while Fran
was off adventuring in the Great White North; bu
on receiving a telegram from Frank, the man ha
put the animals in a livestock car on a train that ha
delivered them to a siding near the Circle C. Fran
and Salty had ridden down from Canada to pic
them up at the ranch, and the reunion betwee
Frank and his old friends had been a happy one.

For a while, Frank had been content to stay ther
and visit with Bob. He'd gotten a kick out of demor
strating gun and rope tricks for the rancher's ter
year-old son. Salty had spent hours telling wilc
hair-raising stories to the youngster, who seemed t
have a knack of his own for yarn spinning. It was
pleasant time.

But eventually, Frank had gotten up one morr
ing and known it was time to move on. That was wh
he and Salty were now ambling along this valley i
a generally eastward direction. Where it would tak
them Frank had no idea.

He didn't figure it really mattered all that mucl

"Are we still goin' to Mexico?" Salty asked. "W
been talkin' about it for a good long time."

"We said we were going to spend the winte
there," Frank pointed out. "It's not winter anymore

t's the middle of summer, and a beautiful one, at hat."

"Yeah, but Mexico's a long ways off. Take us a retty good spell to get there, especially since you lon't believe in gettin' in no hurry. I figure we hould start thinkin' about headin' in that direction."

Frank nodded slowly and said, "We can do that. tart thinking about it, I mean."

"You're a dadgummed deliberate cuss, you know hat."

"A man gets that way when the years start piling p on him."

Salty snorted and said, "There's been a heap nore of 'em pile up on me than on you."

They could have bantered like this for hours, ocking along peacefully in the saddle in the midst f this spectacularly beautiful scenery.

Unfortunately, trouble reared its ugly head in he form of an outbreak of gunshots somewhere ot far away.

Both men reined their mounts to a halt. Salty ooked over at Frank and said, "Oh, Lord. You're hinkin' about gettin' in the big middle of that uckus, whatever it is, ain't you?"

"I'm curious," Frank allowed.

The shots continued to bang and roar. They were loser now. Frank's keen eyes suddenly spotted novement in a line of pine trees about two hundred ards away.

A second later, four men on horseback burst out f the trees. They lashed at their mounts with the eins, urging every bit of speed they could out of he animals.

"They're headed for them rocks!" Salty exclaimed

Frank saw the clump of boulders off to the lef and knew the old-timer was right. The rocks offered the nearest cover for those fugitives.

They might not make it, because an even large group of riders emerged from the pines about hundred yards behind them. There were more tha a dozen of these men, and they were all throwing lead after the four fugitives.

Most of them were using handguns, and Fran knew the distance was too great for such weapons A few of the pursuers had Winchesters. The sharpe cracks of the repeaters mixed with the booms of th revolvers. A lucky shot might bring down one of th men fleeing toward the boulders.

"What're you doin'?" Salty yelped as Fran reached for his own Winchester.

"Figured I'd even the odds a little."

"We don't know who those hombres are," Salt argued. "Might be owl-hoots, and that could be posse after 'em."

"That's why I intend to aim high," Frank said a he levered a round into the Winchester's chambe and lifted the rifle to his shoulder.

He knew Salty was right. It wasn't very smart t get in the middle of a fight when you didn't knov who the sides were or what stakes were involved.

But when Frank saw four men being chased by fi teen or twenty, the sense of fairness that was deeply ingrained part of him kicked up a fuss. H just didn't like to see that.

"Aw, shoot!" Salty muttered. "Well, it's been more'

a month since anybody tried to kill us, so I reckon we're overdue."

He reached for his own Winchester and pulled it out of its sheath.

Frank aimed over the heads of the pursuers, who appeared not to have noticed him and Salty, and pressed the trigger. The Winchester cracked and spat flame.

Now that the ball was open, Frank didn't hesitate. He cranked off five shots as fast as he could work the Winchester's lever. Beside him, Salty's rifle barked several times as he joined in.

The pursuers must have heard the shots, or at least heard the bullets whistling over their heads, because they slowed suddenly and started milling around in confusion. That delay was enough to give the four fugitives a chance to reach the safety of the rocks. As they disappeared behind the boulders, the men who had been chasing them swung around to face the new threat.

They charged toward Frank and Salty.

"Uh-oh," Salty said as he lowered his rifle. "I don't think they're firin' warnin' shots, Frank!"

Salty was right about that. He and Frank were the prey now.

Chapter Two

"Come on, Dog!" Frank called as he jammed the Winchester back in its sheath and hauled Goldy around. From the corner of his eye, he had spotted a small knoll about fifty yards to their right. That was the closest cover he and Salty could find.

Leading Stormy and the pack horse, the two men pounded toward the little hill. It was barely big enough for all of them to crowd behind it. As they reached the knoll, Frank sensed as much as heard the passage of a bullet close beside his left ear.

The varmints were getting inside the range.

He swung behind the hill and instantly dropped out of the saddle, pulling the rifle from its sheath as he did so. His feet had barely hit the ground when he charged ten feet or so up the slope and threw himself down on his belly. He yanked his hat off so the crown wouldn't stick up over the top of the knoll and get ventilated by a bullet.

It was a good hat, and he didn't see any point in letting it be damaged.

Also, the grass growing on the knoll would make it harder for the gunmen to see where he and Salty were. The old-timer bellied down beside Frank and thrust the barrel of his Winchester over the top of the hill.

"We still aimin' high?" Salty asked in a scornful tone that made it clear he didn't think that was a very good idea.

"Reckon we'd better," Frank said. "Those fellas could still be lawmen."

"Mighty trigger-happy badge-toters, if they are," Salty muttered. He squinted over the barrel of his Winchester and squeezed off a shot.

Frank did likewise. He had lowered his aim a little, hoping that some bullets whizzing around their heads would make the men think twice about continuing this fight.

One of the riders suddenly threw up his arms and half-fell out of the saddle, catching himself at the last instant. The man slumped on the back of his horse, obviously badly wounded.

Frank was about to say something to Salty about not following the plan when he saw puffs of powder smoke coming from the rocks where the four riders they'd seen earlier had taken shelter. Those fugitives were taking a hand in this game, and considering that they had been the object of the chase to start with, Frank supposed he couldn't blame them.

With the four men in the rocks and Frank and Salty behind the knoll, the gunmen were caught in a crossfire. First one, then another, and then the whole group yanked their horses around, as they must have realized what a bad position they were in. They spurred their mounts and galloped back toward the trees.

Salty lowered his rifle and crowed, "They're lightin' a shuck!"

"For now," Frank agreed as the men disappeared into the pines, including the one who had been wounded. "We'd better be careful, though. They might double back and try again. I think we'll stay right here for a while."

"Really? I figured we'd go talk to those other fellas and find out what this is all about."

"If they want to palaver, they know where to find us. They're probably pretty curious who it was that pulled their bacon out of the fire."

Curious, maybe, but definitely cautious. Long minutes crawled by with no sign of the four men emerging from their cover in the boulders.

But then one rider appeared, guiding his horse with his knees and holding his rifle ready in both hands, and the others trailed slowly out of the rocks behind him. They were on the alert for trouble as much as the first man was.

Nothing happened, though, as the four men rode across the grassy flat toward the knoll. Frank and Salty watched them come. When they were about twenty yards away, the men reined in, and the one in the lead called, "You still up there?"

"We're here," Frank said.

"Who are you?"

"Could ask the same thing of you, Mister."

The man sheathed his Winchester. He took off a flat-crowned brown hat and sleeved sweat from his forehead. He appeared to be in his mid-twenties, a well-set-up young man with brown hair and the sort of permanent tan that indicated he spent his days working outdoors.

Without putting the hat back on, he looked up at the top of the knoll and said, "My name is Hal Embry. My father is Jubal Embry. This is his range we're on, the Boxed E." Hal turned in the saddle and waved his hat at the other three men. "These are three of our hands, Bill Kitson, Ike Morales, and Gage Carlin." The young man put his hat back on. "Now you know who we are. Reckon it's only fair you return the favor."

"I'm Frank. My pard is called Salty. Just a couple of rannies riding through these parts."

"Well, we're surely obliged to the two of you for taking a hand in that fight, Frank. If you hadn't, Morgan and his gunnies might've done for us."

At the mention of that name, Frank stiffened and glanced over at Salty with a frown. The old-timer shrugged. It wasn't like Morgan was such an uncommon name. There were plenty of hombres carrying it around, all over the West.

Hal Embry went on, "Why don't you come back to the Boxed E headquarters with us? I know my pa would like to thank you, too, and we can offer you a mighty fine dinner in partial payment of the debt. Our cook's the best you'll find in Montana." A sudden grin split the young man's face. "She's my ma."

Salty scratched his beard and said quietly, "I could do with a home-cooked meal. It's been a few days since we left the Circle C, and trail grub just ain't the same as woman-cooked."

Frank felt an instinctive liking for Hal Embry, and the men with him seemed to be sturdy cowhands of the type he knew well and admired.

Besides, he wanted to know more about this man called Morgan, who evidently led a crew of killers.

"All right," Frank called down to Hal. "Hang on, and we'll join you."

He and Salty went down the hill and retrieved their horses. They swung into leather and rode around the knoll, leading Stormy and the pack horse, and Dog came with them.

As they came up to the other men, Frank saw that the three punchers were keeping a watchful eye on the trees. They were being careful, too, in case the gunmen came back and started shooting again.

Hal Embry nodded and said, "I'm pleased to meet you fellas. Just passing through these parts, you said?"

"That's right," Frank told him.

"You don't happen to be acquainted with a man named Gaius Baldridge, do you?"

"Guy Us," Salty repeated with a puzzled frown. "What in tarnation sort of a name is that?"

"Latin," Frank said. "The ancient Romans used it some." He had unexpected bits of knowledge in his head because he was an avid reader and always had a book or two in his saddlebags.

"Well, as far as I'm concerned, it's Latin for low-down snake," Hal said. "You don't know him, then?"

"Never even heard of him until just this minute," Frank replied with a shake of his head.

"That's what I figured, since Brady Morgan works for him and that was Morgan and his men you were shooting at. But since you just rode into this part of the country, it was possible Baldridge might have sent for you."

"To do what?" Frank asked, although he suddenly had a hunch that he might know the answer.

"To sign on as regulators for him."

That was what Frank expected to hear. It must have taken Salty by surprise, though, because the old-timer exclaimed, "Regulators! You mean we just waltzed right into the middle of a dad-blasted range war?"

Hal smiled thinly and said, "I'm afraid so. Baldridge is an old open range man. He doesn't like it that my pa filed an official claim on part of this valley last year and moved out Baldridge's stock. He's been trying to run us off ever since."

"And he brought in regulators to do it," Frank mused. "Most of the time, that's just a fancy name for hired killers."

"Brady Morgan and his crew sure fit the bill," Hal agreed. "But there's no need to sit around here all day jawing. It'll be nigh on to supper time before we get back to the house."

He lifted his reins and turned his horse. Frank and Salty fell in beside him. The three cowhands brought up the rear, spreading out some and riding with their rifles across the saddle in front of them.

"Those gunnies jumped you for no good reason?" Frank asked.

"That's right," Hal said. "The boys and I were just checking on the stock in this part of the valley when

Morgan and the others showed up and started shooting. We lit out, but I don't figure we would have gotten away if you and Salty hadn't pitched in and given us a hand."

"They still outnumbered us by quite a bit."

"Yeah, but we were forted up good in those rocks, and it wouldn't have been easy to roust the two of you from that knoll. Plus we had them between two fires. Morgan may be a lot of things, but he's not a fool. Once he saw the layout, he knew he'd suffer some heavy losses, even if he managed to kill us all. I guess he figured it'd be better to wait and try to wipe us out some other day."

Frank nodded. Hired guns were nothing if not practical. A hired killer would risk his life for wages. That was part of the job. But he wouldn't do it foolishly. Frank had known plenty of them even though he had never sold his gun himself, his reputation to the contrary. He fought only for causes he believed in.

"You said this isn't open range anymore," he commented to Hal Embry. "I haven't seen any fences."

"We haven't gotten around to fencing off most of the Boxed E just yet. Barb wire costs money, and we're sort of cash-poor. And to tell you the truth, my pa is enough of an old-fashioned cattleman that he doesn't like the stuff. He's a little slow to change. It took my ma and my sister quite a while to convince him to file a claim on the land legal-like, but he finally saw that that's the way things are going these days. The land's ours, all right. The claim's on file official and proper down in Helena."

"I don't doubt it," Frank said.

"Yeah, things are changin' all over," Salty put in. "Most of it sticks in my craw, too."

"You'll get along with my pa, then," Hal said with a grin.

True to the young man's prediction, the sun was almost directly overhead when the six men rode up to the ranch headquarters. It was a nice-looking layout, Frank thought, with a two-story, sturdy-looking log ranch house, a bunkhouse and barn made of whip-sawed planks, and several pole corrals. A smaller pen near the ranch house held a couple of milk cows, and someone had put in a vegetable garden, too. There was nothing fancy about the Boxed E, but it had a comfortable look about it, as if a family could make a good home here.

If they got the chance.

Several shaggy yellow dogs came bounding out from the barn to greet the newcomers. They stopped short, their legs stiffening and the hair rising on their necks as they spotted Dog and caught his scent. Growls came from deep in their throats, and the big cur answered in kind.

"Dog!" Frank said. "Easy."

The ranch dogs approached warily. Considerable sniffing and circling went on, then Dog turned his back on the others and strode on next to Frank and Goldy, his disdain for the other dogs palpable.

The ranch house had a big porch along the front of it. As the riders approached, a heavy-set man with thinning gray hair and a gray goatee stepped out of the house with a double-barreled shotgun in his hands. From the man's powerful bearing, Frank guessed this was Jubal Embry, the owner of the Boxed E.

"You all right, Hal?" the man asked in a challenging tone as the riders drew rein in front of the porch. "One of the hands said he thought he heard some shots coming from the west pasture a while ago."

"He did hear shots," Hal said. "Brady Morgan and his gun-wolves jumped us while we were checking the stock over there. Might've done for us, too, Pa, if these drifters hadn't come along and helped us out."

"Drifters," Jubal Embry muttered. Then his eyes widened abruptly in recognition, and the shotgun in his hands came up. "Hal, you damned fool!" he shouted. "That's Frank Morgan, the gunfighter! He's Brady Morgan's father!"

Chapter Three

Frank didn't know what was more of a shock: having that scattergun pointed at him, or hearing that he was the father of a regulator, a hired killer.

Frank had one son, Conrad Browning, who had been led by tragedy to abandon the life of a successful businessman and now roamed the Southwest, using the name Kid Morgan. And there was a girl down in Texas named Victoria who *might* be his daughter. Frank wasn't sure about that, and Victoria's mother had always refused to say positively one way or the other. Victoria was confined to a wheelchair, the victim of a bullet intended for Frank himself, but she was married to Frank's old friend, Texas Ranger Tyler Beaumont, and he knew she was doing well. Every so often, one of her letters caught up to him.

Those were his only two children, as far as he knew, although to be honest he had been with other women from time to time over the years. None of them had ever said anything to him about being in the family way. But maybe they wouldn't have.

And he hadn't learned of Conrad's existence until the young man was nearly grown, he reminded himself. Was it possible that he had other offspring out there somewhere?

He had to admit that it was.

Those thoughts flashed through his head as he looked down the twin barrels of Jubal Embry's shotgun. He hadn't budged since Embry pointed the Greener at him. He didn't want to give the rancher any excuse to jerk those triggers.

"Pa, wait!" Hal said. "You must have it wrong. These hombres helped us."

Embry squinted at Frank over the shotgun's barrels and said, "Are you denyin' it, Mister? Are you Frank Morgan or not?"

"I'm Morgan," Frank said. "But I never heard of anybody called Brady Morgan until today."

Hal stared over at him.

"I trusted you," the young man muttered.

"Are you loco?" Salty burst out. "You trusted us for good reason! We kept those no-good varmints from gunnin' you!"

One of the ranch hands spoke up, saying, "That's true, Mr. Embry. As soon as they saw what was goin' on, they opened fire on Baldridge's regulators."

Hal glared at Frank and asked, "Why didn't you tell me your real name?"

"I did. Frank's my real handle. But once you started talking about somebody else named Morgan, I thought it might be a good idea to wait a while and see what else I could find out about what's going on around here."

"Well, now you know," Embry said. "That blood-thirsty whelp of yours is workin' for Baldridge and tryin' to run us off land that's rightfully ours. But he can't do it. He can't get rid of us without killin' us."

"I believe you," Frank said. "But Morgan's a common name. Just because the man ramrodding Baldridge's regulators is called that, it doesn't mean he's related to me."

"Then why does he keep goin' around tellin' everybody he's the son of the famous gunfighter Frank Morgan?"

Frank couldn't answer that, so he just shrugged and shook his head.

"All I can tell you, Mr. Embry, is that Salty and I didn't know anything about any of this until today. Not about Baldridge, not about the trouble you've been having, and for sure not anything about this Brady Morgan."

Doubt began to appear in Hal's eyes. He said, "I suppose he could be telling the truth, Pa—"

"You think it's a coincidence they showed up just as those gunnies were tryin' to kill you?" Embry demanded. He didn't lower the shotgun. "Don't be so blasted dumb. It's a trick, that's what it is! Baldridge is tryin' to slip these men in amongst us, so they can work against us."

"I don't see how—"

"Did they shoot any of those regulators?"

"Well . . . no," Hal admitted. "I think it was Gage's shot that plugged one of them. Looked to me like they might've been firing high."

Embry snorted.

"Ain't that a surprise," he said. "I swear, boy they've pulled the wool over your eyes! But the can't fool me." The shotgun's barrels shook slightl from the depth of the rage that possessed the mar holding the weapon. "Get off my range! Get ou now before I blow you both out of the saddle like ought to!"

"You're makin' a mistake, Mister," Salty said. "You got it all wrong."

"I don't think so. Now *git!*"

Frank lifted Goldy's reins and said, "We'r going."

He was angry, too, but he could see that he wasn' going to able to change Jubal Embry's mind. Cir cumstances had conspired to convince the ranche that he was right, and he wouldn't be swayed, n matter what.

"Hal, get in the house," Embry went on sharply "You three, ride along with Morgan and whateve that old pelican's name is, and make sure they ge off our range. If they give you any trouble . . . shoo 'em!"

Hal looked over at Frank and said, "I'm prett mixed up about all this, but I appreciate what yo did for us."

"You're welcome," Frank said with a faint smile.

"Hal!" Embry roared. "Now!"

Frowning in embarrassment and anger, Hal dis mounted while Frank and Salty turned their horse away from the ranch house. Frank saw that severa more punchers had emerged from the bunkhouse and the barn. The men watched with wary, slittec eyes as Frank and Salty rode past. They had heard enough of Embry's bull-like bellowing to believe that these two strangers were enemies of the Boxed E.

"Maybe this'll break you of the habit of goin' around tryin' to help folks," Salty said as they rode east and the ranch headquarters fell behind them. "That's the most surefire way of gettin' in a heap of trouble I ever saw."

"Seems like when you and I met, I was trying to give you a hand," Frank drawled.

"Yeah, well, that was different."

The three cowboys trailed behind them, rifles still held at the ready. But when they were out of sight of the ranch house, one of the men nudged his horse up alongside Frank's mount.

"Gage Carlin," he introduced himself. He was middle-aged, with the raw-boned, weatherbeaten look of a veteran cowboy. "For what it's worth, Mr. Morgan, we're obliged to you, too, like Hal said."

"Thanks, Gage," Frank replied. "And also for what it's worth, I was telling the truth back there. I don't know this Brady Morgan, or Gaius Baldridge, either."

"My bones say you're tellin' the truth. Can't go against the boss, though. No offense."

Frank nodded and said, "None taken. I've ridden for the brand in my time, too."

"Not for a while, I expect, judgin' by the stories I've heard about you."

"Not for a while," Frank admitted. "But some of

those stories you mentioned were likely just big windies."

"Some, maybe. Not all, I'll bet."

"No," Frank said, "not all."

They rode on for a while, and finally Salty asked, "Is there a town somewhere the way we're goin'?"

"Yeah. Settlement called Pine Knob. Didn't start out as much, but it's growin'."

"Does the railroad pass through there?" Frank asked.

Carlin shook his head and said, "Nope. Closest train station is in Great Falls. But there are a couple of good eatin' places in Pine Knob, and a decent hotel if you're lookin' for a place to stay." The cowboy grinned. "And some nice saloons, too."

Salty licked his lips and said, "Now you're talkin'."

Frank was still curious and asked, "Where does Baldridge's range run?"

"He has the whole eastern end of the valley," Carlin said. "Pine Knob sits in between, right on Loco Creek. Folks call it that because of the way it twists around so, but it runs generally north and south and cuts the valley right smack in half."

"Baldridge used to run his stock from one end o the valley to the other?"

"Yep. But he never filed claim on any of it excep the land his headquarters sits on, at the far end of th valley. Miss Faye is the one who figured that out."

"Who's that?"

"The boss's daughter. Smart as a whip, she is. probably shouldn't be sayin' this, but she got th head for business that Hal didn't. He's a top han

and as good a ramrod as you'd ever want to work
for, but . . ."

"I understand," Frank said. Hal Embry could
handle the day-to-day details of running a ranch
but didn't know how to go about doing so prof-
itably.

Like most cowboys, Gage Carlin was talkative
once he got going. He continued, "Yeah, Miss Faye
found out her daddy could file on the range and
wouldn't have to share it with Baldridge's B Star
spread anymore. We've always had trouble with
Baldridge tryin' to hog the grass and water. Once it
was done, we pushed all the B Star stock east of
Loco Creek. Baldridge pitched a fit, but there was
nothin' he could do about it. Not legally, anyway. So
he filed on his half of the valley and started tryin' to
crowd us out with regulators."

"Ain't there no law in these parts?" Salty asked.

"Pine Knob's got a marshal, but he don't take no
sides in what goes on outside of town. And a deputy
U.S. marshal gets up this way from Helena now and
then, but you can't count on him bein' around
whenever there's trouble. Folks still handle most
problems on their own."

Frank nodded. That was the way it had been on
the frontier for a long time, and despite the inex-
orable advance of so-called civilization, it was likely
to remain that way for a while longer, too.

"We've had potshots taken at us before," Carlin
went on, "and there's been trouble in town between our crew and Brady Morgan and his men,
but today's the first time they've tried to out-an'-out

murder some of us on Boxed E land." The cowbo
shook his head regretfully. "It probably won't b
the last."

"No," Frank agreed, "it probably won't."

They rode over a shallow ridge, and Frank spot
ted some buildings on the flats about a mile awa
where a line of cottonwoods marked the twisting
course of a stream.

The men reined in, and Carlin pointed.

"That's it," he said. "That's Pine Knob."

"Why in blazes do they call it that?" Salty asked
"I don't even see a knob, let alone one covered wit
pines."

"Well, it's not much of a hill," Carlin explained
"and you can't see it because it's on the other sid
of the creek, past the settlement. A few years ago i
was covered with pines, but then folks came in an
started the town, and they cut 'em all down fo
lumber to make the buildin's. I guess you could sa
the name's all that's left of the original pine knob."

"If that don't beat all," Salty muttered. "Folks ar
too quick to tear down and build things that ain't a
good as what was there to start with."

"You could be right, Mr. Stevens. But I gott
admit, I do like havin' a place closer than Great Fall
where a fella can get a drink."

"Well, you may have a point there," Salty admitted

"We'll head back now. You fellas will keep goin'
right? You don't aim to make any trouble for th
Boxed E?"

"That's right," Frank said. "You have my wor
on it."

"Good enough for me," Carlin said with a nod. He turned to Morales and Kitson. "Come on, boys."

The three men turned and rode back toward the ranch headquarters.

"We didn't get that dinner the Embry boy promised us," Salty said. "And I was sure lookin' forward to it. What say we find us a hash house down yonder in the settlement, get a surroundin' in our bellies, maybe wet our whistles, and then ride on? Might be able to get out of this valley by dark."

"I thought you might want to spend the night," Frank said. "Fill up on something besides trail grub and sleep in a real bed for a change."

Salty looked over at him for a long moment, then abruptly jerked his battered old hat off and agitatedly ran his other hand through his tangled white hair.

"Dadgummit! I knowed it, I purely did. You can't just ride away, can you? You got to mix in and get to the bottom of this whole range war mess. You got to find out what the story is on this Brady Morgan varmint!"

"Wouldn't you be curious if you found out you might have a son you didn't know about?"

Salty pulled on his beard and said, "I just might. I wasn't always a scruffy ol' billy goat, you know. I used to have a way with the ladies."

"I don't doubt it. Anyway, I didn't say we were going to get mixed up in any range war."

"You didn't have to say it," Salty replied with a sigh. "I've rode with you long enough now to know how trouble follows the Morgan clan."

He heeled his paint into motion.

Frank rode after Salty. He hated to admit it, but the old-timer was right. For decades now, trouble seemed to follow Frank wherever he went, and from what he knew of Conrad's life now, the same was true of Kid Morgan.

He supposed he couldn't expect things to be any different with this Brady Morgan . . . whoever he was.